4 Janes

PRAISE FOR *4 JANES*

"*4 Janes* is an inventive and heartbreaking epic that reimagines the iconic character of Jane Eyre, exploring how one enduring figure transcends space and time. Spanning continents and eras, Marian Yee reveals how belief, love, and resilience echo through the ages. A tribute to the transformative power of reading."

—Michelle Min Sterling, *New York Times* bestselling author of *Camp Zero*

"Four very different Jane Eyres lead parallel lives in Marian Yee's *4 Janes*, an ideal read for the Brontë fan longing for more. Exquisitely written and populated with captivating and surprising characters—from the madwoman in the attic to Ho Chi Minh—this genre-bending novel illuminates the tender soul at the heart of one of literature's most beloved classics. Vivid, modern, and inventive."

—Caroline Woods, author of *The Mesmerist*, *The Lunar Housewife*, and *Fräulein M.*

"In illuminating prose, Marian Yee beautifully reimagines Charlotte Brontë's *Jane Eyre* for the modern reader. *4 Janes* weaves the lives of four seemingly disparate Janes—from a missionary's wife in Calcutta to a bookseller in Vietnam—and brings them masterfully together over centuries and continents to answer the timeless question: What does it mean to love, and how do we know when we've found it? These Janes look and feel different from the Victorian Jane we know, but their passionate spirit and universal longings capture our hearts all the same."

—Rosa Kwon Easton, Amazon bestselling author of *White Mulberry*

"In *4 Janes*, Marian Yee accomplishes an astonishing feat of literary acrobatics with consummate skill and enormous entertainment value. Like a master juggler, she dazzles by keeping multiple plotlines and points of view, a large cast of characters, and different time periods flashing before our eyes without a single pause or fumble. I can only marvel at her near-miraculous dexterity, especially in her reimagining of an iconic novel and its beloved heroine for the twenty-first century. Readers of the nineteenth-century novel will treasure this book, but so will anyone who cares about the possibility of extending the genre into our own fractured, intersecting times and places. *4 Janes* is a tour de force of storytelling creativity, a richly imagined fantasy, and a wonderful read."

 —Mark Sullivan, author of *Slag*, *Best American Essays* prizewinner

"An engrossing multidimensional plot with deep insights into human nature along the way . . . A treat of a read!"

 —Andrea Nye, author of *Socrates and Diotima*

"[*4 Janes* is] about the nature of time, karma, wrath of god, and quantum physics, the parallel world theory: For every decision not made, there exists a world in which it was. And of course, being seen . . . Brava, brava, brava for how many minute moments and details reappear and find themselves significant in the light of a new setting. We turn to a different facet and suddenly what was small is critical . . . There was never a moment of predictability. There was never a moment of boredom. There was also never a time I wanted the book to end."

 —Fran Lebowitz, literary agent and editor

4 Janes

A Novel

MARIAN YEE

Little
a

Published by Little A, Seattle

www.apub.com

Amazon, the Amazon logo, and Little A are trademarks of Amazon.com, Inc., or its affiliates.

EU product safety contact:
Amazon Media EU S. à r.l.
38, avenue John F. Kennedy, L-1855 Luxembourg
amazonpublishing-gpsr@amazon.com

ISBN-13: 9781662544521 (hardcover)
ISBN-13: 9781662537912 (paperback)
ISBN-13: 9781662537936 (digital)

Cover design by Zoe Norvell
Cover image: © Christie's Images / Bridgeman Image; © Rawpixel.com, © Kseniia Dizdar, © Amelia Design Art, © Sandra_M, © OlyaSenko / Shutterstock; © Tania Cervian / Stocksy

Printed in the United States of America

First Edition

For my parents, Bake Quin and Suy Kue

Jane Eyre Rivers, 1851–1853

"Reader, I married him."

Chapter One

Marseilles, France, 1851

Jane Eyre is dead.

The plain gold band on my finger is the sign of her demise.

I am Jane Rivers now. Or, more accurately, Mrs. St. John Rivers.

Mrs. St. John Rivers. I try on the name like a pair of new calfskin gloves. The syllables glide along my tongue smoothly enough once I get over the little bump at the beginning. Then I study the small hands lying calmly in my lap. They are encased in soft, pale-yellow leather, and like my new name, they seem to belong to somebody else.

I have been a missionary's wife for barely a week.

I wait at one of the fashionable coffeehouses on La Canebière, surrounded by wonders: gilding, mirrors, paintings, tapestries, and a large revolving clock in the center that gives the time on three continents. They bring together the charms of this port city as if in miniature. I look about, my senses heightened: The drink served here is not to my liking, but I savor its rich, smoky aroma.

For these moments at least, I sit alone. St. John is at the purser's office, seeing to our cabins and passage. We arrived at this bustling French port last night, and were deposited, along with the English mail that had departed on the London train with us, in a damp heap along the quay. This followed a Channel crossing that was in itself a trial. I spent most of that time huffing short, shallow breaths and moaning miserably into my handkerchief while my stomach roiled. St. John held my hand dutifully while I battled nausea, but I could not entirely dismiss a sense that his patience was forced, that he hid his disapprobation at finding me such a poor traveler before we had even ventured beyond Europe.

No matter. Now all is near ready. We have said our goodbyes. I wait with our few belongings, only the baggage we will need on the crossing, hardly enough for a journey of nearly two months. Fortunately, our present needs are few, and the rest of our trunks will be sent along. In our haste to depart we left them to Diana and Mary—his sisters, my cousins—to assemble, to cord, to nail the cards that would direct them to our final destination. They will chase us from port to port until we are reunited—only six weeks from now!—in India. At that point, we will open them with a sense of wonder that such luxuries and extravagances exist; we will puzzle what to do with calfskin gloves and fur muffs in the blazing heat of a sun-drowned continent.

As I wait, I return to the book I laid aside and open it to the point where a folded sheet of paper divides the unread pages from the finished ones. The paper is nothing more, or less, than the very letter that started me off on this journey, having arrived for Mary two months ago from a friend in ——shire. As Mary shared its contents with Diana and me, one set of ears heard, with distant concern and casual curiosity, the misfortune of others that did not touch upon itself, while another set heard the end of the world.

It was news of a devastating fire at Thornfield: The entire estate had been burned to the ground, and no one there had survived the destruction. *No one.* God forgive me, there was only one who mattered in that moment, only one whose death meant my own. I could barely bring myself to whisper his name. *Edward.* I recall Mary's voice droning on, then pausing; Diana's sharp *oh dear.* Was it for the news or at my fainting dead away? I was told afterward that I had collapsed in a wordless heap.

I have no recollection of those hours, those days (five, they told me) immediately following, when I drifted in a haze of blankness. Feeling fled me; I was disembodied, perceiving only strange scraps. A slight stirring in the current of air let into the sickroom. Fragments of hushed speech floating in and out of range. Gradually, shadowy forms constellated into people coming in and going out, though one body remained the longest, hovering near my orbit like a constant moon. As the boundaries of my vision drew in, the blurred edges slowly sharpened into clear features: twin orbs of blue that floated, then settled upon a finely boned visage.

"Jane." The eyes probed my face. "You know me."

"Yes, St. John."

He heaved a sigh. "You have been gone a long time."

"I have been right here," I said, bewildered. "In this bed. I have not moved." Indeed, I felt stiff all over, for I had been practicing the pose of a corpse.

"Stay," he gently implored.

"I am right here," I repeated.

"Nay, you were drifting again, Jane. To that place you have been these past five days, five years, it seemed. Sorrow's shores. Come back to the living, Jane."

And then I remembered.

He held me, that was all. He sat by my bedside hour by hour. He sent his sisters away, which I regretted, for I would have been comforted by their presence. And yet his tender solicitude was the most soothing thing of all. I cannot say that I slowly climbed out from the pits of hell of my own volition. I was rather dragged out by the ankles, inch by inch, through St. John's persistent ministrations. I was soon strong enough to take brief walks, St. John offering a strong arm to support me, though most days were inclement and I sat by the window. There, too, he was my companion, silent, giving me space. My mind was a blank. But it was healing, if healing is a steady putting down of layers upon thin layers of renewed flesh to build a barrier between the gaping wound and the world. That fragile armor was almost rent when he came to say goodbye.

"Jane, I leave in two days."

I had thought I was strong enough to continue existing, but his words proved otherwise. Could I truly survive the loss of another soul? I clutched him, speechless. He gently pushed me back and bent down to kiss my brow. He lifted my chin so my eyes could not escape his.

"I asked you once if you would come with me. Here you will wither away in sorrow. Come and be by my side as we do God's work together. Have a purpose in your life. It is the best way to heal your heart. I have asked you before. I will not ask again."

I waited for my answer, the no. Nothing came. He was right. I had refused before, with all my heart, because I once believed that to enter into a loveless marriage was to exist in a state of living death. Now I was too tired to resist. I had come to learn that there are many ways to exist with a dead heart.

Early the next day, I left my bed. The morning was gray and grim as we quietly slipped out of the house. The sky stayed leaden when we knelt before the pastor and the clerk summoned hastily from the neighboring shire. No one else was there.

Reader, I married him.

And when the modest gold band was slipped upon my finger, the look in St. John's eyes hardened; his whole being solidified into stone and lead. An unyielding support. A foundation. A future to build upon for God's glory. The sky was an iron banner when we left the church. I was glad for its sure cover, as I was for St. John's anchor: Without them, I felt I might very well float away.

I finally discern the source of the pounding rhythm that has been echoing in my head. At first I thought it was the tramping feet of café customers coming and going, restless passengers waiting for embarkment like myself. But it is too steady, and it has been growing in volume.

It is my heart.

To its terrifying rhythm, a black wave breaks over me. I am drowning in darkness, part of me seduced by its promising oblivion, but resisting, unwilling to succumb altogether, gasping for air, reaching out wildly for what—for a reason to continue—for a saving hand. Just as I go under, that other hand grasps mine. Salvation comes to me in the form of a perfumed handkerchief thrust beneath my nose, and a lovely, refined voice accented with gold flecks and laced with concern.

"My dear, breathe."

The scent, a heavy floral bouquet edged with spice, invades my nose. It is an aroma so foreign to my senses that it seizes hold of all my thoughts. Helplessly, I breathe it in, at the same time clinging to the gloved hand squeezing my own. Another breath, and I open my eyes at last to look upon my savior. What a vision I behold: a pair of eyes so dark that they absorb the gaze of the onlooker, a finely boned nose ending in delicately flared nostrils leading the viewer to sensuous lips so puffed that a line along the apex dents the rosy pillows. A firm chin and glossy twines of black hair. Silk, feathers, lace, gold frame the whole. But none of these are needed; they are indeed superfluous to the picture of perfection.

"Breathe," the voice flutes.

I straighten and gently put aside the handkerchief held in the lavender calfskin gloves.

"I thank you for your kindness. I'm better now," I tell the angel.

She smiles. I now see something above an angel. A goddess. A shaft of light from the café's high windows chooses at that moment to break behind her head, crowning her with a glowing halo.

"Am I dead?" I find myself stuttering.

She laughs. "I'm dead too! That's why you can see me."

The heavenly stranger allows me a moment to recall myself, then discreetly offers me a drink from a silver canteen that she has fetched from her black lace pouch. When I shake my head, a little shocked, she tips her head back and takes a swallow for herself.

"It's wonderfully reviving. I do recommend it, my dear."

Indeed, her cheeks acquire a divinely subtle blush of delicate pink, like the underside of a white rose petal. Her eyes glint.

"How quiet and pale you are. Can I not offer you anything?"

I thank her for her kindness, and shake my head no. Putting away her canister, she now turns her entire attention to me, studying me with an uncanny intensity. To put her off, I inquire politely, "You are traveling to the East as well?"

She nods. "I go to wed my betrothed in Calcutta. And then we travel on to Shanghai."

"So far!" I can't help remarking. The distance to India already seemed like a journey to the end of the world. "Our own journey extends only to India, to Calcutta as well."

"It doesn't matter how far you go," she says mysteriously. "There's only one destination. That's why I always carry my coffin with me."

I pull back as if in danger of being stung by a viper. Ungodly woman! Instinctively I look around to make sure that no one has heard. Especially St. John.

"Is it a custom from your parts to do so?" I inquire cautiously. It at last occurs to me that the lady might not be from these parts.

Her head nods while her mouth utters, "No."

The disparity confounds me.

"I am from Spanish Town, Jamaica. I am what you English call a Creole. The servants call us white cockroaches. As for traveling with my own coffin, I mean myself, my body. I am entombed in it."

"Yet a living heart beats within." I humor her.

"Inside, that organ is dead too," she says. "The unloving, unloved heart cannot live."

"You do not love your betrothed?"

"I am chained to one who is not my True Love. Just like you."

I am saved from responding to this vexing claim when we are approached by a small, odd figure who stops and kowtows deeply before the woman.

"Phan Văn Tiến, my servant." The almost child-size figure bends at the waist for me as well. When he straightens, I see at once that this is no child, but a smaller man than I am used to encountering, whose bright, uncanny eyes when they meet mine raise a sense of uneasiness in me.

"Tiến is from Cochin China," the woman explains. "He is my translator, guide, shopper, cook, guardian, masseur, tormentor," she says fondly.

"Madame, we will embark presently," he informs her.

"It is time to load the coffin." She giggles.

Truly, she is mad, I think. Her beauty, intelligence . . . corrupted and wasted. Yet it is I that she looks upon with sympathy as she rises. "He is kind to you, your True Love?"

"He was. In his way." Only after the words leave my lips do I realize that I have confessed what my heart had sealed. I was not speaking of my husband. My heart stutters a beat upon that realization. But why not humor the poor woman; we will likely not cross paths again.

"'Was'?"

"He's gone."

"Why do you think so?"

"He died in a fire," I whisper.

"And he did not rise from the ashes? In my experience, the dead never stay put." She sighs. "Especially the restless ones separated from their hearts' dearest."

But I have had enough of her gabbing, and to my relief Tiến gently takes her by the elbow and leads her away.

Chapter Two

Indian Ocean, 1851

The missionary's wife flew over a foggy field strewn with broken bodies. When the smoke cleared, figures crept from the edge of the wood, like little ants. One or two approached a crumb-size body and carried it off. She could smell their tears. The air rumbled, and the ant people went still; then they dropped their dead and ran for cover. The ground detonated. The air cleared. The field was empty.

She woke, dredged in grief and guilt. She had failed to recover the body; she had held the legs while silent tears streamed down her face, determined to take the corpse back, to take him home. Who? The body had dissolved into the smoke. If only there were something solid. Something to cling to.

When dawn finally broke, the missionary's wife was relieved. After a restless first night in the narrow berth of the second-class cabin, dawn was a refuge. Dawn was relief. And if at dawn one took oneself on deck to watch the sun crack and spill its yolk into the calm, gray water, one might feel that survival was possible if one found something solid, something solid yet filled with air at its core so it stayed afloat when everything else sank.

She made her way to the main deck. At this transmutable hour, everything inhabited a slippery existence: She was hardly surprised when the shadowy form before her resolved into a woman leaning over the railing, clutching a scarlet shawl around her shoulders as she watched the pale rays of light streak across the sky. The missionary's wife hesitated. Too late. The woman at the railing turned and fixed her.

The smile that lit up that face was ravishing, a radiance that made the dawn shrink in comparison. And the laughter: It summoned bells, songbirds, the smell of spices, the weight of tropical heat bending huge heads of carmine flowers along a dusty road.

"I just chased away a curate!"

She laughed again. Darkness shattered. "He fled so fast he almost outran his soul!"

The missionary's wife could not help the smile that stretched across her tight, reproving lips. The image of a scandalized, frightened curate fleeing this outrageous force of life—and it could be any one of the handful of clergy on board bound for missionary work in the East—momentarily overcame her better judgment. "Shameful," she said, uncertain whether she meant the woman, the curate, or herself. At the same time, she wondered what her husband would make of the irreverent bon vivant before her. "Do you not fear for your own soul?"

Those black eyes shimmered at her. "My dear," she said breathlessly, "had he succeeded, his soul might have found companionship with my own—wherever it is, flitting about somewhere over the ocean. Lonely and in need of a friend." She paused. "Like you."

The missionary's wife drew up her shawl, frowning. "I assure you, I am fine and perfectly happy as I am. Nor am I friendless, as you assume." And yet she had the sensation that a hand had reached across a wide sea as she floundered, unmoored—a hand that offered not safety, for she was beyond rescue, but recognition.

"Oh, don't be angry! Though when your visage puckers up like that, your eyes come alive at last."

This was not to be borne. The missionary's wife made to go. Yet she hesitated before turning back. "What did you mean before, when you said . . . that the dead never stay put, especially the restless ones?"

She had spoken to this black-eyed stranger only once before, in the café at Marseilles. There had been no sight of her afterward in the rush to embark on the short voyage across the Mediterranean—most of it spent belowdecks in wretched seasickness—or then in the chaos when they made landfall at Alexandria in the middle of the night. The entire overland route had appeared as a hellish landscape. Then, at Suez, they had embarked on another steamship, which would take them to their final destination, to Calcutta.

"Only the ones with unfinished business."

"Pardon?"

"The restless dead, the ones with unfinished business. They live on."

"Yet would that not be all of us? Who among us possesses the fore-knowledge to settle our affairs before our death?"

"Only those who know that we are already dead and so are able to live."

Was it tiring for her? the missionary's wife wondered. Did it make her head ache to sort out the signs and portents? One thing always meant another. Nothing was what it appeared to be. People were con-tainers of loneliness and fear.

"Your servant is looking for you." The missionary's wife pointed to a thin face peeking from behind a stack of coiled rope.

"I will see you again. À bientôt," the woman said gaily, taking the offered arm of her assiduous servant.

Left alone, the missionary's wife looked vacantly at her hands, at the plain gold band on her finger. *Jane Eyre Rivers,* she reminded herself. *That is who I am. A bit of light to be carried to a dark continent to help bring the Word of God to a people in need of Him. To help my mate, my . . . husband. Yet. How can I help anyone when I can barely help myself?* Calcutta seemed still a far way off. So too did England. Then the hand reaching out across the wide sea flashed across her vision again. Her own hand reached out instinctively to clasp it before she caught herself. A lost soul at sea, she told herself, only that. *Then there are two of us.*

Belowdecks, before the twin doors, the missionary's wife paused. Which one was hers again? Ah yes, the one on the right. They were fortunate, St. John had said, to have rooms side by side in lieu of a shared space, as they might have had in first class. She roomed with a mother and her grown daughter in a cabin so tiny that two had to wait in the passageway while one took a turn dressing for dinner; her husband berthed with three Australians in an even smaller space. Had St. John not seemed so satisfied with the arrangement, she might have admitted to herself that she preferred it this way too.

Side by side. That was how she had imagined their bodies laid out in space, ever since their wedding night. Was it possible to be made love to without being touched? Somehow, St. John had accomplished that at the —— Hotel. How else to account for the virginal feeling she had not shed since that night, when he had executed his husbandly duties in the same cold and intentional way he performed his religious ones?

Embraced by ice. But I was once held by fire. And inside that flame, how I burned.

The door on her left swung open.

"Ah, there you are, Jane. I knocked on your door earlier. Let's to breakfast. I had the misfortune to meet the most appalling woman on the main deck this morning, and I feel the need to wash away the memory of that encounter with a strong cup of tea."

Sunlight striped the wallpaper, streaming through the branches and leaves of the potted plants, when we entered the saloon. It was still early, and there were many empty tables. A small two-seater, partly screened by a potted fern at the end of the saloon, offered a space of discreet dining. I was glad when St. John steered us in that direction, for I hoped to avoid my chatty cabinmates.

I cast a wary eye about as we crossed the room. Close. Almost at our table. But a foot away.

"There you are!"

The woman materialized from thin air, impossibly appearing from behind the potted fern, where a moment ago there had been, I could have sworn, empty space. I glanced anxiously at St. John's face, saw it stiffen in distaste before freezing into a mask of wooden indifference. Ignoring St. John's cold reception, she slipped a slender arm through mine so that I was now trapped between my husband and his antagonist. She used her momentum to smoothly pivot us back toward the center of the saloon.

We approached a round table where three gentlemen were already seated. They rose and bowed. Tiến pulled a chair out for his mistress, then to everyone's surprise seated himself beside her. The other diners shifted uncomfortably. "This is rather . . . unusual?" one of the gentlemen ventured.

"The purser declined to allow my servant to eat at the table in the first-class saloon, so I bribed him for a seat here!" Had she held to her assigned seating, she would have eaten earlier and we would have been spared her presence. But if the gentlemen felt put upon by the eccentric whims of the wealthy woman, they did not voice their objections. I suspected her true motivation was to invade our company. I held my tongue.

An awkward silence followed, broken by one of the gentlemen, a portly Englishman to my left, exclaiming, "Beastly heat!" It was indeed unpleasantly warm even though the sun was not even near its zenith, promising a scorching day.

The woman smiled radiantly at the diner. "It will get much hotter, my dear."

The gentleman swore softly as he fanned himself with a stiff folded napkin. I realized that none of us had been introduced and that St. John, sitting back in his seat, arms crossed, was not even trying to be civil. The beginnings of a headache pecked at my temples. I turned to the portly gentleman. "I am so pleased to meet you, Mr. . . ."

"Winters. At your service." His head bowed officiously over the back of my hand. When he raised it, his eyes fixed eagerly on the woman across the table. She smiled and extended her arm to him.

"The soon-to-be Mrs. Edwin Sayre. But do call me Madeleine. You must all call me Madeleine!" Her gaze rested warmly on me.

"I am happy to see you again," I murmured. "We met earlier at Marseilles before embarkment," I explained to St. John.

"Tiến always says I have a gift for picking up strays," the woman said brightly.

The other gentleman was Mr. Richardson, and a nameless thin, gray, quiet man in an officer's uniform completed our company.

St. John now turned his disapproving eye on me. "You had not mentioned a prior meeting," he said coldly.

Indeed, I had not. And I now hoped fervently that the soon-to-be Mrs. Edwin Sayre would not go into details of the encounter, when she had found me at my lowest point. The woman, to my relief, only widened her smile, but said nothing more. I was also beginning to realize that St. John had not spoken of his own prior encounter with Mr. Sayre's betrothed earlier that morning. Or was this not the "appalling woman" he had spoken of earlier? The one who had left such a distasteful impression that only a strong cup of tea could restore his equilibrium? Hoping to redirect the conversation altogether, I turned to Mr. Winters. "Are you going on voyage for business, sir?"

"Indeed," Mr. Winters replied. "I have business in Bombay and Canton."

"Oh, but I believe this steamer will end her journey in Calcutta?" I asked in confusion.

"Indeed she will, but I am disembarking before then, at Aden, when the ship stops for coal. From there, I will ship out again on an East India Company steamer for Bombay to purchase my goods, then on to China."

"My future husband undertakes similar travels for business, Mr. Winters. Pray, do you also traffic in illicit dreams?" Mrs. Sayre said.

"Indeed, Madame, I trade in a healthful, medicinal balm. The opium calms the agitated nerves and soothes an upset stomach by putting those heathens into a sweet sleep. It is more valuable than gold!"

St. John, who never suffered bores or fools gladly, used the cover of business talk to attend to his own thoughts.

"And how did you meet Mr. Sayre, pray tell?" I put in a little desperately when the conversation stalled.

The enigmatic future Madame Sayre smiled blandly.

"Indeed, he snatched me up at a bargain," she said laughingly. "I had just been tossed aside by another Englishman who deemed my bloodline tainted beyond redemption. I was staying at a convent in France when Edwin stopped to visit his sister, who was also residing there at the time. When he learned of my circumstances, and my resources, Edwin was happy to step in and seal the deal, especially when my dowry was doubled for his trouble."

"That is without a doubt a good business deal, a real bargain indeed," Mr. Winters agreed without irony.

I was at pains to find an adequate response. "But as for your prior engagement, that Englishman was surely a lout," I finally said.

"Indeed he was. But a magnificent one, as it were. I think I am half in love with him still."

I was aghast. "His loss was Mr. Sayre's gain. Were but it mine," Mr. Winters offered gallantly. His self-satisfied smirk was hard to bear. When I peeked, I saw that St. John was finally listening to the talk, and his face had a thoughtful expression as he regarded Madame Sayre without the icy aspects it had held before.

"Madame," he finally said, solemnly, gently even. "To bear one's lot with equanimity is no small thing, yet it is not God's wont to have His subjects suffer without bringing them to a higher place."

Something in me jolted. Was he beginning his work here, now, with the soul of this Creole woman as his first conquest?

Madame Sayre turned a dazzling, breathless smile upon him. "You will not win a convert in me, my curate," she said. "With nothing to live for, no love, no future, I but think of my entertainment and my food!"

She slipped a savory slice of sausage into her mouth, then licked the grease from her shiny lips with the tip of a pink tongue. I was mesmerized. Even more so when I glanced from one to the other and saw that St. John and the future Mrs. Sayre also glowed. Something in my soul quavered. If they were to do battle, which light would stamp out the other? Or was it my own that would be obliterated?

St. John and I approached our next meal with trepidation after the first breakfast with "that woman," as he immediately took to calling her, but found our worries banished. It seemed that a High Anglican missionary and his snobbish wife had complained vehemently to the steward, who had then removed Madame Sayre and her servant (for it was the seated servant that had offended) back to the first-class saloon, and consequently a nondescript missionary couple had replaced her. I found myself missing Madame Sayre.

Yet why, too, did I fear meeting her again? In the days that followed, I slipped into a period of heat-laden solitude. I took to wandering on the promenade deck when others tried to sleep away the hottest hour belowdecks. I went up to the port side of the hurricane deck, which was reserved for second-class passengers and empty because of its exposure to the sun. The change in climate was still jarring: When we'd left England, it was late October; passengers shivered on deck in their heavy wool coats. By the time we embarked on the second steamer at Suez, a ship twin to the first except that it was manned by turbaned, dark-skinned seamen in white cotton suits rather than heavy blue serge uniforms, we'd stepped from the beginning of winter directly into summer. Everyone had thought I would shrivel up and perish in the unrelenting heat of the East. But to my own surprise, I found I could bear it. Though I knew it would get even hotter than this, I found I could endure high temperatures without fear. Strange as it was, the trick was not to resist. Resistance came in holding to a picture of the weather as it should be for a proper Englishman and thus being inconvenienced that the world did not organize itself to accommodate that preference. It was hot, that was all; it was supposed to be hot.

Charting my wandering itineraries across the decks, I was able to go for seven days without encountering *her*. But even on my guard, I was not prepared enough, apparently. She made a frontal attack when I was on the look-out for an ambush. I opened my cabin door one morning, and there she was.

"Come," she said breathlessly as she slipped her arm into mine, effectively capturing me. "The sun is just about to peek over the horizon." How did she know that I had gotten into the habit of rising almost in darkness to wander around the sleeping passengers on the main deck just before the lascar seamen came at dawn to eject the sleepers so they could scrub down the oak surface? I tried to gently disengage, pleading the need to attend St. John. "I have a greater need of you. In God's eyes, the greater need is the one that must be addressed."

I did not think that was written in the scriptures, and I was about to demur, but the woman pressed my captured arm closer to her side, and I was led to the main deck. There, she had instructed Tiến to arrange two deck chairs that flanked a table set for tea.

Madame Sayre handed me a steaming cup, then sat back with her own brew. I braced myself for her endless gibberish, but to my surprise, she was silent, looking out at the water. I sipped uncomfortably, determined to say nothing to encourage conversation. "But this is delicious!" I found myself exclaiming.

I glanced over at Madame Sayre, expecting a smile of acknowledgment, but was startled to see tears streaming silently down her cheeks. I held my breath. She did not wipe them away, and eventually they stopped and she sat in silence, with dew-lapped lashes edging her shuttered eyes. We sat wordlessly like this for so long that I wondered if she had fallen asleep. At last she blinked, stirred, then turned and smiled gently at me. Still saying nothing, she rose as Tiến soundlessly appeared with a silk wrap, which he draped over her shoulders before leading her away.

Alone on the deck, I mused over this odd encounter, where we had done nothing but drink tea silently together. It was only when I reached my own cabin some minutes later that I realized how peaceful and disburdened I felt. Some ache so deep inside me that I had not realized it existed had dissipated, as if I had been enwrapped in some silent embrace of total sympathy. As if she had said, without words: I see your heartache. For that was what it was.

In the confines of my cabin, I took a breath, at last, and then another.

I no longer sought to avoid Madame Sayre after that. Nor did I seek her out. Sometimes she suddenly appeared by my side, most often when I was alone, staring into the waters or sky. We would nod pleasantly to each other and share a moment in silence. Always, I left relieved that the interaction was no more than that, and then, too, I felt strangely eased. I did not want more. On the other hand, I was troubled by St. John's reactions to the Frenchwoman, as he now called her. Even though she was Creole, not French. "The Frenchwoman is an abomination," he insisted. "The Frenchwoman's soul is severely compromised, shrunken, or possibly nonexistent." Amid these words meant to minimize her, she somehow materialized more insistently in my mind: I pictured a tiny Madame Sayre with a hole edged in black lace where her heart should have been. Even in my imagination, she wore her debasement with effortless elegance.

"Why do you vex yourself over her?" I asked him. As we strolled arm and arm on deck, we passed that same lady with her steadfast servant. Madame Sayre flashed a brilliant smile, and St. John tipped his hat, but his lips pressed so tightly together they turned pale. I lowered my eyes. Indeed, as I became calmer, St. John seem to grow more agitated.

We continued to promenade, but it did little to soothe him. At one point, he turned furiously to me. "You are to have nothing to do with that Frenchwoman!"

"My dear, I don't!"

"'Tis well, Jane. You are nothing like her, and it is best that way."

I wondered at his passion. I was perplexed, too, at how he yoked us in opposition as if we were two sides of the same coin. Being confined on this ship was bound to enhance our anxieties and bad habits of mind, I supposed. I found my own turmoiled thoughts easing as we journeyed farther from the source of painful memories. I was relieved that it was not otherwise, that I was not eaten alive by them. To be truthful, Madame Sayre helped.

I didn't even know that I was seeking her out until Tiến appeared suddenly at my side in the way that he did. "She cannot come today, and sends her apologies."

I concluded that she must be among the adventurous passengers who had ventured ashore, along with the mail, to explore the novelties of Ceylon. We had only just anchored that morning. St. John had expressed an interest, but I had noted the beginnings of a headache and pleaded for a day of peace and rest lounging on a deck emptied of most passengers. Yet would she go without her trusty servant? Was she ill, then? To my concerned question, Tiến shook his head. "Though she prefers to align her star with yours above all others, there are times when she is distracted by a wayward celestial object."

The servant had an odd way of speaking, but it warmed my heart strangely to hear that it was my company above all that she preferred. Or perhaps that was just Tiến's silver, heathen, lying tongue. As though he had read my very thoughts, he smiled and said, "Not every word spoken by a heathen is a lie."

"But some are?"

"Only the ones that soothe."

"Such as the ones you have just spoken."

"Such as this: Your journey will be a smooth one."

I pondered his enigmatic words as I made my way back to my room. On the way, I thought to stop at the saloon and beg a tray of tea to bring back to my cabin: The headache was getting worse. A group lingered at the entrance, and rather than make my way through them, I went around the corridor to make use of an obscure back entryway I had discovered in the course of my wanderings. Rounding the corner, I was brought up short, almost colliding with two figures entwined in a passionate kiss. "Oh! Pardon me." I backed up in haste. Her smile was smooth and beautiful. No triumph or treachery shone in her eyes. Only a sadness, I thought. His shocked face was something else to behold. I could not read the expression. So many thoughts crossed that fine facade in seconds: dismay, regret, rage hardening into righteousness. My tray crashed to the floor. I didn't care. I fled from Madame Sayre and St. John.

The pounding at my door had finally stopped, but not the one in my head.

I thought I must have slept, for the next thing I knew, the cabin was in complete darkness, save for the glint of starlight through the port window. Silence and darkness soothed me. My body had calmed at last. Now, movement was a matter of unlocking one limb at a time. I must have been on the floor for hours, in the same position from when I had barred the door, shoved a chest against it, then backed up to the far wall and collapsed, holding my head to shut out the pounding from within and without. St. John's muffled roars still echoed faintly in my head: "You will let me in, or I will break down the door!" I had never heard him so furious. Now I heard nothing but silence. Perhaps the world had ended. I knew not. Nor cared. I only wanted to slip off into oblivion.

The walls of the chamber are booming as they expand and contract. The room is alive. No, it is my heart. I am inside it. Locked inside, while behind the door seductive voices beg to be let in: We will love you, we will wash your tears away, we will treasure you and see to your every need, we will soothe, we will stroke and caress, we will break down the door if you do not open it, how dare you lock us out, it is our right.

It is St. John. It is Rochester before him, when I left. That marriage was a sham; he was not free to belong to me. Oh, his fury when I barred my door to him. The pounding, then, as well.

Men pounding on my door, furious men, self-righteous men, men who felt they were owed more. And the price paid by ridiculous women who believed in honor, truth, loyalty. But who will pay, I cry out, my back to the wall, fists over my ears, who will pay if not me?

I awoke again, hours later. Now sunlight streamed through the portal window. I had been in this room a full day and a half, I calculated. My cabinmates had stayed ashore overnight but surely would be returning today. Under different circumstances I might have relished the rare occurrence of having the small quarters entirely to myself, but at the moment I barely gave it thought as the demands of my body captured my attention. My thirst I was able to slake from a pitcher of water, but the hunger I could do nothing about. I was surprised that I still felt things like thirst and hunger after the death of my soul. The demands of the body kept me going. So I was not dead.

I opened the door a crack and had taken two steps forward when a shape separated from the shadows and pounced, grabbing my wrist.

"Jane."

In my weakened state, I could offer little resistance when he dragged me into his room and slammed me into a chair. I stared at him sullenly as he paced the small, tight quarters, if one could call the step-turn, step-turn action pacing. He dragged trembling hands over his head until his hair stood up in wild disarray. His entire countenance was distorted by discontent, disgust, dismay. I had never seen St. John in such a state. He was unrecognizable. I might have pitied him. I did pity him. Until he spoke.

"I was possessed."

This did not seem to bode an acceptance of responsibility, culpability, but I held my tongue.

"Homer's tale of sailors possessed by siren song, minds and hearts taken . . . driven to madness, taken from themselves. Those were not tales, Jane, I know now. I was almost one of those unfortunates."

I listened wordlessly.

"It began as a desire to save her soul: When I encountered her on her promenades, I would take pains to accost her and deliver small drops of the Lord's words to lead her back to the right path. She seemed receptive, so more and more I sought her out to that end, for I saw that it was a festering sorrow that had led her astray, that her entire character was a kind of mask for her pain." (I had to wonder, then, how many masks Madame Sayre had in her possession. For I had seen that one too.) "At first she resisted with glib and mocking words. Then she became silent and seemed to listen. Then she wept and avoided me. That only made my seeking of her more urgent. I see it all now, as clear as day: the path she took me down. I followed willingly, like a fool, like a lamb to slaughter. I became more eloquent than I had ever been in my life as I pleaded with her, argued with her. I reached such heights, Jane!"

Indeed I could picture it, as she stroked him and seduced him, using his own vanity to bring him to a height of passion. I was fascinated and appalled.

"I know now, more than ever, why I married you, why we *had* to marry. It was to check my arrogance. I thought to save the devil from himself. Instead, the devil seduced me. I would have fallen, if not for you!"

"I saw *you* kissing her, not the devil," I said icily.

"Was she not the devil incarnate?"

"If she were, then you must name every woman a spawn of Satan." It looked, for a moment, as if he were prepared to do just that, when he thought better of it.

"Not every woman, Jane. Not you."

And it came upon me: St. John did not think of me as a woman. And with his next words, he said as much.

"You are more than a woman, Jane. You are my mate."

"I did not know that marriage to you rendered my sex and my existence obsolete."

He stared at me in surprise. "Obsolete?" he demanded. "Do you think your work for the Lord a nonexistent thing? My entire life, existence, is dedicated to no greater task on this earth, and I am humbled indeed to learn that it is a task I cannot do without you!"

"Because I keep a check on your lust?" My tone could not have been less sarcastic. "By my utter lack of feminine charms?"

He viewed me, aghast. "Have I not done my husbandly duty?"

On the first night, mechanically, his mind, I suspected, elsewhere. Preoccupied with memories of his first love, the fair Rosamund, perhaps. Even in my inexperience, I knew I was not getting all. Not even close.

Yet behind this memory was another, where a perfunctory kiss deepened into an embrace of lips, where warmth and wetness, the hard and the soft, came together in the most tender and solicitous joining. I clung to this memory, proof that I had once been held, that I had been touched with love and desire. I was suddenly struck by the symmetry: he and I both enraptured on this voyage by what the other was not. Our hearts captivated by phantoms.

I turned to him. "You will never share my bed, St. John. You will be my husband in name only. Is this not what you truly want?"

He stood very still for a moment, head bent, eyes closed. He went to the door and opened it, his expression hewn from stone. "What I truly want? Jane, you do not begin to know."

In the echoing silence he left in his wake, it finally dawned on me, what I had chosen when I chose a life with St. John Rivers. I could deceive myself no longer. None of this was surprising. I had chosen this: to be nothing. I now had the rest of my life to live with it.

Calcutta, 1851, a Fortnight Later

Coffin after coffin descended the steep gangplank of the *Hindustan*.

The missionary's wife, standing on the main deck, shook her head to dispel the sight. Instantly the coffins morphed back into people disembarking onto the shore. Was that a straight, proud back, a fall of jet-black hair? Madeleine? No. Her heart slammed against her chest. Perhaps the fleeting image had been an effect of the heat, which wrapped around her like a stifling cloak. They had arrived in Calcutta. St. John appeared, took her diffidently by the elbow, then guided her forward. They were very formal with each other. She could barely look at him.

Instead, she thought of the note she had found in a small packet in the bottom of the drawer. Someone had known that this was the drawer that held the last items she would pack up. Someone small, quiet, a discreet spy, had slipped in, identified *her* drawer, and left this parcel to be found exactly at this moment. It held a sheet of paper, folded atop a single lavender glove.

> By the time you read this, my dear, I will be gone. Do not look for me in Calcutta. You see, I disembarked at Madras and never returned to the ship. Edwin will be most disappointed. Will you? I dare not ask for forgiveness on my behalf, but please forgive St. John. He is another one with a battered heart. Are there not enough of those already? But do as you like. It is a new world. Break your chains or endure them. I am finally free of mine. Free to learn how to live and love as I wish. I do not think it will be an easy lesson. Your friend, if you wish it to be so, Madeleine.

Something was set loose within her. It felt unruly, vast, like the ocean even though she was finally on land. The freedom to live and love as one wished. But how did one forge a path through the wilderness and confusion of the heart? And if the roads diverged, which passage was the correct one: a love that ennobled, one that consumed, or the one that took flight?

The missionary's wife clutched the lavender glove in her hand, clenching it tightly as if to a lifeline, as if it held a hand that attached to an arm that hinged to a shoulder that led to a head, a head that bent now and whispered in her ear: "My dear, breathe."

She took a breath.

And then another.

She moved forward into her new life.

Chapter Three

Calcutta, 1851

The air between us was still strained as we settled into our boarding-house, run by a Mrs. Porter. Still, we had attained a kind of truce. We trod carefully, allowing each other as much space as possible in our contained living quarters. When we lay down to sleep, it was each to our own side of the bed, with an impenetrable barrier between, two coffins side by side. Having been released from our marital duties, he had not pressed the issue. In the deepest hours of the night, as my body steamed, when the last thing one might want was a warming touch upon one's overheated skin, I yet despaired that I would ever be touched again. I lay awake. The sweltering heat softened and blunted the edge of my senses; the perspiring air moistened every inch of my frame. I felt myself expanding and swelling in the damp, feverish darkness, my body pulsing and throbbing in a rising rhythm that mounted moment by moment until I thought I would erupt.

Plagued by such restless nights, I clung to Mrs. Porter's promise, made on the first day we boarded with her: "If you have any sharp feelings, my dear, this country will grind them down within a year." She should know, good woman: Apparently she had been here running these lodgings by herself since her husband died twenty-seven years ago.

Now that we had landed, St. John was eager to throw himself into the work he had come to do. He had already called on the bishop, returning each time restless and unsatisfied, as the bishop had not informed him yet of where he would be stationed. But at last, we were to dine with him and his wife that night. "And we shall not leave until I know where we are going," he vowed.

For my part, I was also desperate for a distracting occupation. It did not matter what form it took. I had not come to India to be a missionary, but to be St. John's wife. Whatsoever that required of me was acceptable so long as it was demanding enough to consume my attention and to tire my body so that I was entirely drained by the end of the day. That night we left for dinner in high hopes of being released from our wretched state of deferral.

I found I had very little appetite for the meal or the company. Indeed, we were not the bishop's only dinner guests. To my left was a commander general; his wife sat across the table, next to St. John. To my right was another gentleman, portly and red faced, who fussed at imaginary crumbs on his lap and seemed generally put out. The bishop's widowed sister and an empty chair to her left made up the rest of the party.

In the abstraction of my boredom, I was hardly prepared for the lightning bolt delivered in words by the good bishop. A strained silence had fallen upon the table when he exclaimed, "But I have not introduced Mr. Edwin Sayre, who joins us, I'm sorry to say, without his wife!" He nodded regretfully at the empty chair. My head rose sharply. My senses were startled out of their slumber. My eyes caught St. John's astonished look as he glanced swiftly at the gentleman across the table and then at me with an unreadable expression, before his gaze lowered once more to his plate.

"The devil!" Mr. Sayre snorted. "What could the woman have been thinking!"

The bishop's sister made soothing, inarticulate noises that expressed her shock and commiseration.

"I was to marry them this morning," the bishop explained. "Only the bride sent a message informing that she had left the steamer at Madras and would not be coming on to Calcutta for her nuptials."

Mrs. D, the commander general's wife, shook her head in dismay. "Well, I never!" she exclaimed. "Young women these days—it will come to no good!"

Mr. Sayre buried his face in his hands and moaned. "I'm ruined!"

"Come, come, my good man! There are other fish in the sea, as they say." The commander general's unsympathetic comment prompted louder moans of distress.

"My money! I was to pay for the opium with our . . . combined assets . . . following the wedding. Oh, why did I not secure the funds beforehand! Only she said she could not bear to think of papers and legalities and monies until we had said our vows, and then it was all mine anyway, so no need to rush."

"But can you not repay your creditors after you've sold your shipment? Tell the bastards they must wait." The commander general was clearly discomfited by Mr. Sayre's tears.

"The terms now demand that I repay at double the loan. There shall be no profit at all!"

"Surely you've suffered a greater loss than your finances, Mr. Sayre," I said gently.

"I lost a bargain. It was too good to be true." He blew his nose.

"If that is how you think of your betrothed, you are each well rid of the other," St. John interjected sharply. I could hear the disgust in his voice. Indeed his feelings matched my own. Of course, I had known of her defection, but until now had not realized how justified she was in seeking her freedom. Our eyes met across the table, and I was held by the clear blue of his irids.

The bishop coughed nervously. "What is lost can be regained, and at greater return," he said fatuously. "Life is but a grand journey on the road appointed to us by the Lord in His great wisdom." His sister nodded benevolently. Mrs. D expressed her general disapproval by emptying her glass of wine in great gulps.

"As we are speaking of journeys"—the bishop turned to St. John—"I must inform you that your mission has been settled." St. John leaned forward eagerly. "You and your charming wife will travel in the commander general's party to the northwest. He will stop at the British hill station at Simla, and you will continue on to Amritsar."

It was what St. John had hoped for; his eyes blazed. "I am grateful for this opportunity to lead—"

The bishop held up his hand. "Where you will assist the village missionary there in his duties," he finished.

St. John went still. Without thought, I opened my mouth to protest. St. John had not come to assist, but to lead his own missionary station. "Nor have you been forgotten, my dear," the bishop continued before I could speak. "Indeed, the governor stationed there and his wife have two fine girls in need of an education. Mrs. P has been greatly vexed at this neglect. She has indeed been writing me a great many letters deploring their condition and seeking my advice. Think how fortunate that I can send an assistant and a governess at one stroke!"

Fortunate indeed to come halfway around the world to do the things we had thought to leave behind. St. John and I exchanged a wordless glance. He would bear it. He had only to prove himself. I read that in his eyes, and more: a question, a challenge—could *I* bear it? My chin rose, my lips set firmly as I gave him my answer: If you can, I can too. And for the second time that evening, a flash of understanding linked us.

Amritsar, 1852, Two Months Later

My inner resolve soon met the external reality of our journey up the country: At our British station stops, the dinners and meetings with dignitaries, the tiger hunts and tours and endless balls, fatigued me. I used the excuse of suffering from a touch of jungle fever to avoid as much of it as I could and grew to love the interior of my tent home by the end. We spent a week at Simla, then left the commander general and his wife and most of the party there when we went on to a small village in Amritsar, our final destination. The station posted there was filled with military and civil officials of the East India Company, everyone, it seemed, still bloated with triumph from the end of the war with the Sikh empire. In an uneasy mix with that triumph was a sense of being on edge: One felt that the unrest had only gone underground, threatening to reemerge at any moment from the soil.

Reverend M, the resident missionary, was most obsequious in his greeting, and Captain P lost no time in conveying the compliments of his wife, who was quite desperate, he said, to get hold of me. "But all in good time." He laughed. "We shall expect to see you all at dinner this evening!"

Reverend M beamed and added, "Mrs. P lays a most congenial table! I cannot imagine how she manages in this wilderness, but then she brought her own English-trained cook from Calcutta!"

We were left to survey the small bungalow, the former living quarters of mid-level lieutenants. In addition to a modest sitting room with a sofa and some wicker chairs, there were two small bedrooms, each fitted with a slim cot fit for a single sleeper. During our march, there had been no question of intimacy, given the utter lack of privacy. Now a wall between us would prevent it. Yet how lonely and cloistered each room felt. Peering into the cell that would be mine, I felt that virginal desolation creeping upon me again. The tour completed, we allowed that it was small but neat, and we were satisfied, even when we saw Captain and Mrs. P's mansion and realized that they regarded us as no more than higher-class servants, really. Reverend M's residence, I would later learn, was little more than a hut.

Dinner that night was a misery. Mrs. P lost no time in presenting me with a schedule to attend to her daughters' education. They were brought in for introduction: The elder Miss P, Luella, was a tall, indolent, yellow-haired girl of fourteen, and her younger sister, Mary, was a thin, sallow-skinned, sullen girl of ten. Neither seemed pleased at the prospect of expanding and grooming their minds. My heart sank as they were dismissed to their quarters. "You will start tomorrow, Mrs. Rivers," Mrs. P declared. "I can brook no delay when every day in these climes is a further erosion of their characters." I sighed inwardly as I relayed my consent; I had hoped for a delay so I could absorb and learn these parts.

"Indeed, indeed," Reverend M gushed. "Any further delay in educating these fine young ladies would be an erosion of their staunch British characters!"

Mrs. P ignored him as she turned to St. John. "You will find the native soul inadequate to your aspirations, I'm afraid."

"Quite right," Reverend M agreed. "We have yet to make a convert, but the presence of the church itself exerts a healthy moral influence among those it hopes to sway."

Not a single convert! I peeked at St. John with trepidation, but he did not appear discouraged or dismayed.

Captain P frowned. "I say, I never saw the point of these sham conversions. You can dress up a Mohammedan or Hindoo in any religious garb you want, but the minute you leave, they revert back to their native dress. If you want God in this country, then the English must stay."

"We can hardly expect otherwise when we seek to impose an alien religion upon them," St. John replied calmly. "Conversion must come from within, and it must be voluntary."

"I am not without faith that the better kind will eventually see the light," Reverend M said hastily. "Indeed, I have recently secured an invitation to a high-class Brahmin family—"

"I don't mean conversion for just the elites," St. John interrupted. "Nor a conversion that dresses up the exterior while leaving the soul untouched. For God to take hold of this country, the Indian must take hold of God and create something new: an Indian Christianity born on this soil that will flourish even when the English have left."

In the shocked silence that followed, Reverend M turned beet red and the captain took on a stony countenance. Mrs. P murmured, "Well, I never!" She called for the servant in a huff and ascertained that it was indeed quite time for the steamed pudding to be brought out.

The weeks that followed did not improve our relations with the English community in the village. In the evenings, we sat quietly studying Hindustani together, and on this night, like many nights previously, St. John was at work compiling a list of Hindustani words and marking notes beside them. The uneven keel of my days went from bouts of restless energy to spells of sluggishness. I wanted the wind in my face, to feel the surface beneath my feet propelling me, wavelike. But that ship had run aground and left us stranded and billeted in this dusty bungalow.

He must have noticed my sighing.

"Why, Jane, what do you have to be miserable about?"

I burst out, "This is not the life I envisioned. I am of no help to you or to anyone!"

I thought St. John would surely berate me for the arrogance of presuming I could make a difference for anyone. But he only looked upon me with a benign, even kind, expression. His lips remained sealed. I was silent for a while as well, but then I finally confessed my own woes. "Mrs. P constantly interrupts our lessons with trivial nonsense. It is difficult enough to gain their attention. The older one is prone to mischief, and the younger follows her lead. I nearly sat upon a gecko today."

"Might it not have crawled upon your seat of its own accord?"

"If it did, it also leashed itself there of its own accord, and left a calling card introducing itself as Monsieur Gecko."

I waited for St. John to offer some advice or guidance, but he only continued to sit in silence.

"Well, St. John, have you no thoughts? What would you have me do?" I finally said to bring the awkward silence to an end.

"Indeed, Jane, what will you do?"

"Do? I?"

From that dark pit of despair within me, a faint light began to shimmer, and I made out the broad planks of a long table. Gradually I saw the square room that it lay within, and a blank wall with a map nailed to it.

I had my answer.

I smiled at St. John. "I shall open a school."

Mrs. P was quite put out to learn that her daughters would be taught in my newly opened school for girls, which was but the back room of our bungalow, but I was adamant. All was now ready. I paused at the threshold. This was not the first schoolroom I had taken charge of. I thought fondly of the village girls I had taught at Morton. I had taken up the task at St. John's request; it was his test of whether I could fit myself to a life of dutiful if dreary responsibility. I had proven myself then, but this was something more. *My* school.

As I looked proudly about, I felt mind and body coming into a pleasing alignment with place. The room had been thoroughly cleaned, the long table polished and waxed, the broken chairs removed and replaced by two long benches that ran along each side of the table. A piece of slate sent for from Simla now hung on the wall where the map had been. A supply of pens, paper, ink had been secured. The opening at the back of the room now held a new door, which I kept open to allow light and air into the windowless room. My pupils, such as they were, entered through the bungalow's front door, crossed the sitting room, and entered the schoolroom one by one. There were four altogether. Having been in doubt of securing even one pupil for my school, I was relieved. Luella and Mary were there: Mrs. P had sulked until she realized that my services could only be had in this setting. Another pair of siblings, younger than the Misses P, were also there. I had asked Reverend M to announce my school to the village families, as it had been my intent to open it for all girls regardless of race, caste, or religion. Reverend M, I later discovered, had only approached the highly placed families, and in the end, none came.

Just as I was closing the front door of the schoolroom, a small child scurried in and curtseyed awkwardly before taking a place at the foot of the long table, where she scrunched down and tried to make herself as inconspicuous as possible. The other girls moved noticeably farther away from her. I recognized her as the Eurasian daughter of a former British official stationed at the village and gave her a warm smile before I went up to the head of the long table. The other young ladies openly snickered at Molly, as I would soon learn the girl was called, and were barely civil to me. To be fair, it was mostly Miss Luella who behaved thus: She was perceived as the head girl and indeed secured that status by claiming the seat nearest to the head of the table, to my right. The others copied her mannerisms, though not quite as openly, and I realized with a sinking heart that my little school was failing before it had even begun. *These are not infants, and I am not their nursemaid,* I rebuked myself. I thought of a stern, harsh teacher from my time at Lowood. Would Miss Scatcherd have tolerated such a crew of rude reprobates? That basilisk? No, indeed! She would have cut them down with one lethal look; she would have ripped out their livers with her hooked claws. I was no monster, but I needed to learn from her example, to seize their contempt and turn it back upon them.

I read from a history and had them compose short pieces based on their memory of events. Luella tipped over a small jar of ink and pretended it was an accident. My headache increased, but so too did my ire. I collected the writings and said I would read them aloud. I began with Luella's piece. As I read, I did not modulate my voice to smooth over the awkward phrasing and poor expression. At the end I paused before I delivered my judgment in a cold voice: the most worthless piece of tripe I had ever come across. I tore the paper in half and flung the pieces onto the ground. Luella's face reddened. Mary, mistaking her sister's silence for scorn, flounced about in her seat and impertinently asked when lessons would be over, for she was famished. I handed her an empty basket and bade her to go out to the back garden and collect some tamarinds. This she was eager to do and bounded out the door, only to hear that door closing and locking behind her. Having been shut out of the classroom, she now was eager to be readmitted, but I ignored her pleading and pounding. *This is my domain, and none may trespass unless I allow it!* A stillness descended upon the room. All looked to me to see my next move, for I had gained control of the reins and might now lead them where I would.

A small noise drew my attention, and I looked over and saw St. John leaning against the front doorway of the classroom, his face unreadable. He said nothing as he turned and left.

At the end of the week, I was passing through the open market one morning, having given the girls a holiday due to some local religious festival, when I came upon a commotion at the end of the bazaar. A crowd was gathering quickly, and I was swept up in the flow, which brought up short before a figure standing upon a box, holding before him a book. The crowd was electrified and pressed forward eagerly. The figure stood very tall and erect, his head turned from side to side as he addressed the crowd. I had heard Reverend M preach in public before, but it was usually near the mosque, and it was nothing like this. When Reverend M spoke in broken Urdu, the people would mill about, puzzled or amused by the spectacle, but all went about their business after the initial curiosity.

I sought a closer look; I discovered it was not Reverend M. It was St. John, standing solid as a pillar, voice ringing like a clear bell as it set forth the Word of God. The crowd came to a standstill. People pointed and gaped. A hush fell, and they listened as if they understood. I did not recognize the words that poured from his mouth. It sounded like and unlike the Hindustani we studied, and I concluded that it must be the local vernacular, the Punjabi he was studying on his own. At the edge of the crowd, I spied Reverend M. He too observed, unhappily.

Later, when St. John returned to the bungalow for tiffin, he sat down at the table in a state of exalted fatigue and overstimulation. After a single bite of rice, he laid down his fork and peered at me. "Were you not at the bazaar this morning, Jane? I thought I might have glimpsed you at the edge of the crowd."

"Indeed I was," I murmured.

"And what did you observe there?" he pushed.

"Nothing but the usual tumult of a market day," I replied.

"Nothing more?"

"Was there some sideshow that I missed?" I inquired in an innocent tone.

"Only that of a clergyman making a fool of himself," he hissed.

I had gone too far in my performance. I took his hand contritely. "Indeed, a fool who delivered the Word of God directly to the people's ears."

His anger subsided. "A noble fool, then?"

I nodded. "The best kind."

"Jane," St. John said warily, "what would I do if you were not here to puncture my pride and lower me down to earth, where I belong?" He looked down at my hand, which was still laid atop his. I removed it self-consciously.

"Why, you would carry on precisely as you do, St. John."

"To my detriment, no doubt, without your waspish wit to sting me into good sense." There was an edge of bitterness to his voice, but he had recovered his equanimity and was able to turn to his meal with appetite. I recalled how I was once able to manage Mr. Rochester's mercurial moods in much the same way. That I could provoke and soothe two such different men unsettled me.

Oh, for a Jane of my own to do unto me what I did for others!

As St. John offered neither criticism nor praise in regard to my school, it was left to me to judge the success of my endeavors. This I was able to measure at the end of a month through my pupils' docile manners and increasing desire to please, which in turn resulted in a slow but steady progression of achievement. Luella's manners were now decidedly more subdued, and her compositions were passable, if still mediocre. Mary was coming along with her sums, the other pair of sisters were picking up French, and Molly, the Eurasian girl, was working her way through an elementary primer. I had come to learn that Molly was an orphan: the offspring of a British official of the East India Company and his Hindu housekeeper, who had died giving birth to the child. The official, against the advice of his peers, had adopted Molly and cared for her as his own until his death from dysentery shortly thereafter. She was now apparently under the care of the official's spinster sister. This situation compelled my sympathy, but what drew me to her was her hunger for learning, for books and stories. I saw myself in these noble desires, and I supplied her as much as I could from our limited library. In return, she rewarded me with her diligence, as well as small gifts of shiny pebbles and colorful feathers. These were moments of connection amid an existence without sure mooring for the girl: Both the native community and the Anglo one appeared to shun Molly, a situation reflected in the debased behavior of her schoolroom peers. Had I not suspected that spreading a protective wing over her would make things worse rather than better for the girl, I would have taken up arms against her tormentors. As it was, I resolved to nurture my bond with her in the invisible realm of my soul.

Molly was a source of light in the mornings, but in that first month I felt adrift after the schoolroom closed at noon. I worked a bit in the garden and kept up my study of Hindustani, now supplemented with Punjabi. Though the hours and days passed, I felt a growing dissatisfaction that I could not name. The initial shock of a new location had settled by now, and a grinding dreariness set in that reminded me of my days at Lowood. Indeed, my environment had changed, yet my life had not: I was as lonely and restless as ever. And so I was hardly surprised when my mind reached out with a mind of its own toward new horizons. These tendencies had been lately accelerating, and one day my mind slipped—or did it leap, rather?—in the strangest way. One moment I was standing in the garden under the tamarind tree, and the next I was peering out at a busy road streaming with people and unimaginable moving vehicles of all kinds. All of it was in motion except for me: I was the still one witnessing from the confines of a narrow room or hut this current of life that was so close yet so far away. Extraordinary—I felt in that strange place a mix of vigilance and longing. But in an eyeblink I was back in the garden, where all was quiet and still; there was barely enough breeze to lift a leaf, and only a faint buzz that could be insects or the hum of traffic on a road heard from afar.

Perhaps the interior of my mind had expanded so strangely because amid my loneliness, it was not society that I wanted, but some purpose. I did not seek out the company of the other English women in the village, nor, after I had politely returned some early calls, did they seek out mine. Instead, I found myself curious about the native women, or rather, about their absence. St. John had explained the situation thus: "The women of this country are kept in a state of what is called purdah, meaning 'behind curtains,' veiled from the eyes of all except their own family. This is achieved by sequestering them. You will see they dwell in zenanas, interior chambers of their homes designated only for them. No man outside the family may look upon them, much less violate that sacred space." Fleetingly I felt a shudder of recognition in St. John's description of a confined and sheltered life, which I shook off at once. Was not the notion of an English purdah anathema to our civilizing mandate? I wondered what such chambers held, how the women there lived and passed their days. Were they entombed, or did they enjoy unique privileges of a protected community: Was it a prison or a sanctuary?

My curiosity would not go long unsatisfied, it seemed. St. John informed me that along with the head missionary we had been invited to dine at the home of the high-class Brahmin whose society Reverend M had labored to cultivate for some time. Captain P and his wife were also invited. While I could have done without these additional guests, such an invitation, I surmised, was rare, and I felt honored.

On our tour of the beautiful house that evening, we were at last brought to the courtyard at its center, lit with lanterns and thrumming with nocturnal insects. It was a veritable Eden. "This is indeed an honor, to be shown a glimpse of the quarters enjoyed by the women of your home," St. John said earnestly.

The Brahmin beamed and rubbed his hands gratefully. "It must not be thought that we are barbarians and that we keep our women captives in dungeons! You see, there is air and light and space!" Indeed there were, but where, I wondered, were the women themselves?

As the Brahmin ushered his dinner guests back to the main part of the mansion, I lingered in the rear, reluctant to leave the courtyard just yet. I had a blessed moment alone and turned slowly around, wondering at the stillness . . . but was I alone? There was a whisper, or was it the wind? That was most decidedly a giggle, far off yet nearby, like water bubbling over stones. Though I saw no one, I suddenly felt the weight of many eyes upon me. And though I felt my feet still standing on the cool stone of the courtyard, I was in a flash back at Thornfield, that feeling of a watching presence, of a life lived parallel to mine yet invisible to me: That woman, poor soul, the wife, haunting the attic rooms. I shuddered and hurried after the others.

That night those unseen eyes invaded my sleep. Perhaps they had spied upon our dinner and found nothing of interest about the stilted conversation or the endless streams of dishes, many of them prepared by Mrs. P's Calcutta-trained cook, whom she had insisted upon loaning to the Brahmin for the occasion despite his own ample staff. Thus thwarted, those eyes might have followed us home hoping for more substantive fare within my dreams. They floated in an ethereal space, older eyes with lines radiating from the corners; younger eyes bright and eager; brown eyes; ones flecked with green and blue; wide eyes fringed with the longest, darkest lashes. Eyes that looked haunted, lost, staring grimly at the blank walls of the attic, swiveling suddenly to fix me with a sharp stare. Again, was I still in Amritsar, or had I been spirited back to Thornfield? Those dark eyes, oh how they laughed at my confusion, softened, sparkled.

No, not Thornfield. Tea shared on the ship's main deck; the sea. They suddenly turned into Madeleine's eyes. Those were hers. They looked right at me even though I could not pinpoint my body in my dream—I was just there. Those eyes looked so deeply into my own that the gaze penetrated my soul and I woke gasping.

My face, I found, was drenched in tears.

The next day St. John said goodbye and laid a formal spousal peck upon my forehead before he mounted his horse and, accompanied only by a single servant, set off to undertake a missionary tour of the nearby villages to propagate the gospel. Reverend M had approved the trip and seemed pleased at the prospect of seeing his rival's back, if only for a month. Watching that tall, straight back grow smaller as it proceeded down the dusty road, I thought of biblical figures who had trod before him into the wilderness, protected only by their faith. I would miss him, I realized. We were like jail mates who had through enforced familiarity come to rely upon the presence of the other. Perhaps all marriages were thus. As for love, I did not allow myself to consider that. Where I was concerned, he maintained a steadfast aloofness, although I sometimes felt as if I were under close surveillance. It was an exhausting dance that we did around each other, and I should have celebrated the respite offered by his absence. Instead of peace, however, I felt strangely exposed. Though unafraid to be alone, I had unknowingly come to shelter within his strength. Another man might fill a room with his presence (I thought of Edward), but St. John would bear the weight of it upon his shoulders; he was the unyielding column: the ceiling and the support. I braced myself for the coming days of solitude.

It was not to be. Two days after St. John's departure, Reverend M flew to the bungalow in a flustered state. "You would not guess, Mrs. Rivers, what an opportunity has been laid before us!" I waited for Reverend M to settle himself. Whatever news he bore would release itself in good time, and it did so after two cups of tea and a few imported biscuits. "You have been requested!" he exclaimed. "Your presence has been requested by that good Brahmin to attend his wives!"

I surely disappointed him with my puzzled response: "Why, whatever for?"

"For?"

"I'm hardly in a position to proselytize them."

"Oh, no, no, no, Mrs. Rivers. I agree with you there!"

"So I am to . . . ?"

"You shall teach them needlework!"

I stood nervously at the threshold of a doorway opening into a dimly lit room, where the servant had left me. This was the zenana where the women of the household lived. There was a stillness, a waiting that I sensed from within. I was tempted to bolt. What lurked there? What could be fearful about a roomful of women? This was a privilege, I reminded myself. No men outside the family had ever set eyes upon these women. And what would I say to them? I clutched my bag of silk threads and wooden hoops. I took a deep breath and stepped forward.

Nothing. Silence. Then I felt the weight of unseen eyes again, the ones from my dreams. A rustling of robes, and then a figure emerged from a shadowy corner, and then another. From all around me now, disembodied eyes floated toward me until I discerned that the darkness of their robes covering every part of their bodies but their eyes and blending with the darkness of the ill-lit room was what made those eyes appear to levitate and move of their own accord. A hush; a sigh; suppressed, nervous, excited giggles. "Memsahib, welcome."

"Welcome."

"Welcome." The greetings echoed softly, brushing against me like curious fingers. No, those were real fingers on my skirt, my hair. I resisted the impulse to bat them away like they were nettlesome insects.

A hand gently took my own and led me farther into the room. As my eyes adjusted to the dimness, I discerned about a dozen robed domes gathered around me. As the only unrobed figure in the room, I felt quite exposed. I imagined myself shrouded as they were, my individuality instantly obscured beneath a sheet of fabric, leaving only the orbs of the eyes open to a small part of the world. I began to feel suffocated and faint, as if I were entombed. My mind jumped: Madeleine's image of people as living coffins. My breath came forth faster and faster now, until I was almost panting.

"She is going to faint!" I heard in soft Urdu. "Give her room. She must have air." The voice that spoke was youthful, but clear and commanding. Instantly, a space opened around me, and the owner of the voice, attached to a set of dark-honey eyes, bade me, in passable English, to sit upon the seat that was brought forth from some part of the house. It appeared that chairs were not part of the furnishings of this room, which was set about with cushions and pillows. A cup of tea was pressed into my hands. "We were told that the memsahib likes tea. Please drink!"

The drink did revive me, and I was able to regain my composure. "Thank you for your kindness," I said to the honey-colored eyes. They smiled back upon me, and it was a wonder that I could perceive that they did so, having only a subtle narrowing and glimmering of the irids to indicate a hint of expression. Remarkable. She was quite young, I guessed, perhaps sixteen. "What is your name?" I asked her.

"I am Abha."

"You are the sahib's daughter?"

"I am his youngest wife," she said demurely. "It is not my right to address you so directly, but I am the only one who knows a bit of English. And the others are too bashful as well."

"So you are also the most courageous?"

The eyes twinkled. "I am the most curious. It was I who persuaded the sahib to have you attend us and to teach us needlework and . . . perhaps more."

"How do you know English?"

"My father learned from a previous missionary. He taught me a bit when I begged him to. Before I was married." Her voice dropped into an almost inaudible sigh at the end of her sentence. The limits placed on Abha went beyond the end of English lessons, I was acutely aware.

"If you like," I offered hesitantly, "I could teach you more English."

The glow that lit up her eyes told me the answer.

"As you wish, Miss Sahib! As you wish! For as you teach us the fine needlework, if it is your desire to converse with us from time to time in your own tongue, who are we to say otherwise?"

I caught at her meaning: Lessons might proceed if I undertook them discreetly. But in truth I saw that this young wife had orchestrated the whole thing despite my perception of her as powerless. Here I was, summoned, deputized, tasked in the most subtle, charming, and efficient manner possible! I smiled despite my misgivings. It was not my wish to deceive the Brahmin or Reverend M about my activities here, but as Abha had indicated, who could object if I conversed in my own tongue from time to time, and if linguistic knowledge was gained from such exchange, then English language lessons were thrust upon the continent by the English simply opening their mouths.

After that first visit, I was only able to sleep just as dawn broke. I turned over in my mind that mysterious atmosphere of lives lived in the shadowy interiors of the house. Abha had assured me that they did not keep their faces covered when alone, that it was in deference to my presence. Nor were sunlight and air forbidden, as the Brahmin had said. Their lives did not seem strange to them; it was mine that bewildered them: that a woman of my status could roam at will, allowing anyone to look upon her face. It was humbling to see myself as an object of pity as well as curiosity.

Thus did I justify my now-daily zenana visits, which I began to look forward to in the late afternoons, past four o'clock, as the day was cooling. A carriage arrived at the door of the bungalow, and I was driven to the Brahmin's house, where I entered the zenana quarters from a back door. My new pupils were fascinated with the needlework and picked it up quickly. They were curious about the details of my dress, and I allowed them to examine its buttons, my breast pin, my cuffs, and all the details of my European costume. They asked how old I was and wanted to know if I had children. When I said no, growing a little self-conscious, they appeared amazed and saddened for me. I quickly learned their names: Parvati, Leyshya, Maahi, Shanti. Nor would I allow them to call me St. John Rivers sahib, but I told them to use Jane. I came to know each from her height, the color of her eyes, her way of holding herself, her voice. Gradually I even grasped the quality of each of their minds as a tangible thing. My initial view of the purdah as an object of oppression was revised as I considered what it would mean to be judged purely on my mind and wits rather than my looks, never to be called plain and dismissed on that account. And how soothing, this society of women, supporting each other rather than competing for men's attention, though I was only seeing one aspect of it, I supposed.

Abha's lively spirit drew me above all else, however, and in turn she put her entire attention upon me. It was a wonder to see her take charge of my visits, with even the most senior matron deferring to her. Abha was a quick learner, and her questions were different from the others'. Above all, she was intrigued with the missionary's work. She had many questions about God. She wanted to know why it was necessary for missionaries to spread God's word. Why did God not make us all Christians, and why does God not use His power and convert the whole world at once, so that there need be no leaving of one's loved ones to confess to Him? I had no ready answer to that and sorely missed St. John's guidance. The only thing I could think to say was how more blessed was he who found God rather than he who was born into a home that already knew Him. That it was like being starved, and not knowing it, then coming upon sustenance. That was an unsatisfactory metaphor. I tried again.

"It is like being in love."

This comparison, too, puzzled her. "What does it feel like to be in love?"

I blushed, then tried to steer the ship along surer channels. "A husband is one's earthly mate and partner. But God is the eternal light that takes one into Himself." I carefully described God's great plan of salvation, if she would only believe in Him and give her heart fully to Him.

"God sees all of me and loves me?"

I nodded at the simple yet fully adequate summary. For did He not see beyond the plainness of my exterior? Did our souls not forge a unity, a world of its own? Did I not fully understand His suffering and forgive and love Him for his weaknesses? But who now was I thinking of—God did not have weaknesses. My mind faltered; my heart stuttered. A hand pressed against my own and brought me back to my senses. "Love seems . . . painful."

Indeed it was. Her lovely eyes held a look of wonder, I thought. I quickly brought our visit to an end, unable to sit any longer with my own thoughts in that setting.

A most astounding moment came three weeks later, our daily exchanges having grown into a kind of intimacy. My cherished pupil must have felt the same desire I did: to reach across the expanse of difference. For that day I entered the courtyard and found a beautiful woman sitting in a chair set beside my own. I gasped. It was Abha. She was radiant. Her face was extraordinary: a perfect oval, high cheekbones, dark-honey eyes, elegant arched brows. She kept her hair covered. "Today we will speak face to face, my friend," she said with a brilliant smile. "Let us speak more of God and of love."

She seemed to glow with an inner light. I smiled back faintly. For I was suddenly afraid for her. She was in search of something. And unwittingly I had given it to her in the course of our "lessons." I was astounded at Abha's progress merely through conversing with me. She seemed to do best just listening and absorbing the cadences of my speech, punctuated with her intelligent and lively questions. ("Is your God not really our God but called by a different name? Is it right to change the religion one was born into?") God offered her a vista, an opening, an escape. *If she finds God,* I fervently prayed, *let Him soothe her restless soul, guide her to make peace with her life as she finds it.* Let a new and larger world expand within her that will lead her to His world in heaven when the time comes.

The next day, the carriage that customarily transported me to the Brahmin's house failed to come; I waited until the late-afternoon sun dipped to the horizon. And the following morning, no pupils came to the school. I found myself idly turning the pages of an illustrated book about birds that I had just that morning found at the bottom of my trunk. It was a book I used to pore over as a girl when inclement weather deprived me and my cousins of our daily walk. I had meant to loan it to Molly, had she come. I could picture her poring over the pages as I had once done. Yet the schoolroom remained empty all week as I sat there each morning among the books, papers, pens, and ink, hoping to see a small face at the back door peeking in. An air of unrest seemed to permeate the entire village. Finally, one evening a commission that included the captain, Reverend M, and the village magistrate arrived at the bungalow. They came to inform me that I was to cease my zenana visits, that the school had been permanently shut down, and that I was to appear before the durbar the next day.

There was no opportunity for me to decline the commission's request: A carriage arrived the next morning at the bungalow to convey me to court. The room I entered was semidarkened by drawn blinds despite the sun's rays already lighting up and heating the day. I could make out three people seated behind a long table: Reverend M, the captain, and the village magistrate were all there. An official placed a seat in the middle of the room, facing the table, and bade me to sit. I could not help feeling I was on trial.

The village magistrate, a thin, gray-faced official, tried to reassure me. "Ahem, Mrs. Rivers, we would like to ask you a few questions."

I nodded, waiting. Reverend M tugged nervously on his clerical collar. The others looked upon the proceedings with stern, impassive expressions upon their faces.

"Did you go to the home of an esteemed Brahmin to attend his wives there?"

"I did so at the request of Reverend M."

"What was your purpose in undertaking such visits?"

"It was my understanding that I was to teach his wives needlepoint in their quarters."

"What else did you do besides teach them needlework?"

"Nothing. We conversed a bit."

"Did you converse with all of them?"

"I principally spoke with his youngest wife, for she knew a little English." My heart was starting to skip along faster by now, and I was careful in my reply to say nothing of English lessons.

"And what did you speak with her about?"

"She had questions about my life and our ways. She was curious."

"And how did you answer her questions?"

"As truthfully as I could. It is not my wont to deceive or lie."

"Did you ever converse about religion, Mrs. Rivers?"

"Yes," I said slowly, "when the subject came up."

"Did the subject come up frequently?"

"She had many questions about God and about a missionary's work. I tried to answer them as truthfully as possible."

The village magistrate leaned forward, his sallow face set in a frown. "Did you ever urge her to give up her own religion and to forsake her own family and people?"

My heart thundered. Had it come to that? My earlier fears had been justified, it seemed. What had Abha done?

"I did not, and I would never urge anyone to do a thing of such monumental consequence and disruption. I merely told her about God's abundant love for all should anyone choose to take Him to his heart. How she heard and understood that, and how she chose to act upon it, was her decision and her choice alone."

"Have you been trained to do missionary work, Mrs. Rivers?"

"No," I said. "Nor was I proselytizing, if that is what you are asking."

"It seems, however, that you have made a convert. The first one in this village, I believe."

The information that followed entered my mind as a series of flickering images: Abha on her knees before her husband, espousing the cause of her Lord Jesus Christ; the Brahmin, in fury, dragging Abha to an isolated room and bolting the door; the other wives gathering and scattering like frightened birds; this world that had briefly been my home now shredded and coming apart at the seams. Soon I was no longer listening. My head spun and my heart was wrung for Abha's sake and her fate.

"This is not a trial, Mrs. Rivers. You have committed no crimes. We have called you here merely to review the facts. But we believe a serious breach of judgment has occurred, with resulting harm to the elites of this community. We must therefore charge you to cease all contact with any of the native women in this village."

"Am I then to choose between staying and abandoning my work, and exiling myself from this place?" I found myself asking.

"The choice is not yours."

A movement stirred from within a shadowy corner.

"It is for your husband to decide."

St. John stepped into the light, with grace and fury, an avenging angel. He took a place behind my chair so that I could not see his perfect face. I bowed my neck, ready for the blow of his mighty sword.

"She will go."

His words smote my heart. They left me numbed and reeling. I tried to think only of each breath, to stay in the moment for as long as possible, for I could not begin to think of the moments that would follow this one, of where I would go, what I would do.

"For you do not deserve her presence here."

A chill filled the room. The silence thickened.

"Nor will I stay. Trapped as you all are in your small-minded ways, terrified rather than joyous at your first convert, you will never reach these people, and you will never hold this mighty country. They will overthrow you in your ignorant pride."

St. John took my hand and led me out the door.

We were silent all the way back to our bungalow. Once there, I barely managed to take a seat before my knees gave up the weight they supported. "St. John, what have you done? I will leave! You must carry on your work here, where you have done so much good!"

"Carry on without you, Jane? I think not."

He began pacing.

"Why did you marry me, St. John? I have not been a help at all, merely a hindrance. Why did you not marry a woman who truly believes in good works, as you do?"

"It is true that you did not come to India with the intention in your heart to do God's work." He paused his pacing to stand before me. "But you do so now with all your heart."

To my astonishment he sank to his knees before me. I was so surprised I could only gape wordlessly for a moment before springing to my feet and bidding him to rise as well with panicked entreaties. His face shone with breathless triumph.

"You have surpassed my expectations, Jane!"

"Indeed, I have done no such thing, St. John," I gasped. "I have merely carried on."

"I watched you. I did nothing to help you in your struggles, though I saw you had them. At times I even threw obstacles in your way. And yet you persevered; indeed, you thrived. You are revealed to yourself as one of God's chosen ones!"

Words eluded me. Was it true? Did I truly have the power to help or save anyone, much less myself? Was Abha helped at all by my work? And what was that work? Had it remained hidden, perhaps she would not have been in this predicament. What right did I have to disrupt her world so? I was not a missionary, nor had I ever wanted to be; I only wanted to answer her questions as honestly as I knew how. That had felt like my work.

Desperately, I clung to my doubt. "But St. John, we are banished from here."

He rose to his feet and went to the window that looked out toward the mountains. "This place?" he scoffed. "It is but a way station." He beckoned toward those distant, mighty heights. "We must go forward and build more way stations, each one an outpost."

In my mind I saw a pathway of tiny lights bravely holding back the darkness, each one a small beacon in a great wilderness. Each one so fragile, but for a lost traveler, offering hope, lighting the way forward.

St. John's voice had become soaring, otherworldly, ringing the air, backed by a choir of angels, muting my doubts. "We will build churches, schools, orphanages! Where I cannot reach, you will enter. You will do zenana work and help build Indian female normal schools. Men and women, brothers and sisters, will be brought to the church. And we will go farther, Jane! Over that great mountain, across the plains, to the heart of China itself, where multitudes await. Together, we will be the torchbearers. With you by my side, I will light the way to all of Asia!"

The pathway of tiny lights flashed back, at once more brilliant and more uncertain in its destination. And I wondered: How far would the road to glory go? Would it take me to a place where I could lay down my pack by the door, leaving it there, for I need never take it up again, a place where the door is open, where it is always open, and I call out softly as I enter, *I am home*, then louder, urgently, as I dash through the rooms, *I am home, I am home*, as I fall at last into the arms of the lover waiting there.

Chapter Four

Rangoon, Burma, 1852

In the end, we did not penetrate the Himalayas; we did not set out on a path to conquer China for God's kingdom. A letter from the bishop on the eve of our departure sent us marching back to Calcutta, where St. John received his appointment to a missionary station of his own in Burma. For a time he struggled quietly with his disappointment, but in the end he vanquished it. "All roads lead to heaven," he said with only a hint of bitterness. "We will get there one way or another."

We arrived at the harbor of Rangoon in June, two months after war had broken out there. Though all major campaigns were on pause, this was a period of simmering unrest—in the city and within myself. I had kept thoughts of Abha at bay during the return trip to Calcutta. Now she haunted my sleep, and I fretted about her, imagined her entombed in darkness forever. Yet in my dreams it was I who was buried alive. We became one, a single soul scrabbling against the compressing walls. I fought and struggled, and her words—*What does it feel like to be in love?*—echoed through my head until I woke up sobbing.

St. John and I, on the other hand, were most definitely not one. We did not even touch. At night in our bungalow, we lay side by side, and I tried to hide my distress. If he ever suspected me, he never said, never woke. By day he was kind. He would bring me a shawl for the cooler evenings, and made sure I had my umbrella when I went out. He read to me, and when his coughing troubled him, I read to him. There was a tenderness in these moments that even now, when I think back on them, soothes a lingering ache in my heart.

At this time, we encountered the Reverend Jeremiah Anchor, who, as a testament perhaps to his name, had managed to secure a small following of English and Scottish expatriates, though not yet any native converts in a country impermeable to Christian evangelism—though not for lack of trying. We had heard colorful stories of this American Baptist missionary when we disembarked in Lower Burma. It was rumored that he went about in the garb of a Buddhist priest, that he spoke Burmese fluently and proselytized in that tongue from a bamboo-and-thatch *zayat*, as the traditional meeting places for Burmese men were called. He had built one for himself by the roadside and cried out to all who thirsted for knowledge to enter.

Propelled by curiosity, at our first opportunity, we betook ourselves to hear the American missionary preach at the fledgling Baptist church in Rangoon. It was a modest space lined with a few benches, with a small podium at one end where the reverend stood, to my disappointment, in the normal garb of a cleric. There were only a few other worshippers present that day, mostly the wives and daughters of Scottish timber merchants.

The American missionary was disappointingly normal. St. John was a man of austere masculine beauty and Edward a dark, brooding troll, beautiful only to me. Reverend Jeremiah Anchor was neither. One could pass him on the street without a second look, so ordinary was he. Of middling height, neither tall nor short; he was not plain, like me, nor was he exceptionally beautiful or ugly. His features were even and not unpleasing: sandy hair, hazel eyes, pale complexion. Altogether forgettable. Until he smiled. One moment, there was a blank slate; the next, a curve of the lips transformed his whole mien, as if a brazier lit within had thrown out a radiant light. Reverend Jeremiah Anchor smiled upon the entire small congregation, yet one felt that the smile was meant for *you* alone. And then he spoke.

"Brothers and sisters, let us pray. And let us pray first of all for love"—it was not till the end that I vaguely realized that he had not mentioned God once—"love of a warm hand, a smile of understanding. Have you felt alone; have you struggled; have you had your heart torn in two; have you cried in the dark; have you cried out *to* the dark: 'Will it be like this forever?'" I felt a prickle at the corners of my eyes, a tear threatened to slide down my cheek, and while some part of me resisted his words, another part was drawn to them as a moth to a flame. "Have you been desolate; have you wondered how you can go on and what you go on for? Have you wondered whether anyone can see your pain or whether you are a walking coffin"—here, I startled—"enduring a living death as you go about your business, numb—the only way you can get through your day? And what kind of life is that? You are waiting, waiting for that someone, anyone who will see you. One who will take your hand. One whose touch will be gentle and warm. One whose embrace and love will envelop your entire body and soul. It will feel like a lover, like a homecoming; it will cry: 'Where have you been, and I have found you at last and I will never let you go, for you are mine and I am yours, forever and ever.'" Quite a few people, women mostly, were openly sobbing. But even some of the gentlemen dabbed discreetly at the corners of their eyes. "Come home then, come, I say! For *he* is waiting." I heard it with the small *h*, and, sinfully, a picture of Edward sprang to mind. "Waiting! And if you are not ready or able to return yet, still yet will he wait, heart open, arms wide. Be you ever so plain to those who can but see the vain material world, know that he sees you as the bridegroom sees his bride. Come, beloved, come to me."

I was no longer myself. I was only that sense of waiting. Yearning. Yearning could not erect buildings, forge towers, shape cities. But it had the power to set one's feet upon a path, to move one forward for however long and by whatever means so long as one could at the end of the journey lay one's head against a warm chest, ear pressed near a beating heart that whispered to one's weary, beaten soul, *You are here at last, my love, you are here.*

The missionary circle being small, it was only a matter of time before we met Reverend Jeremiah Anchor in person. And of course, he had seen us at his sermon. We had only attended the one, but the reverend's powers of observation and memory were keen. It was he who sought out St. John, and the two had agreed to read Burmese together. On this they both wholeheartedly agreed: that the key to the native's heart was through his own language. Indeed, as they spent more time together, St. John found more to approve of in the reverend. "He lacks proportion, his idealism will be his undoing, he is undoubtedly a sentimentalist, impractical in the extreme" was St. John's judgment. "And yet I like the man." Though, his methods were wrong, St. John insisted, "wrong, and they will bear no fruit, I daresay. It is one thing to wander into the wilderness a songbird, attracting the wild things with notes of charm. Imagine, Jane, he thinks it's a matter of saying: 'I'm going—will you come too?' And to *anyone* who will listen. No thought of a community and the leaders needed to move a people. The moment he stops chattering, the crowds will disperse like chaff in the wind. It is quite another thing to lay the groundwork, build an enduring structure of worship, something that will last beyond our mere personalities and presence."

I did not tell St. John how rather comforting the former scenario was, how free and open it felt, that his own vision of solid structures of worship made me think of cages. I reveled in the contradiction of the American missionary's name: Anchor—an object of immobility, yet his words inspired images of a ship with all its sails unfurled, harnessing the wind to speed across the ocean. I nodded my agreement at St. John, but I did not think that Reverend Jeremiah Anchor was harmless. He was dangerous. Because I knew that, I took him seriously from the start, and as a result, though I was moved, I was not seduced. St. John, on the other hand, condescended to him but quite immediately fell in love. A week after he read Burmese with Reverend Jeremiah Anchor, that name seemed to crop up in every other sentence uttered from St. John's lips. Granted, it was usually to condemn him for a fool, but it was always followed, I noticed, by an indulgent smile.

My own days were unorganized, and in the mornings, if it wasn't raining yet, I often walked about the city, wandering aimlessly. I was never molested by the Burmese or the Buddhist monks, though the children would sometimes follow me out of curiosity, always at a safe distance. The heat eventually drove me back to what I thought of as our headquarters: Our living space felt more like a barrack than a home as patrols of militia maintained the business of keeping the city pacified. The mood of Rangoon felt like the swollen clouds. There was an air of suspension, of waiting, that made the English soldiers uneasy and sharp in their dealings with the people. I quavered at the thought of us finding ourselves in the midst of an outright rebellion and renewal of fighting, though St. John did not think that would happen. "There is some murmur of it, but not to worry," he assured me. "The Burmese court has been well ground under the heel of the British."

We were to stay in Rangoon until the rainy season ended, then head south. Reverend Jeremiah Anchor, who had just returned from the south, was sojourning in Lower Burma but planned to return as well. Our paths, it seemed, were inevitably converging.

One night St. John brought the reverend home to dine with us. I had steeled myself for this meeting, having avoided and deferred and delayed it, finding numerous excuses, including St. John's own health, which was poor at the moment, he having never fully recovered from the cough that had beset him upon our return from Amritsar. But I could postpone no more; indeed, St. John was starting to give me quizzical looks. Now my guard was up. He could storm against my fortresses, but they had been fortified by a determination to turn aside the penetrating gaze, the lingering handshake, and the seductive smile. I was prepared, I say.

So when none of it came, I was disarmed. His smile was warm and mild. The handshake was indeed held on his part for a fraction of a second beyond my readiness to release it, but it was perfectly within the boundaries of the seemly and the discreet. "You have a most delightful and orderly home," he remarked politely. I thanked him for the kind observation. "I hope you've found the weather amenable." I conceded that I had, and I wondered if the rest of the evening's conversation would proceed in this bland and conventional vein. "How is Burma to your liking?" he asked. If I told him that I found Burma to be a seething hotbed of repressed resentments and fear, would he take me seriously? I told him it was a charming country. The reverend eyed me sharply at that, as if he were taking my measure. It looked like he might say something more, but instead, he smiled enigmatically and did not press me further in the end. This was not the vapid cleric, after all; but nor was it the romantic saint. I was relieved, but dare I say, let down as well?

I was silent during most of the meal as St. John and Reverend Jeremiah Anchor argued in a passionate but friendly way about the merits of institution building as opposed to proselytizing from the ground up. For Reverend Jeremiah Anchor, even the zenana was too privileged: He would storm every soul where it stood. It was clear to me that despite their differences in views, the two regarded each other with much respect and even fondness; that a friendship had sprung up—that rare kind forged on difference, in temperament, outlook, disposition, rather than similarity. It was St. John's coolness in contrast with Reverend Jeremiah's warmth; the intellect against the heart.

Over coffee, I sank a little deeper into the shadows. I was content to bask quietly in their company and hoped for more days together before our inevitable separation. I was not prepared for the reverend's question.

"And you, Mrs. Rivers, what is your heart's work?"

I startled from my reveries and pardoned myself hastily for my inattention. "I am content to follow St. John and make a home for him in whatever way I can," I murmured.

St. John frowned. Reverend Jeremiah Anchor leaned a bit closer. I braced myself for the onslaught of suggestions of good works I could be doing for Him rather than just him. For weeks now, St. John had been urging me to set up another school, to visit Burmese women in their homes, to set up socials and teas. And each time I had demurred. Each time I had thought of Abha, of her fate and my role in it.

Already I had started to feel weary, and selfish, and unwilling to say what I truly felt: Who is anyone to tell another what to believe, whom to love, how to live and why? I bowed my head. I waited. After a moment or so of silence, I looked up. Greenish-hazel eyes gazed upon me evenly. A warm smile beamed beneath those clear, mild orbs. His words, too, when he saw he had my attention, were gentle and mild. "It is well," he said, "very well to attend to what is near at hand, to do so with all one's capacity and all one's heart and mind, and soul." His smile broadened. Light played in those green irids, like a meadow warming beneath a ray of sun breaking through a bank of clouds. I thought of Saint Francis as he walked in the fields listening to the birds, who, in their love for his gentle ways and the crumbs left for them, followed. The meadow in my mind then blossomed with small white flowers and hovering bees, and the springy grass beneath my feet tickled my back when I lay down and watched the birds wheeling in the clear blue sky above. The simple beauty of life opened before me.

All this I somehow saw as the vivid green eyes smiled at me.

St. John shook his head as he shut the door upon our departing guest. He did not need to speak, for I could perfectly interpret his judgment from his stiff back and repressed sigh: poor fool. For a fleeting moment I wondered: Did he mean me?

Yet some fools could be indulged. The Reverend Jeremiah Anchor was such a one. St. John continued to meet with him to study Burmese grammar, discuss the political situation, argue about the best way to reach converts—whether to lay the foundations for a mighty house or to wander free and storm every soul where it stood, whomever one found along the path. I did not see much of the reverend. St. John continued the work in his mission station, and I settled as best I could into my own work, which was seeing to our small household, writing letters to Diana and Mary, reading fitfully when the sun and heat kept me indoors and under the shifting punkah. And brewing the pungent tea that St. John drank to soothe his cough. The dusty, brooding city did not have much else to offer.

On one occasion, driven by restlessness, I ventured to deliver a basket of mangoes to the monks who lived along the edge of the river. I had heard, too, that Reverend Jeremiah sometimes preached near there. Though there was a fledging church in Rangoon, he seemed to prefer a more itinerate approach, often preaching at open markets or near a mosque. Do not think that I sought an encounter. Indeed, I thought to avoid meeting him by coming at an hour of the day when he was likely to be preaching near a mosque on the far side of the town.

As I got closer to my destination, a sudden squall sent me rushing to the shelter of a *zayat*. This one was empty, and I took shelter just inside the open entryway, where I sought to while away the time until the rain stopped. It was common during this time of year for such moments of downpour to erupt and then just as suddenly to subside. I listened to the soft hiss of water and inhaled the damp, heavy air. There was water everywhere, yet within me, I felt calm, as if I were in my natural element. The eastern climate was one of extremes—water, heat, both at once—but I continued with the adaptive attitude I had cultivated in the solitude of the steamship's decks: The most helpful response was to accept what was offered, to adjust one's mind as much as one's body. It was what it was; we were the uninvited guests. Who were we to curse the heat? When I thought of the moors and raw fields of England now, it was not with a feeling of nostalgia and longing, but with a sense of having passed through a prior state: shedding one skin, or life, and taking up another, yet still in a raw, unformed state of becoming.

"Must home always be where we stop, plant, harvest, sow again, take possession? Can we not pass through, observing, greeting, inviting, but going forward always, toward a final resting place?" It was Reverend Jeremiah Anchor. How had he managed to suddenly appear beside me without my hearing his advance? The thought startled me. His bare head was dampened from the rain, and he held a covered basket in his arms.

I took hold of myself and turned to him. "To what end, sir? Do we not all long for a home of our own, to settle?"

"Life is the journey home. And when we arrive, we will settle for good." He smiled; I was in the meadow again. Bees hovered above my face, then darted off among the small white flowers floating in a sea of green. My back pressed against the cool ground. I was hidden by tall, swaying grassy stalks as I stared up at the birds circling in the cloudless sky. Then I blinked. How unsettling. Back to the damp heat and Reverend Jeremiah gazing meaningfully at me.

"So we must not make ourselves at home too soon?"

"Certainly not before our time," he said. "To move is to live."

I waited for him to say more, but now he was silent as we stood side by side. I held myself stiffly, aware of his nearness, erecting an invisible wall between us, which he shattered with a casual brush of his knuckles across the back of my hand as he turned a bit before the view. The touch was like a lit flame racing along an artery that led directly to my heart, which ignited and threatened to burst through my chest, so explosively did it hammer. I felt my cheeks flare with heat. My breath hitched. I tried to disguise my reaction with a demure cough. He laughed softly as he shifted the basket of provisions he carried, delivered, no doubt, by some helpful church lady whom he was just now trying to get away from. Confusion transmuted to anger. "Do you mock me, sir?"

"By no means," he said soberly, quietly. "There is no one I respect more, Mrs. Rivers. If I make you uncomfortable, I apologize profusely."

I said nothing, looking straight ahead. After a pause, he continued. "If I may ask you a question," he said gently. I hesitated, then nodded. "Why are you so afraid of influencing another person?"

My eyes shuttered. He had put his finger on it: my fear, my nightmares since we left Amritsar, my punishment and personal hell. *What have I done, what have I done to you, Abha?*

I saw her look back at me, dark eyes wide with compassion and concern. *You gave me a new thought, and it changed my world; is that so bad?*

I told her, *It is dangerous to fall out of our worlds.* Or was it myself I was talking to, I who was now rising in defiance against the smallness of my life and reaching for further horizons?

After a moment he spoke again: "Forgive me for saying so, but you react as if you're guilty of committing a crime."

My eyes remained closed, my face turned away from him, but I could feel tears pushing against the lids, finding a corner for a drop to leak out. Air rushed around my face. "If there is a story you need to tell, rest assured I will listen without judgment. If it will ease your heart to do so." That was all he said. It was enough. I nodded slowly.

"I can't tell it yet," I choked out. I felt him accepting that. The rain had stopped, and he offered to walk me home by way of the monks' dwelling. I demurred, but he walked alongside me nevertheless, and I found I was not averse to his company.

Not too far from my bungalow, an ugly scene unfolded before us: an officer beating a Burmese man, who cowered under the blows and groaned; the officer cursing when his cane finally broke against the man's back; the reverend watching beside me with an intensity that drew a scowl from the officer, who stalked off; then the reverend dropping his basket to run forward, kneeling beside the moaning man on the ground, speaking to him, helping him to his feet. The Burmese man kowtowed respectfully to the reverend before limping off. I caught his eye, then the reverend's. I didn't know what to make of what I had just witnessed but felt the weight of significance in their exchange.

"You were kind to offer him comfort." We were again walking side by side, mostly in silence. I wondered what St. John would have done. I knew he often preached the need for tolerance, but I did not think he would have stopped and spoken to the beaten Burmese man. The reverend nodded stiffly, and I noted the grim set of his mouth. A drizzle started to descend upon us. My curiosity finally overcame me. "What did you say to the unfortunate man?"

He stopped in his tracks and turned to me, compelling me to face him fully. His eyes were clear and penetrating. "I said nothing, Mrs. Rivers, that a human being would not, or should not, say to another in pain: That I am sorry. I see the pain and the injustice. And God sees it too."

My breath suspended. So simple. Yet enough. Why spend hours constructing a sermon when this was all one needed to say?

"And for this they follow you in the multitudes?"

He smiled. "I do not know about the multitudes following me, but who would not want to know that her troubles are witnessed, that she is not alone?"

I blushed and turned away. The *she* was strangely personal. "I assure you, if you are speaking beyond the general, that I am untroubled, nor in need of witnesses if I were not so."

We were now upon the porch of the converted barrack, our clothes streaming, when he stopped me before I could go in. His eyes danced. "Mrs. Rivers," he said, "excuse me for my impertinence, but your troubles are perhaps just beginning." He took my hand. "And I assure you that it will be my honor and privilege to be here to witness them." With a smile, he raised my hand to his lips, which were warm against my suddenly cold skin. Nor did he release it after pressing a soft kiss there. A second kiss, as light as the brush of a butterfly's wing, followed, alighting briefly upon the corner of my mouth. I felt my whole body seize up. When I breathed again, he had already turned and left.

I could have imagined it, I thought. But from the corner of my eye, I discerned a movement at the window and knew without seeing him that it is not a dream when another is able to witness it.

When I entered our residence, St. John was sitting in one of the cushioned cane chairs, absorbed in the printed columns of a local newspaper. He did not look up as I shook off my wet shawl and smoothed my damp hair. "You are home early," I said to him. "I hope nothing is amiss." He made no answer, so I made my way toward the bedroom to change. But before I had crossed the room, he lowered the paper and eyed me sardonically.

"Not *too* early, it seems."

I stopped and turned slowly to him. "I beg your pardon?"

"It is not too early in the day, it seems, for a tête-à-tête with the good reverend."

I blushed, and in my confusion I took refuge in indignity, for I, at least, had done nothing wrong! "If you mean Reverend Jeremiah Anchor, I met him when I was walking near the river and sheltered briefly at a *zayat* during the rain. It seems he had just returned from preaching nearby, and he kindly walked me home. That is all of our tête-à-tête."

St. John carefully folded his newspaper and laid it upon his knees. "Be careful, Jane. With the good Reverend Jeremiah Anchor, an innocent walk is never all that it appears."

"Whatever do you mean?" I flared. I had never seen St. John act jealous. I was baffled.

"The good reverend has a silver tongue, which he has lent to the Lord's service. But that is not all it has been used for." St. John paused.

I felt a hollow ringing in my ears that grew steadily louder as I contemplated his words. It was anger, I realized in time. I resolved to take a firm hold of it and push it down. But my voice quavered nevertheless when I replied: "Do you accuse him of being a seducer?"

He eyed me curiously. "Do you never wonder why, among our set, he has so many followers of the female persuasion? His sermons are love letters to hungry hearts."

I thought of the basket of provisions that the reverend had held in the *zayat*. And it occurred to me that St. John was jealous not of me, but of Reverend Jeremiah.

"I saw him speak kindly to a Burmese man who was beaten in the road by an officer," I said haughtily. "If to be a seducer is to treat everyone alike with decency and in doing so to earn their gratitude, then I suppose you could call him that."

"Any fool can be kind. Any fool can make another like him for being so. But the Lord does not need fools and charmers. What happens when such a one moves on? The world is left as it is, and there are no churches or schools or orphanages to shelter those who remain behind. That is the hard work, the real work. To leave behind something solid after we depart from this earth and return to our maker, not mere footprints that will fade and disappear forever."

I thought of his half-finished school, the subscriptions he had painstakingly gathered for an orphanage. These were indeed worthy and lasting legacies. Then before my eyes, the walls of whitewashed buildings cracked, the roofs caved in, and the buildings crumbled into dust swept away by a great wind. What *could* last? A building, a memory of a kindness? Could love be enshrined in mortar and brick and cement, or did it only thrive when set free? And why did my thoughts turn to love? I wondered wildly. What was *that* about? The world was filled with people. And yes, people needed homes and shelters. But people also needed kindness.

St. John had returned to his paper. Did I speak that out loud or merely think it? I hastened to bed.

A fortnight later, it was St. John himself who raised the specter of the reverend. "It seems, Jane, that your little admirer had better be very careful in his dealings of kindness toward the locals, for he is under suspicion of acting on their behalf to overthrow the governing class." A recent headline from St. John's newspaper appeared in my mind's eye: **Native Unrest Growing Under Sympathetic Eyes of Foreigners Will Not Be Tolerated.** It was an English press; of course there would be prejudice not only against the natives but also against Americans and Scots. I had recently become aware, too, of whispers in the back of the church; Burmese bystanders bunching in small, tight groups at the market; minor riots breaking out, then quickly dispersing before the red-coated soldiers arrived. The streets were tense, amplifying my own restlessness.

"How can they think that?" I demanded. "He is only preaching, like you." Really, I wanted to slap some sense into him, but the next moment he was racked with coughing, and I hurried instead to bring him a soothing cup of honey-laced tea. Lately, this had been happening more and more, and though I urged him to rest and decrease his activities, he took the opposite tack and drove himself so hard it alarmed me. It was as if he sensed that he was running out of time and feared to leave his work incomplete: The ghostly ruins of whitewashed buildings briefly rose and faded in my mind like a distant memory.

But his words alarmed me too. Should I warn Reverend Jeremiah? Did he know he was under watch? I took to walking past the vicinity of his *zayat*, hoping to encounter him again, but to no avail. Finally, some weeks later at the market, there was a commotion at one corner, and I found myself at the edge of a crowd listening to the fiery speech of the American curate. He stood upon a crate, bareheaded, oblivious to the heat; the language I did not understand, but his gestures, his expressions, I could read. He spoke *to* the gathering of Burmese people, not at them; they listened, at first in wonder, then with growing warmth.

Then there were shouts as red-coated soldiers approached, confusion as the crowd sought to disperse.

Within that confusion, Reverend Jeremiah Anchor caught my eye and hurried to me. "Jane, I thought that was you at the edge of the crowd. But we must leave at once," he said hastily. He took me by the elbow and led me down an alley.

"Reverend," I said breathlessly, "I have heard, and you must have, too, that the authorities suspect you of organizing an insurrection!"

He laughed unconcernedly. "Disagreement is always seen as insurrection from some quarters," he said.

"But you must be careful. You must lie low, or you must move on." I unexpectedly felt my heart give a little lurch as I said that. It caused me to stumble, and the reverend came to a stop to steady me, and in so doing, looked me full in the face.

"You think I should go?"

"For your own safety, you must!"

He searched my face. "Would you come with me?"

For a moment, I thought I had misheard him. "What are you asking?" I finally stuttered. "I am married; are you suggesting that I abandon my husband, my duties?"

"That is of no consequence."

I was stunned. Did he love me?

"Your duty, your real duty, is to follow your heart," he said.

It was thrilling, a reality of lawlessness and disregard glimpsed. Did I love him?

"What would happen if I came with you?"

"We would go forth, side by side, spreading love, God's love, moving onward."

St. John had wanted to forge onward as well, across the Himalayas, into the heart of China. But his dream was not to do so as a will-o'-the-wisp, merely passing through. He wanted to leave cities behind him and to lay a road before him. Opposing this, the principle that organized Anchor's life: to inspire and to move on. In truth I did not entirely agree with this approach. But just now the choice seemed stark: permanence or a sea of possibilities, the monument or the journey, the latter possibly without end.

"You must be careful," I said again. He looked surprised, as if his charm had never been thwarted before, or perhaps I only imagined that. I took my leave and hurried the rest of the way home on my own.

All that week trepidation pulsed in my chest even as the unrest increased in the streets. At the end of the week St. John confirmed what I had hoped would not happen: The reverend had been arrested. "I fear it will turn ugly," St. John said when he told me the news. He did not sound smugly self-satisfied as he might have done, having predicted the outcome weeks before. He was in fact enraged. "The fool, the fool! To involve himself in a tussle that did not concern him!"

"But surely the authorities will not harm him," I cried.

"He prevented an arrest, so they arrested him instead. But it is not him but his supporters who will suffer. Already there is a military ship in the harbor prepared to remove him from the country. But the Burmese will think that the English mean him harm, that they will take him away to be executed, and they will riot on his behalf. It is just what the military wants: an excuse to move in and subjugate the people and claim the land. Your reverend has played right into their hands!"

The only thing that stopped a full rampage was a fit of coughing that finally silenced him and sent him to bed with a pungent compress that I prepared for his chest. His labored breathing made me uneasy, but while St. John slept fitfully, I slipped out in the early morning and made my way to the prison house. At first the guards would not let me speak with the reverend, but when I threatened to come back with St. John, they relented and allowed me a brief audience. When they brought me to his cell, the sight of Reverend Jeremiah Anchor with a bruised eye and scratched cheek aroused my full indignation and fury. I turned on the guard and demanded that he open the door and allow me to attend to the reverend's hurts. The guard patted the key dangling from his belt and declared that I might speak to the prisoner but that I could have no other access. He left us, promising to return in five minutes.

"How dare they lay a hand on you," I bristled. The reverend smiled when he saw who stood on the other side of the bars.

"You've come," he murmured. "I've been dreaming of you, and here you are." He seemed very calm; outside, chaos reigned.

"Listen to me." I spoke in rapid and low tones. "You must recant, you must tell them you were wrong to arouse the natives, and you must promise not to do so again!"

In answer the reverend stroked my fingers, which I found were clenching the bars so tightly that my knuckles had whitened. His feathery touch loosened my grip and sent shivers down my spine. "Jane," he said softly, and my knees shook. "You must not fret. All that is happening is happening as it must. If the natives are aroused, it is because it is time for them to be so. It is naught to do with me. I am only God's instrument. I cannot repress my words or myself. Indeed, I cannot repress saying that I want you, Jane."

His whispered words roared inside my head.

"I did not come to hear that," I said faintly. "I did not come for this."

"No? You did not come for me?"

"I—yes—but I did not come to speak words of . . . love . . . but to implore you to save yourself and your followers while you still can!"

"What good to save oneself for a world without love?"

I was snapped awake by his words. He was now the snake in the Garden of Eden; that creature, too, spoke with a silvery tongue.

"I must go." I snatched my hands away and pulled back.

At the same time, the guard had returned to escort me out. I stumbled against him as we left, and he kindly offered me a seat to rest upon before I left the prison house. I declined, apologized for my clumsiness, and departed quickly.

St. John had risen from his bed and was awaiting me when I returned to the house. I shut the door and leaned against it. Our eyes locked across the room as he waited for me to catch my breath from my hurried flight home. "Please," I said. "You must help him. In doing so you help the people as well. Bloodshed will be avoided if you help to free him and send him away." I held out my hand: The jailer's key lay in my palm. I had unhooked it from his belt when I stumbled against him earlier. St. John's grim silence when he regarded the key was terrifying.

Finally he spoke: "Do you think I have not already tried to intervene by all lawful means?" He paused at *lawful.* "But it is no use. The outcome has been determined." His acceptance of the matter maddened me.

"How easily you succumb to the world as it is, St. John. I had thought it was your passion to change it."

He rose and came toward me, but I stood defiantly in his path, ready to take the full blow of his wrath. He gripped my wrist. "Is it justice that seduces you, Jane? Have I failed you as a man? Will you join his harem? It is odd, Jane"—and I stiffened at the mockery I anticipated in his voice, but it was not what came out—"how you shine when you are angry. When you are enraged, there is a light unleashed from deep within you that is almost blindingly beautiful." The final word stung in its alienness: When had it ever been attached to my name?

He took my fist, drawing back each finger like a petal until the key lay exposed upon my opened palm. He could not have hurt me more if he had lashed me with a whip.

I whispered hoarsely, "It is unkind to mock my plainness in this manner."

Ignoring me, he strode to the door. "If I am not back by the end of the day, you must prepare for the worst, and send word to the bishop of Calcutta."

Snakes with silvery tongues; a towering column of flame; Abha dancing in the street in the pouring rain, beckoning me to join her; Madame Sayre looking on with her mysterious, sad smile: These were the images that invaded my troubled sleep, achieved after a day of waiting. I woke up with a start. Outside, the pounding of running feet, punctuated by a sharp snap of gunfire in the streets. I smelled smoke; the town was burning. Finally, the door burst open and St. John staggered in. He leaned against the frame as a spasm of coughing racked his entire body. And I saw with alarm the blood-soaked handkerchief that he clutched in his fist as I helped him to a seat.

It took him a minute to recover his breath. "It is done. The distraction I arranged drew off the guard, and I was able slip in and free him. He is on his way south with a few hours' head start before the military sets out after him."

"And he agreed to go?"

"Scampered off into the dark like a thief."

"But he will not be pursued and caught?"

"Fear not." St. John looked at me curiously. "Like Saint Francis, he will be aided by all small creatures whom he has befriended. You are relieved?" I startled at his comparison of the Reverend Jeremiah Anchor to Saint Francis, as if St. John had caught a glimpse of how I privately viewed the man.

But he was right: I was relieved. I wanted to fall to my knees before him, to kiss his feet in gratitude, but I only nodded as I sank back into my chair. I was fatigued to the bone. It was time to retire to bed.

"You will miss him?"

I froze. St. John rose.

He stood, towering over my chair. Swiftly he grabbed my arms, gripping them like gauntlets, and lifted me from my seat, and the look upon his face was dark and unreadable. *He will crush me,* I thought wildly, but it was not fear that coursed through my veins—it was exhilaration at the tight, imprisoning grip. He touched me, for once, and I felt it to my core. My body thrilled to that hard touch, my breathing came out ragged, almost a sob, and his kiss when he smote me with it was violent, searing, coarse, and fierce. Burning.

Rangoon, Burma, January 1853

A new year. There were rumors that the country would soon be annexed by the British Empire. We had meant to leave in late October, at the end of the rainy season, but tarried because of St. John's poor health. I watched the Burmese women bending over the bank of the Rangoon River, washing their clothes in the brown, silty water. They were always bending, I noticed, over laundry, over rice, over children. My own back ached: Earlier that morning I had been bent over a basin, filling it convulsively with the remains of last night's meal. The river gleamed beneath the rising sun; the women's chatter drifted over my brooding thoughts as I walked along the river's edge. Time moved relentlessly before me like that flowing water that fed from an unseen origin and ran on into an unknown destiny.

I had been a missionary's widow for barely a month.

And I was here today to make a decision. But my thoughts would not settle. Nor would my feet as I walked on and on beside the river. Fishing boats trawled atop the waves. Birds wheeled overhead. At last I sat down upon a bit of rock perched on a sandy patch, pulling my skirts around my feet. The war was over, if it could be called that. Burmese troops were routed, and Lower Burma was now part of British territory. It was time for me to leave as well, before the March heat swept in. But where?

I retrieved three letters from my pocket. I had been carrying them about for days. The first one I looked at had English stamps and had been forwarded by Mary weeks ago. I opened it gently and smoothed the creased page and reread it yet again.

Dearest Jane,

My sources finally found a trace of you, and I learned from them that you are married and living abroad. If this missive reaches you, it conveys that I wish for nothing but peace and happiness for one whom God knows is more deserving of these than any other. That is all, Jane. And yet I must add one more thought. Though you are the wife of another man now, in my mind and in my heart, you are a small Mrs. Edward Rochester who dwells within the house of my soul. And there you shall ever reside, for my heart, though broken, belongs wholly to you, and none other. Free of all matrimonial ties now, I will never contemplate taking up that bond with another female unless it be with you, and you alone. Should you ever break your ties with one I am sure does not deserve you, I see no dishonor in that, for I have never recognized the bonds of the law before those of the heart, as you know. I make no pretense that I am deserving of your hand, but I will forever remain incomplete without you here by my side. Leave that blasted, forsaken Asiatic continent. England's cool climes call. Come home, Jane.

Your former master and devoted slave,

Edward Rochester

First, shock. Edward had not perished in the fire as I had thought. He lived. He still wanted me! Then, an expanse. There were an ocean, a continent, and a whole other life between us. I was no longer that Jane who would return without hesitation to be a homunculus by his side. That Jane wanted safety, love. She turned without hesitation to the first one who offered it. Now I found myself filled with ambivalence. It was not that I craved adventure. But, like Abha, I perceived that a wider world, greater vistas existed. Was it possible to return?

My hand smoothed over the front of my dress. No bump or swelling impeded the downward sweep of my palm. Yet. If I did return, would Rochester cherish the child that I would bring back? Would we both belong by his side, or would I be divided between two loyalties? I felt a fierce, protective claim for the knot of life within me.

Did he suspect it on his last night on earth? Did St. John, his glazed eyes already turned toward the world beyond, know that he was leaving two lives behind? So eager was he to embark on that journey that his mind was already halfway there while his body lingered and burned despite all the cooling cloths I had draped over his fevered parts. I remembered how I had touched that body as I cared for it, my fingers trying to memorize every contour even as the soul within drifted away. My own body burned with the memory of that night of fiery contact a month ago. In the end, he wanted me—at least he had that night. And I had wanted him. That night he had loved me with his heart as well as his body. Now he was beyond my reach. How would he live on? The work would continue; structures would be erected; St. John's footprints would not be washed away with the tide of time.

I palmed my still-slender midriff. He would live on there too. Though in both cases, he would not see his work grow. *Send some word from heaven,* I prayed silently; *tell me what I should do.* I waited. And after a time, I sighed and picked up the next letter. I opened that one and admired the elegant penmanship before rereading the rather breathless prose.

My dear Jane,
I know I should address you as Mrs. Rivers, but in my
heart you are Jane, and I say your name over and over

again, and always with gratitude, for I know it was you who orchestrated my freedom—he said as much when he flung open the prison door and practically booted me into the night like a common criminal. But no matter, I made my way south, where I speak to all who will listen as I have always done, and the ladies have given me aid as well, as they have always done, and so I have some jewels, a satchel of sandwiches and provisions, and even some promises to slip away from their husbands and join me as soon as I am settled. I now find myself on a ship returning to America; but I vow to come back, and when I do, won't you join me? There is room for you as well. We will be a new community, and it will be the ladies who will lead, I am convinced. There is need for you. I need you. And should you come, I await, always, with my arms and heart wide open as

Your humble servant,

Jeremiah Anchor.

And why not? Why not join those good ladies? There would be more. Why not join and be part of something larger than myself? I imagined a train of strong, devout women leading the way, beating back the dark, clearing the path, opening it for the Reverend Jeremiah Anchor and his seductive oratory. (St. John's sardonic voice rang in my ears: *His sermons are love letters to hungry hearts.*) But it made my back ache more, truthfully, the thought of all that silent female labor: the work of laundering the household linens and dirty clothes, supporting a religious cause, carrying a child. All essential, worthy duties, no doubt, these ancillary services for others. Was it wrong to want something more? Was it selfish to desire something just for oneself, a singular love that was an end in itself? And what form would that singular love take?

The third letter released a whiff of flowers and sunshine when I unfolded it.

> After a time we left Canton and crossed into northern Indochina. Presently we are in Annam, but we will soon head south to Cochin China, to Tiến's home. I do believe that little man has been leading me there ever since we met. He is a sly one indeed, and yet he has awakened me from the dead, and perhaps stealth was the necessary means of doing so, as we were surrounded on every side by those who wished to keep me confined in my coffin. His home, he says, is a country invaded and broken, but it will fight back and remake itself into something whole and new. He says he must leave me soon, but he will not go until I am strong enough to take up the fight. Daily, I get stronger in spite of myself. Today I walk along the Perfume River, and I wonder if you wander beside another Asian river as you read this, and, if we walk far enough, whether our paths will eventually cross and we will meet once more.

I refolded Madeleine's letter and put it away with the others. Where would I go; whom would I meet; how would I now fit into the world? The Rangoon River had no answers for me as I gazed into the flowing current. On a parallel course, almost touching in the ancient city of Prome, the Irrawaddy rolled through Burma. One day, through the needs of commerce or nature, these two bodies of water might join in mid-course. For now the Irrawaddy ran until it forked into tributaries that seeped into the Bay of Bengal, merging with the Rangoon River as it poured in from the Andaman Sea, both connecting with currents of the Indian Ocean, linking to the South Atlantic, then the North Atlantic, carried past the eastern coastlines of the New World,

Reverend Jeremiah Anchor's home, then swept into the Gulf Stream past England, some part of it threading through the English Channel, meeting the River Thames as it spilled into the North Sea, rushing onward to the Norwegian Sea, the Arctic Ocean, the East Siberian Sea, faster and faster through the Bering Strait, joining the North Pacific Ocean that touched the East China Sea, uniting with the South China Sea, which kissed the mouth of the Perfume River as it flowed at last into the arms of the Rangoon River, from where, looking up, I gazed back into eyes that looked across time and distance and moving water, into mine.

Boston, 2008—Vinh

What is she thinking, he wonders, as he always does when he walks past the picture of the woman looking out over the banks of a long, silty river. She looks oddly familiar, somehow, in her flowing Victorian dress. And the landscape, too, half recognizable from another life.

But he doesn't linger to ponder over it this time. Tonight he is a little late getting started on the rounds of his midnight shift, so he hurries through the first floor but pauses as usual in the Raphael Room on the second floor to look at Pesellino's *Virgin and Child with a Swallow*. There are plenty of paintings of the Madonna and Child at the Gardner, but he is drawn to this one. He likes how the Christ child gets to protectively hold something warm and small of his own while her hand rests elegantly on the baby's chubby thighs, instead of fingering the toes like so many other Madonnas'. There is something more intimate in that gesture. The deep-set niche in which they sit intensifies the intimacy. It frames them. No, it presses them together, defining a space of their own. They are at the center. But she looks sad and distant, like she suspects what's coming and is steeling herself for it, even if at the moment she is caught up in the small, warm life in her lap. And the way the baby holds the bird echoes that. It is all such a delicate, fragile moment.

But tonight, Pesellino's mother-and-child doesn't charm him. It's a lie. The illusion of a receding sculpted wall behind the figures is a lie. It has all been a lie: the illusion of a family, a mother, a child. An absent father, somewhere. Lies, lies, lies. They are just flat blobs of color, dark against light to create a lie of shadow, of a space that bodies could inhabit, come together in.

He continues his rounds. On the second floor he stands in front of a pair of empty frames, giant blank eyes left by the thieves who stole the Rembrandts in 1990. *How old was I then?* The place is as famous for what it's missing as what it contains, he's reminded in this room. The frames were left here per the founder's decree that nothing be changed in the museum after her death. They are signs of loss. And of promise: someday to be filled again. He stares at the wallpaper behind the frames. That seems honest, at least. Wallpaper doesn't try to pretend to be expanding space, tunneling into the wall behind the painting, suggesting a world, a moment caught by the painter, every one an impressionist, freezing that moment in their paint.

As he looks, it becomes his own body, not the wall, that seems to stretch back. Space opening up, a street, movement, streaks of light, spots of color here and there with a fleeting glimpse of a sandaled foot on a bike pedal. *Go faster, Đức!*

In his memory light splays through shadows: Across a busy road he sees a shack; the open window makes a frame. There are a woman and a child sitting together, looking out. They lean toward each other as they look. They're not centered in the frame, but sit off to the side. Still, yet part of the movement, held in the wind of activity that swirls down the open road. You have to look for it. You can barely make them out in the busy scenery. But there they are. *Mother and Child.* He takes a pencil out of his pocket, unfolds the flyer he picked up earlier. The back of the page is blank. He makes a mark. Then another.

Trần Thị Trang, 1984–1994

Chapter One

Huế, Vietnam, 1984

Trang picked up her book and opened to the page she had arrived at after weeks of slowly struggling through the text. The girl in England had left the home of the unloving rich lady and was about to take a long journey to attend a school far away. It was dark and cold as she waited. The child was anxious and a little frightened, but also excited. It was a new beginning. She felt the wind of possibility on her face. But Trang closed the book. She should be reading the Bible, she thought. At the same time, she wanted to know the world a little. She wanted to know who Jane Eyre was. Each page was a battle, and the world that Jane lived in was baffling. So why did it also feel so familiar?

She was still partly in the dark moorlands with Jane when she looked up at the Huế boulevard and waved to the spy. No wave back, as usual.

"How do you know he's not a poet, or a novelist who's observing our lives for his book?" She had been so absorbed in her thoughts that she hadn't noticed Father Martin walking up to her bookstall.

She laughed. "What writer would trouble to make a book from our small, insignificant lives? He must be a spy or a lunatic."

Father Martin pointed to the book she had set down when he came by the bookstall: the used abridged copy of *Jane Eyre*. She placed her hand over the cover instinctively, protectively. "Sometimes small, insignificant lives make the best books of all," he said. "Besides, we don't know what he is writing or even if it's words at all. He may be illiterate, just making marks on his pad." Ciphers, she agreed. He was indeed all mystery, a ghost. Ten years ago, the spy appeared in a frayed, drab uniform that had since been patched in so many places that the original garment was barely visible. Some leftover soul from the war, people thought, with no home to return to. Perhaps he was a former Việt Cộng who had drifted here after the Americans left, as so many others had done. The afternoon was when he usually took up his post across the street, near the alley where the bicycle vendor stacked her rows of three-speed Chinese-model rentals. He just stood there. For hours. Jotting things down in a notebook with a soft brown cover secured by a rubber band when he wasn't writing in it. If he was a spy, he wasn't a very good one. He didn't bother to hide what he was doing. After a while, she forgot about him. He became part of the landscape of shifting people. He stood out a bit at first because he didn't move. So then he became the part of the shifting landscape that was still.

"No, my little dreamer, I don't think he's a spy *or* a lunatic." Father Martin laughed. "I will see you later for evening prayers. Bring your friends. And your sister," he added hopefully.

Trang looked fondly after his tall, receding back. She did not have the heart to tell him that neither her sister nor the other workers in the row of shacks and stalls along the avenue had any interest in attending Father Martin's prayer meetings or Masses or Bible studies. To please him, she had tried to persuade them to join her. Most had only attended one function—the time when the church had offered a free picnic lun-cheon after service. Her sister Loan had not liked the short, curved noodles coated in pale cheese or the sweet beans swimming in brown sauce. She had complained for days of the taste that stuck in her throat, and she had continued to make fun of Father Martin's sandy reddish hair and waxy face. *He is like a ghost with human clothes on,* she said. *He's not real.*

Trang wanted to slap her. Whenever Father Martin stopped by their bookstall on his way to the church, Loan would smile at him and blink her big eyes. Father Martin would speak hopefully about the church schedule and events. Trang berated Loan for leading him on. "I would go," Loan said contritely, "but I can't bear to sit that long."

"But you sit here on the stool all day," Trang pointed out.

"I can't bear that either," Loan said.

Later, Loan persuaded the chatty bicycle lady across the avenue to allow her to help rent bicycles and mopeds to tourists. And that was when Father Martin started saying pointedly, "Bring your sister." He was alarmed that a girl with so much spirit might be easily misled by interacting with so many foreigners. She had been safer at the humble bookstall that sold postcards and bootlegged copies of textbooks to the university students. They must try to persuade her to walk upon the right path. Trang thought that was hopeless, but she wanted to please Father Martin.

My little dreamer.

Father Martin's parting words that afternoon repeated in her head. His words often invaded her reality when he was not there, taking her back to the day she first met him. He had stopped by the stall for a stack of postcards. By that time, it was only she and Loan. The dirt road that several of her father's shops once lined had broadened into a wide boulevard; from the perch of her own bookstall, she now watched the stream of traffic flow by. Occasionally, it threw something interesting her way, like the tall stranger who appeared one day.

"Are you American?" Trang had inquired. The sandy-haired man was what she later learned was a "ginger." But it was not at all like the color of the spicy, biting, yet warm and sweet-flavored root she minced and sprinkled into her cooking. He had light-blue eyes, almost gray, with pinpoints of black dots, rimmed with pale lashes. His skin was not used to the sun and reacted by breaking out in flaky patches. Overall, he was rather pink. "You should wear a hat," she advised. His skin turned a brighter shade of red. She was fascinated.

He dipped his chin in agreement. "Yes, but that would make me look even more like a tourist. Actually, I live here now." He put his hand out. "I'm Jim Martin. I live behind the church." She looked again at his casual clothes. No collar. Yet there had been talk of a new curate to help and eventually replace old Father Anderson, who was due to retire at the end of the month. "And what is your name?"

"I'm Trang," she said.

"You have such a nice smile. Are you, I was wondering, by chance Christian?"

But of course he would ask that. He was a clergyman, after all. She felt a little disappointed, nevertheless. He wanted to add her soul to his collection, that was all. It was not the first time she had heard this question, and she sometimes wondered if her eagerness in greeting the foreigners who made their way to her shop somehow made her out to be an empty vessel in need of salvation. For they were always some-how a little disappointed to find that she already was a Christian, and they subsequently moved on. Any fleeting excitement that this new-comer might be interested in getting to know her vanished. "My family, yes," she said carefully, "but not so much now. Not much time," she explained. She gestured around them. "Busy." Even though there were no buyers as far as anyone could see, no one queuing to buy her dusty picturesque postcards of Hạ Long Bay. He handed her a small card.

"Perhaps you might have a little time this Sunday to renew your acquaintance with one who has never left your side," he said with a smile.

"Yes." She nodded. "But what are the postcards for?"

"I thought I would give them out as prizes for the children in Bible study class, to motivate and encourage them," he said.

"They will just sell them," Trang said. *And there is already enough competition,* she thought. Yet she was thrilled. Unlike the others who had moved on quickly, he had stayed to talk with her. *We are having a conversation! In English!* She knew that there were probably numerous mistakes in her speech, blushed to think how many, worried about her accent, but was determined to push her embarrassment aside. When would she have this opportunity again?

He frowned, perplexed. "Do you have a better idea?" She had noticed how worry drew a fine line between his brows that vanished when he smiled shyly and dropped his chin.

"Just tell them they are doing a good job," she said. Just look into their eyes, she thought, with those light-blue orbs, shining with heavenly light, see into their souls, say you did well, child, you did well. They will follow you wherever you lead them, just as I would. She hadn't said any of this out loud when those thoughts popped into her head, of course. Even if she had tried (she'd rather die, first of all), her words would never have been as fluid and intimate as her heart's speech.

"It's what you say, not how you say it." *(Had he read her mind?)* "And I can see that you are wise beyond your years, as your name, Trang, implies." He had studied a bit of Vietnamese, he confessed shyly. "I will be blessed indeed to have you as part of our congregation."

She was named Trang, she had been told, because even as a baby, she had possessed the qualities associated with that name: an odd, quiet, serious demeanor, someone deep into her own thoughts. But she preferred a secondary definition where the name Trang referred to "page" or "chapter." She imagined herself as an unfolding story, even though at the moment nothing interesting was happening in her life, and to be honest, she was afraid that nothing ever would. So she tried to make something happen for herself in the *Jane Eyre* book: Sometimes she traveled in her mind to a strange, cold land where she walked beside thick bushes called *hedges* and looked out at open, blank fields dusted with snow.

From a distance, she saw Loan. Trang blinked. Again, it took her a moment to separate her thoughts of the book from the physical world around her. That was Loan, but not walking through a field dusted with snow. Loan was slipping through the stream of moving bodies along the busy avenue. She reached the bookstall, a little breathless and pleasingly flushed. Loan had always been a beauty, with those bright eyes and plump cheeks. "John Wesley has invited me to visit him in Sài Gòn!" She laughed breathlessly. John Wesley was an American whiskey merchant who often stopped at the bicycle rental to chat with Loan when he was doing business in Huế. Trang's first thought was *Oh, Father Martin will not be pleased. That John Wesley. It will come to no good.* Then she realized that she was not pleased either. "Oh Loan, no! What would you do there?"

"He will set up a new restaurant in the city! When it's ready, he wants to show me."

Trang did not believe it. John Wesley had never struck her as more than a chatty, self-interested man. Yet Loan clung to his every word about his exploits as a traveling salesman for his company. Half his stories must be made up, Trang thought. "You girls speak good English," he would always say with a wink when he stopped at the bookstall sometimes to chat with Loan. Trang despised him. She saw in his chirpy compliments evidence he was indifferent to anything besides himself.

And it was as she had guessed: Father Martin did not like it. "That scoundrel! We must find a way to dissuade her from going, to give her attention and energy to the church!" Trang hung her head in shame, thinking again that she had not been able to get Loan to attend any of the services or teas.

"I'm sorry. I failed you, Father," she whispered.

"Oh, Trang! Theresa. You've never failed me—no one works harder than you."

She loved it when he used her Catholic name. It felt so intimate, almost like a physical caress. When he used "Trang," on the other hand, it had begun to feel that he was further away. But he was glum after hearing the news, and for a while they both stared at the road full of people streaming in both directions as the sun began to set. It was cooler these evenings now that the typhoon season was over.

"Christmas is coming," Father Martin said thoughtfully. No one cared much about Christmas, but Trang thought of how Christmas in her book came with white powder floating from the sky, drawing rooms lit with cozy fires after the characters came in just at twilight from raw and chilly walks. *Welsh rabbit. Roasted onion.* She could taste it. She was enchanted.

"I know what we should do," Father Martin said suddenly, excitedly. Trang waited, breathless. "Let's have a Christmas party!"

Trang's job was to recruit the guests. *If I could only perform miracles, like Jesus,* she thought, *then they would follow me in droves.* That was blasphemous. She banished that thought at once. One guest at a time, then. She started with her neighbor, the owner of a stall on her left that was almost indistinguishable from her own. The only thing that differentiated one stall from another was that behind the cheap toys and trinkets one might sell pornographic magazines, if you knew to ask for them; another might have illegally imported liquor or cigarettes. Many had a few bootlegged copies of *The Quiet American*, but only Trang's stall overflowed with books and so could properly be called a bookstall. It included some textbooks, courtesy of Father Martin's help in making a connection with the university—she didn't sell that many but was grateful for this distinction and took pleasure in talking with the few Huế University students who stopped by to get used books for their classes or sell the ones they no longer needed. That was how she had come by *Jane Eyre*, a cheap, abridged copy originally meant for an English literature class.

Bring your sister.

Trang sighed. When did the refrain start? It was that week, a year ago, when their mother's stomach cancer had taken a turn for the worse and she could not tolerate Loan's restless care. "It's worse than sitting in this shack," Loan herself had complained. So they had switched their schedules, and Trang had sat with their mother during the day at the charity convalescent hospital while Loan took over the morning and afternoon shifts at the bookstall. "Your Father Martin says hello and hopes our mother is feeling better. He says you are a saint," Loan passed on. So they had talked, Trang thought with annoyance. By that point Trang had already come to cherish the dimple on his cheek that deepened whenever he smiled at her during Mass, at Bible study class, at volunteer events and fundraisers. But it was more than that: She admired Father Martin for the zeal of his belief, the way his pale-blue eyes brightened with ardor when he talked about God. What would it feel like to have those eyes turned upon her in that way? The moment she had thought it, she had blushed in shame. She felt her soul burning for something she couldn't name yet longed to reach.

Next to whatever that feeling for Father Martin was, there was death. She guiltily found herself counting the days left in their mother's life. She hoped they would not exceed fourteen. In her mind, two weeks was when people started forgetting their old reality. Sure enough, their mother had passed on after fourteen days, and the sisters had resumed their regular routine at the bookstall. When Trang thought of that time, she still dipped her head in shame. They were truly orphans then, and the past slipped even further away. Memories of loss, one after the other, became fainter and ghostlier in the passageway of her mind: First her father had disappeared during the war. When the gunfire quieted down, he had slipped out to check on the half-dozen shacks and stalls they owned back then and never returned. There was no body to recover. A lost father. A city in rubble. Then the memory of their mother slipping away from her sanity and being taken in by the nuns, leaving her and Loan alone, well before the cancer. The two of them had clung to each other, but eventually Loan had been sent to a Catholic orphanage, and Trang herself packed off to distant relatives in the north who had treated her coldly and suspiciously and, to curry favor with the Communists, left her at an orphanage as well.

That was a loss of self, and Trang had felt as if she were disappearing. She called them the "not-enough years": not enough food, not enough warmth, not enough kindness. She had not disappeared, though, subsisting on something other than bodily nourishment—her imagination, fed by scraps of stories of other worlds, other lives.

Until Loan came for her. One day she had turned up at Trang's orphanage, had demanded her sister like a crazy lady, taken her back to Huế, where she had found work after leaving her own orphanage. It was not much, but the owner of one of the shacks said that Trang could work there too. He even let her sleep on the floor of the shack at night to prevent thieves from breaking in. Lying on a straw mat on the hard ground every night, Trang could hear the rats scurrying from one corner to the next. Loan would have slept on the floor of the shack with Trang had there been room enough for two. There wasn't, so Loan shared a crowded room with other workers at night, but she came to the shack every morning with hot tea, and the sisters worked together during the day.

The shack belonged to them now. Something solid, a room of their own claimed in the city streets. And it was no longer a shack, no longer four walls tacked together, barely standing. They had improved and enlarged it, increased the merchandise. It now looked more like the other merchants' stalls lining the boulevard. Trang liked being there: She could afford to rent space in a room in a house like Loan did, but she preferred to sleep on the floor of the stall. Sometimes, often after she'd been reading late into the night by the light of a candle stub, the strangest dreams would slip into her head. There was one in particular that haunted her, and, when she woke, left her disoriented for the rest of the day. In this dream she was in a cold land where a woman in a stone-and-wood house slept in a bed and dreamed, and in that woman's dream she hovered over another woman asleep on a pallet on the floor of a shack in a warm land, dreaming. When Trang woke from this dream, she felt temporarily weightless.

Bring your sister.

A cool breeze fanned her head, and her heated thoughts loosened their grip on her heart. Her unruly, unchristian heart. But enough of that. Repenting, she turned to the task given to her: get partygoers. She accosted the owner of a shack on her right.

"No."

"But there will be free food."

"We will miss the holiday tourists."

"There will hardly be any. Not many, anyway."

"The food is no good, and they will expect us to come every week after that."

"No," she lied, "it is just a party."

"Well, I do need to go with my daughter to Sài Gòn for a new dress for her. I need to keep her out of trouble."

"I'll watch over your shop for you while you're gone."

"We'll be gone three days."

Three days of looking after her neighbor's shop as well as her own was too tedious to bear. "Yes," she agreed. She tried to hide her annoyance. She suspected that in their place she would refuse as well. She understood that for them time spent at the church felt like another job, but one that didn't pay for the work of worship. That the work of worship should not require remuneration did not make it feel less like unpaid labor.

To the shop owner two stalls over on her left: I'll clean your house next week. The owner two shacks down on the right: I'll give you a dozen old postcards. Okay, twenty. She managed to get five promises of attendance at the Christmas party, and her time for the next four weeks was completely booked. *Six,* she thought. *I must get at least half a dozen for Father Martin.* She looked up in despair. Then she marched across the street, startling the spy, who jumped when she tapped his shoulder. He hastily tucked his notebook inside his shirt.

To every offer in exchange for his attendance, the spy merely shook his head. Finally: "I'll let you use my life in your story." It was the most useless thing she could have offered. Her life was nothing, of no interest to anyone, not even herself. And he could use it anyhow, write whatever he wanted about her, and she couldn't stop him. He hesitated, then started to turn away. Exasperated, she grabbed his elbow. The spy yanked his arm free in alarm and scuttled back. A few steps away, he peeked over his shoulder. His eyes narrowed in suspicion.

"Maybe."

The guest of honor refused to come.

"But everyone will be expecting you."

"Who's everyone?"

"It will be fun!"

"I don't have time for *fun* right now."

This puzzled Trang, for it seemed like Loan did nothing but live for fun. She remembered how when they used to get crackers for Tết, Loan would always tear away the paper and devour hers right away, while Trang would hide her own as long as possible to preserve the sense that something *good* was coming.

"I'll give you anything."

"Anything? Would you give me your Tết sweets?"

One year her New Year's treat had disappeared from its hiding place. Trang had suspected Loan at once, and her face had turned bright red and her whole body had trembled with her desire to *hit* Loan, to strike her so hard in the face that she could feel skin split beneath her fingers. Loan had stopped protesting and stood there staring at her in shock. And she had said, very quietly, *Go ahead. You can hit me.* As if she were giving Trang a gift to replace the one she had taken. Of course, Trang couldn't do it after that. And that had been another kind of theft.

"Anything."

"I need money."

Trang felt her throat tighten as if the cords on her neck were purse strings. Why had she not known that Loan would ask for money? Loan who spent every extra dong on useless luxuries like hairpins and cheap perfume.

"I'll do all your shifts for a week. And we'll still share the profits for that time. But I can't start until I've paid off all my time for the other shopkeepers."

"I need money now."

Trang felt panic rising. It was a black cloud that formed at the base of her head and spread tentacles around her skull and down her back. Yes, she had money. It was money she had quietly put away all year, sacrificing sweets, lotions, undergarments without holes, all manner of small needs, just to see the pile of money grow from a thin wad to the thicker stack that she kept rubber-banded and hidden in an envelope under a stack of old magazines in a corner of the bookstall. The savings felt like a dream. She needed it for the retreat to Hội An that Father Martin was taking a handful of congregants on next spring. It was a city not too far from Huế, just past Đà Nẵng, but she had never been there. She had never been on a retreat, especially not one with Father Martin. She could not give up any of it. Especially to Loan.

"Two weeks. And you can keep all the profits."

"That's not enough money, and I can't wait two weeks."

"No! Name something else. I don't have any money."

Loan looked at her then, and her face tightened. "I know you have money. You never buy yourself anything, and all your things are old. I make as much as you and I am always having to get things."

That's because you are frivolous and you waste all your money, Trang thought. She kept her mouth closed.

"I really need the money. I have to get a bus ticket to Sài Gòn. I'll pay you back, I promise."

"Is John Wesley's new restaurant open?"

"No, there's been trouble about getting funds for that, but he is working on it. He will show me around the city, though. He says it is much larger than Huế, and full of possibilities. I just need a vacation."

Trang did not like it. "What will people say?"

She meant, What would Father Martin say? And Loan knew it.

Trang did a mental calculation. A bus ticket would only put a small dent in her savings. But she would make Loan promise to pay it back before the spring retreat.

"Fine, I'll lend you money for the trip. But don't leave until after the party. How much do you need?"

Loan named a price that was double what Trang had in mind. "Surely a bus ticket doesn't cost that much!"

"I want to get my hair done." *Vain fool. And does a hairstyle really cost so much?* "Wait, there's more. I want you to get your hair done too. Cut and styled. Nobody wears it long anymore. And all you do now is just tie it back like a curtain. I want you to buy a new dress. To look like a modern woman."

"I can't afford to!"

"All that money you saved?"

"It's not for silly, frivolous things!"

"So you admit you do have some money! Well, I'm not going to the party with you dressed in your old skirt-and-blouse church outfit. You're not a nun."

It was Trang's best outfit, the one she wore every Sunday and to every church function. The white blouse was always bleached, starched, and ironed, and the dark skirt brushed and tidy. "What's wrong with it?"

"You look so plain in that. I'm sure Father Martin would approve."

Trang blushed. What was wrong with looking plain? It was respectable. And they were going to a church party, after all.

Loan just waited, arms crossed. Trang made further calculations: bus ticket and a hairstyle for Loan. A new dress and hairstyle for herself. She sighed. That was pretty much her entire trip savings. She could find a dress in the parcels of discarded, donated bags of clothing for the church. They would go to the cheapest hairstylists. And the retreat wasn't until the end of spring. There was time to save more.

"Yes, agreed," she said reluctantly.

Loan's face lit up with a broad smile, and Trang noticed how her dimple deepened and her dark eyes brightened, and she had a sudden glimpse of why John Wesley and, for that matter, Father Martin were captivated. She was too. The regret would come later, a taste of ashes and bile.

In the end, the figure in the glass did not repulse her. She wasn't able to take in her reflection all at once with the handheld mirror, so she started at her feet. The sleek, pointy-toed black city shoes were slightly raised on kitten heels. Sturdy nylon pantyhose stretched over a solid pair of legs up to the knees, which barely peeked from beneath the dress's modest hemline. The skirt of the dress flared slightly. Small white flowers danced across the delicate peach fabric, which pinched in at the waistline to structure a demure figure that she had tried her best to disguise with a sensible green cardigan. The cardigan hid her bare arms, which the sleeveless summer dress exposed, but it did not cover her throat, which was revealed by the low V neckline. She had rectified the situation with a white silk scarf knotted at her throat, batting Loan's hands away when she tried to remove it. Loan had gone over the pile of donated church clothing with Trang and pulled out this dress herself, casting aside the long, high-necked navy dress that Trang would have chosen.

Finally, she took a deep breath and raised the mirror to her face. Chin-length hair, freshly cut, feathered at the sides and blown, brushed, and sprayed to a stiff helmet. Layered bangs framed her eyes. Loan had made sure they did *not* cut the bangs straight across her forehead as Trang had directed. Gone were the long curtains of black hair bunched together by a rubber band. Trang had refused the lipstick and rouge. But bright, dark, eager eyes lit up the face in a way that no makeup could. She peered timidly at the stranger in the glass, who peeked back shyly. She was still plain, not at all—and never would be—like Loan.

Wide cheekbones tended to flatten rather than sculpt the round face; short, stubby lashes trimmed small eyes, which gazed with a keen, hungry expression out at the wide avenue. But there was something there. Even Trang could not deny it. She looked, as Loan had promised, like a modern young woman on her way out to a party.

It was dark. The bookstall had been closed early. Trang waited in front, impatient. It was just like Loan to be late. She braced herself to be met by a luminous beauty. Even though Loan had not purchased a new dress in the end ("I already have something I can wear"). Trang brushed her hands down her skirt self-consciously. She wondered if Father Martin would notice her own efforts to honor the party. Or would he think she was trying to be someone else, someone like Loan?

She looked up and saw a small child navigating the slackening stream of bicycles, and she knew instantly that the child was heading toward her bookstall with a message. And she even knew what the message would say. She sighed as she read Loan's note: *I'll be late. Go ahead and I'll meet you at the church.* She gave the messenger a coin and sighed again, annoyed. Trang did not want to walk in alone dressed like this. Loan would have deflected attention away from her and absorbed it for herself. But it was getting late: She had to go; she had promised to help set up. She made her way, walking carefully in the tight new shoes.

She was not the first to arrive. Father Martin was already there, arranging the long benches against the wall. She quickly went to help him. "Why, Trang," he said brightly, "you look ready to go to a party!" She blushed happily, relieved, touching her hair bashfully.

"You look ready to deliver a sermon, Father."

He smiled. "Not very festive, I'm afraid. Do you think people will dance, if there is space in the room?"

Trang could not imagine any of the guests she had corralled into coming doing anything that resembled dancing. "I even prepared a tape," he said eagerly.

She read aloud the songs written on the cassette cover: "'Jingle Bells,' 'Rudolph the Red-Nosed Reindeer,' 'A Holly Jolly Christmas,' theme song from *Chariots of Fire*?"

Father Martin looked sheepish. "It's cheesy, I know, but I just love the swelling chords." Twisted streamers hung from the low ceiling. The modest church room looked like a plain girl with cheap ribbons in her hair. A long table pushed against the wall was set with platters of cut raw vegetables and bowls of creamy dip. Popcorn and corn chips filled colorful plastic bowls. Trang helped set up towers of Styrofoam cups for pitchers of iced tea. She could not imagine anyone eating any of this. The party would be a flop. She began to sweat beneath the cardigan. "There." Father Martin looked about with satisfaction. Then his expression turned anxious as he peered at a damp spot in the ceiling. "I've been keeping an eye on that." Trang nodded in concern as well. Typhoon season was over, but sometimes an unexpected storm still ripped through. There was a rumbling now, in fact. She wasn't sure if that spot would hold up either. But yes, it would, she reassured him. *Something* had to go right tonight.

The guests began to trickle in. Trang was relieved that the empty room was filling up, even though everyone was avoiding the center, so the room still felt empty. Nor was anyone eating. They glanced skeptically at the platters of food. "Music," she said to Father Martin.

"Right you are," he said gaily. Swelling chords from *Chariots of Fire* vibrated the room. Father Martin went from guest to guest, greeting them enthusiastically. They stood limply in a line against the wall, as if waiting for vaccination shots. Every now and then he glanced expectantly at the door. Half an hour passed. Two guests quietly slipped out when no one was looking. Trang desperately whispered into the ears of each guest that if they left before the party was over, she would not fulfill her end of the bargain. They were sullen. No one even bothered to pocket the popcorn or corn chips. "A Holly Jolly Christmas" chirped into the void. Father Martin had already greeted everyone and was now making the rounds again and re-greeting. Outside it started pouring, which kept more guests from leaving for the moment, thank goodness.

"Goodness, she'll be soaked!" *What?* Then Trang remembered. Loan. Oh yes. And where was she? She would save the party, which was starting to wither under the wholesome holiday tunes. *Please, please,* Trang thought. *Get here soon!*

A child stood at the doorway, afraid to come in. The rain had plastered his hair against his head, and his large eyes shone shyly. Trang saw him, and her heart sank. It was the same messenger who had brought Loan's first message. She beckoned him in, and he whispered in her ear. She could sense her face drooping in disappointment, and she felt Father Martin suddenly at her side. "What is it—what's wrong?"

She turned to him, shame heating her cheeks. "Loan is not coming. She's going to Hồ Chí Minh City to meet John Wesley."

Father Martin's face turned dark. "That is indeed a calamity. The child will surely be misled or corrupted by that blackguard!" Trang found it hard to think of Loan as a child. But Father Martin drew himself up. "I will not allow it!"

"What are you going to do?" Trang had never seen him look so determined, so . . . heroic. *Not for me.* She couldn't keep the thought from deflating her admiration somewhat.

"I'm going to the bus station. I'll stop her before she boards!"

As soon as Father Martin dashed out the door into the night and the rain, the ceiling over the corner collapsed, water spewed through, and the lights guttered out.

Basins, buckets, bowls, Styrofoam cups: Guests rushed to gather receptacles to catch the falling water. A line formed to pass each filled container from hand to hand up to the door, where the water was thrown back into the rain and the emptied vessel passed back along the line to be filled again. Someone started to sing an encouraging song. It was taken up by all the line workers. Then the rain stopped suddenly and the water slowed to a trickle. Just as the Christmas song crackled to an end on the cassette player, Michael Jackson's "Thriller" blasted through. Someone must have switched tapes. The light blinked in time to the staccato beat, creating a disco vibe. Gyrating bodies suddenly filled the floor, arms flinging out in stiff, robotic gestures.

Trang watched in amazement, her back against the wall, holding a Styrofoam cup filled with fish sauce and chili flakes (someone had produced a bottle of the pungent liquid and filled the cups with it). People were dipping popcorn and raw, cut vegetables into the sauce. It improved the food tremendously, Trang had to admit, as she popped a hot and savory kernel into her mouth. Word seemed to have rushed out, and people were appearing at the church in droves. Bouncing, bobbing bodies filled all the previously empty space. Each time the song ran out, someone would rewind the tape, and "Thriller" would punch out its irresistible throbbing tempo again.

If only Father Martin were here to see what a success the party was! Though she wasn't sure this was the party that he would have had in mind. In fact, the whole thing had a hellish quality to it that excited her. *Thrilled* her, like the words of the song. All of Huế was here tonight, breaking out of its skin. Even the spy. When his face popped up before her, Trang wasn't even surprised. It was that kind of night. He silently handed her a folded sheet of paper.

"What's this?" She already knew.

He shrugged, then turned and vanished between the shaking, shadowy bodies.

Trang unfolded the paper and tried to read the words between the pulsating stabs of light. It wasn't easy. Words flashed in and out. *Sorry. Couldn't. Promise. I'll pay back. Please try. Someday.*

Trang crushed the paper into a ball and shoved it deep into her dress pocket. She watched the dancers with their heads thrown back, eyes closed, swaying, jerking. The music dulled to a thudding, muffled beat in her head. The beat synchronized with her heartbeat, growing louder and louder until she feared it would reverberate into the walls and ceiling and bring the church crashing down upon their heads. There was no air. She had to get out.

Stumbling, pushing her way between twisting bodies, she found the exit at last. Outside, she took in deep, gulping lungfuls of air. Only when she no longer felt like her chest was crushed against her spine and the air was able to flow freely again did she begin to calm down. A red glow arced in the dark below her, sending sparks to the ground. Her chin dropped, and she saw the spy crouching there. His sandaled foot pivoted on the heel and smothered the sparks into the dirt.

Startled, Trang spoke sharply. "Well, what have you got to say?" He shrugged. "How about: What a wonderful party! I did that. I made that happen—all those people in there enjoying themselves. I worked hard!" She was furious. Neither Loan nor Father Martin was there at the party that was meant for them. The fury flared up for a moment, and was just as suddenly smothered, tamped down like the spy's cigarette butt. She closed her eyes and leaned back against the building.

"I don't care for parties," said the spy.

The cool night air soothed her flushed cheeks. The wall behind her thrummed faintly. The spy rose from his haunches, and they stood quietly side by side.

"She's gone away," she found herself saying quietly.

The spy shrugged again. He dropped the stub of another cigarette on the ground. "Someday you will travel further than your sister ever does." He walked off into the night.

With that, a cold, wild plain opened up in her mind. Blue mountains loomed in the distance. Fields of long grass bowed from a sweeping wind. Overhead, a night sky spread, open, pinned with stars. The rain in Huế had stopped an hour ago. She blinked. For a moment, it seemed, two worlds had collided. She recognized the view from her dreams, from her book. *Jane Eyre*. She was right here, she had to remind herself. In Huế, this night, in her own little world. Was it enough?

Later, back at her bookstall, lying on the thin bedding, feeling the hard earth floor pressed against her back, grounding her, keeping her from crashing through the tin roof and falling into the stars, the words of the spy lingered in her ears and folded into her dreams.

Someday you will travel further than your sister ever does.

Chapter Two

Trang liked to come here when the unshed feelings filled her so much they threatened to explode, taking down everyone near her as well. She had never reached that point, though she imagined it would be like the war. She had heard the stories: flattened homes, bodies buried in the ashes. And she had seen and known the aftermath of people who never came home, or people with stumps where there had been limbs, people who wandered with hollow, empty eyes. Much of the destruction was now covered over, rebuilt, hushed. But she felt the ghostly presence of that violence sometimes. The spy, for instance. Sometimes she saw his soul limping beside him, as if the war had blasted it out of his body.

It took an hour to break free from Huế's traffic congestion, another hour on the quiet dirt road that bore her farther and farther from the noise and rush of bodies. A moped would have gotten her here in twenty minutes. But who had extra money for things like that when the rusty old bike still worked? It was dry enough that the mud did not catch in the wheels as she cycled along the dirt road that turned and suddenly opened out onto a wide, flowing field. Coming to this open patch in the late afternoon was a soothing ritual that she had not performed in a while. Small houses nestled at the edge of the other side, but no one from the village ever came out here.

So she was startled when she saw the figure standing there in the tall grass, his back to her, facing the distant settlement. She paused at once, not frightened. Just curious. She could tell right away, even without seeing his face, that he wasn't from around here. It wasn't so much his clothes, though it was true that they didn't look cheap and refurbished like everyone else's clothing looked. No, it was more the way he just stood there, so upright, so still. Like part of the landscape. That alone would have marked him as different: No one around here just stood around doing nothing. Who had time for that? Nor was it a relaxed stance, she could tell even from a distance. She could feel the tension of a focused concentration so intense that it sucked up all the air around it. Moment by moment the tension built, mounted, drew force, readied for a monumental strike. It must come out! It must come out! She thought she might faint. She dared not move. She hardly breathed. And oh! The release when it broke out, and somehow, in the same instant, a guttered, strangled cry from the figure, as if he still tried to hold it back even as some force hooked and dragged it out of his depths.

A name, repeated three times.

An incantation or a tether to a soul lost on the other side of the world. It was not a human sound. Or perhaps it was the most human sound: a snarl of raw pain, longing, need. Would there be a response? She would never know. She turned and fled on the bike.

The head of the match scratched along the strip of red phosphorus and powdered glass, and Trang watched it flare into brightness before it guttered down to a steady point of light. All week she had been haunted by the piercing cry of the stranger. She could not get it out of her mind. The memory of the man in the field baring his soul to heaven had finally driven her here today, to the church. His cry had forced her to confront her own heart and what it cried out for too.

She lowered the tip of the flame to the candle's slender wick. Shadows skittered about the corners of the church. She was lighting a candle for Saint Abha. There she was in the corner, a small painted figure of a small, pious woman. Trang knew the story by now: She was the first believer in her

Indian village, converted by an English missionary's wife over a hundred years ago, then shunned by her family. She escaped, wandered, became a missionary herself, traveling far and wide, and eventually arrived here, at this chance place so far from home, where there was now a small house of worship devoted to her. Trang felt a strong affinity for the little saint. It was as if a line connected them, though Trang couldn't quite grasp it.

Suddenly, the candle went out. The darkness out there felt as deep as the one inside her. Trang shuddered. She closed her eyes.

At first I was afraid in the darkness too, the voice said. It was velvety, like the night, smooth, with a hint of amusement. *I was lost in it, lost in my despair. But deep, deep inside me, I sensed a light, and I knew I was not alone. I held on to that light with all my might.*

Trang felt tears prickling beneath her shuttered lids. She felt herself leaning into the voice, into the void, floating there, ready to be taken into Abha's world, into Abha's time, memory, experience, as she had been drawn into the land of snow and moors and pastures in her dreams.

I bribed the guard with the gold rings in my ears and bangles on my arms. I fled into the night. I left it all behind, my husband and master, my sisters, my home. I shed my silk garments for rags and trousers, sheared off hair that had never been cut before; if I could, I would have stepped right out of my skin. Everything was strange and miraculous. Disguised as a lad, I apprenticed myself to a traveling merchant and followed the caravan across moonlit deserts scattered with gleaming animal bones, beneath a sky domed with stars. We arrived at last in a port city, and I saw the ocean for the first time. Oh, what a world, what a world is out there! I left the merchant and stowed away on a ship. When the crew discovered me, I was put to work, as if that were a punishment, as if I wouldn't have scrubbed the deck raw, until my hands bled, just to be there, upheld upon a land of water! But it could be cruel and murderous as well. A storm overwhelmed the ship, shredded the sails, cracked the vessel in two, poured the crew into the gnashing waves.

Trang was trembling; she reached out her hand as if to catch hold of a drowning soul.

If He had not held my hand, I would not have survived that terrifying and mighty baptism, the voice continued. *And when I was finally flung onto the shore, half corpse, my feet touching solid ground at last, I was born again. I took my first step into a new world, a new life. I knew then there was not anything I could not do, that I would not do. For Him.*

Oh, Abha, Abha. Trang felt her own soul wrung.

Saint Abha had journeyed so far; Trang longed for the courage to take a first step forward. She dipped her head in shame. She didn't want to ask for too much, more than she had been given. But some part of her wanted so much more. That part, it seemed to her, sometimes took matters into its own hands, as when her spirit leapt from her body at night and covered vast swaths of space and time. In one of her dream travels, she thought she had even found her father, then witnessed his death. In life, she only remembered him vaguely, or at least parts of him: a kind, tired smile, warm breath that blew across her face when he lifted her up in his arms. In the dream-vision, he knelt, alongside others, in the rubble of a ruined city street, head bent, eyes closed, mumbling a prayer right before the soldier shot him in the back of the head.

Father, I was with you.

She could not call these experiences dreams. They felt too real. Maybe these astral journeys were preparing her to step out of her own narrow life. She was ready.

She relit the candle and watched how shadows danced around her. The flickering light steadied, and her own mind became more focused, bringing her back to her world, to this place of sanctuary. She found she could not concentrate enough to pray. She had never met Father Martin here at the church at night. But she was so familiar with this squat, yellow building in the day that she had no trouble moving about it in the dimness. She thought of all the days she had come to worship, to help Father Martin build up the small Catholic community that found refuge here. Here her own submerged faith had been retrieved from its forgotten, buried place inside her.

But was that right? She wondered even now about the actual object of her passion: her faith or Father Martin? He always called her his right-hand helper, his co-missionary. What could be more noble than to be a mate, a partner to this man? But would he look upon a mate, a partner, the way he looked at Loan? That was how she longed for him to look at her. It was the look one bestows upon the bride who glides down the aisle modestly hidden behind her veil, slowly flowing toward the bridegroom who is waiting, breathless. He lifts the veil, and she looks up shyly, barely able to breathe herself; his expectant eyes cloud; brows press inward in a puzzled frown . . . Not you . . . the other bride. There are two of us? Amid the imagined ceremony, she did not notice, but there, beside her all along, a silent, spectral double. Delicate hands lift the lacy film, though she already knows who is beneath that other veil. She squeezes her hands into fists, shattering the image of the double brides.

It is time to end this, she told herself.

At first, Trang had written the letters just to put Father Martin's mind at ease: *Forgive me for not coming to the church party; I am well and living in Hồ Chí Minh City now. You must not worry about me.* But she had not expected Father Martin to press a return letter into her hands and in an urgent voice say, "Please deliver this to your sister." She had opened the letter, of course, and been moved by the power of his plea: to return, to seek the way of the Lord, who loved her. He begged her to turn from the sinful, corrupting city and live like her sister in the light. And then she could not leave such a heartfelt plea unanswered: *All is well. You must forget me. God travels with me and protects me.* That should have settled it, but Father Martin did not give up. Back and forth the letters went, and Trang found herself pouring her heart and thoughts into the replies, in her stuttering English: her desire to travel to a foreign land, her fears of existing forever trapped within four narrow walls. His replies: Trust in the Lord; doors will open to Him, a world that expands into infinity.

And finally, the letter that made her realize she had to act: *I love you; please come back.*

She had written back: *I am here now. Meet me at church tonight. We must talk.*

For she would confess. And Father Martin would forgive her transgression, he must! It was so innocently meant, but she had let it go too far, had enjoyed speaking to him through the words of another woman whom he had opened himself up to in a way he never had with her or anyone else. That was love.

It was so dark in the church as she approached the confessionals, opened the door, and stepped in. Would he ever forgive her for not being Loan? Would he banish her? She trembled in the darkness, started to feel suffocated, almost missing the soft footsteps. Then the door creaked open. Father . . . *shh* . . . but I have to confess . . . A finger on her lips, palm on her cheek, breath against her face, lips on her ears, oh, and all words slipped away as she closed her eyes and went down into the darkness.

Dear Loan,

Please accept this letter from your sister. She has kindly agreed to be my emissary for this difficult communication between us. I cannot find the words to express my shame and remorse over the unfortunate events of two weeks ago when we had arranged to meet and to talk. I don't blame you for fleeing after that night or for your continual silence since then. I don't know if you are still here in Huế or have gone back to Hồ Chí Minh City. Trang says you prefer not to reveal that. Your sister is such a blessing. Without her steadfast belief in me . . . but she does not know the depths of my depravity. If I could only reverse the events of that night! I have hardly slept or eaten much since then.

But I've been in constant prayer, and the Lord at last has given me a glimmer of light. My child, though I do not deserve it, He tells me to beg your forgiveness for my transgression and to open myself to love. I confess I don't know what that means. All I know is that I want to say this to you: forgive me, forgive me, forgive me.
—Father M

Dear Father M,
Please, nothing to forgive. Nothing bad happened. For us, like water, love flows. Let love carry us. With open hearts and minds we face each day.
—L

Dear Loan,
I think you are wise beyond your years. And generous, and kind. The first time I ever saw you was months before Trang introduced us. You were with her at your bookstall, and you were defending her against an obnoxious American customer who had demanded some free postcards after purchasing a box of cigarettes. Your sister was in tears, but you were adamant and fierce. You sent that American packing. I remember your voice: loud and strong as you protected your sister. At the time, I thought: that young lady has almost too much spirit, and will surely get herself in trouble one day. She would benefit greatly from guidance from God, a community that nourishes patience and cooperation. Your sister, for instance, though

meek, is a humble servant of God and finds peace, I know, in her submission to Him. I sense that if you came closer to Him, peace could be with you too.
　　—Father M

Dear Father M,
That time you remember in your letter. One correction. The customer did not ask for free postcards. My sister gave postcards as bonus for his big purchase. Because that customer bought a whole carton of cigarettes, not just one packet. Also she gave away the cheap out-of-date postcards. But I butted in and yelled even though I did not know anything, and the customer left and did not buy anything. So you are right: I have too much spirit. Trang is not meek. She has spirit and passion too: a lot!
　　—L

My Dearest L,
Your defense of your sister and belittlement of your own actions just go to further prove how right I am in my assessment of your character and achievements. Your modesty is beguiling. I admire you so much. And so it pains me to say this next: we must cease to communicate as we have been doing. I can no longer endure the monstrous hypocrisy of my actions. Let me be clear: it is entirely on my own shoulders. I alone bear the responsibility of guiding my flock, and in that I have seriously misled one particular member. We must pray. I especially must pray day and night for forgiveness and

guidance. I pray for help in bringing relief and light to as many as I can in this dear country that I've come to love so much. And you, I beseech you, come into the light. Come out of the darkness we created, out of the corruption we created. I will think of it one last time as I write, and then I will think of it no more. Please, dear Loan, if you on your part decide rightly to have no more to do with me, heed these words, my last to you. I have arranged to meet my superior, Father Xavier, next week in Berlin, where I will confess my sins and await his decision. This is my last letter to you. God be with you.

—Father M

Trang frowned when she read the letter. And then she felt such an ache in her chest that she curled her hand into a fist and started pounding there like she had seen her mother do when she heard the news about their father. She still thought of that night in the church when their bodies had met, but it was through the letters that she felt close to him. The intimate reality they had constructed through shared words was what she would miss the most.

She waited. A few weeks later when he came back, he was subdued. He often looked into the distance when he preached, pausing in mid-sentence as if suddenly sidetracked. When he looked at her, his gaze would slide off her concerned face with an embarrassed, sad expression. And true to his word, he would not take any letters from her written by "Loan." Meanwhile, real letters from Loan to her piled up. Here was another one, arrived just today. Trang unsealed it warily. But this time she did not bundle it away with the others. This one made her hands tremble as she read and reread the Latin-scripted Vietnamese words slanting down the page in Loan's childish but firm handwriting:

Dear Sister,

At first I thought my letters were getting lost in the horrible Sài Gòn postal service. But last week I ran into our old neighbor's daughter who had just arrived, and when I asked her how you were doing, she said you were well and always reading a book or a letter. So I know you are getting letters, and you must be getting mine. Why do you not answer? The truth is, though I tell everyone I am very independent, at the moment I need help, and there is no one else to turn to. Please take a bus to the city. How many times must I beg you to come? I am losing my patience! Just today I accidentally broke a glass, and then I cried for over an hour. I think I cannot go on like this much longer. If it is because you are concerned that your precious Father Martin has need of you more than I do, then I will write him that this is not the case. Why should you work so hard for him when your own flesh and blood has asked you to come? I am so angry at him! And you know what I am like when I'm angry. Please come soon.

—Loan

That caught her attention. Because she did know what Loan was like when she was angry. When Loan was angry, she was capable of anything. She remembered Loan chasing a thief down the long boulevard, dashing through the crowds and making bicyclists swerve and curse. And the day Loan showed up at the orphanage and demanded that they release her sister. It was possible, very possible, that Loan would do something impulsive now. She could do anything. Trang immediately wrote back.

Dear Loan,

I will arrive on the noon bus at the end of the week.

—T

Sài Gòn made her dizzy. The moment Trang stepped off the bus, she felt a wave of anxiety washing over her. All her thoughts of herself as a woman of travel and adventure vanished, and she wanted no more than the safety of the four narrow walls of her bookstall. Not that it was so different from Huế. The bicyclists here were just as unyielding, swerving around her at the last minute. The beggars pegged her as a new arrival and extended their palms and cursed her when she ignored them. There were more foreign faces, of course. That was to be expected. What Trang did not expect was the force of life here that did not heed her at all. Foreigners and locals alike hurried about their business, and she realized how invisible and lost she felt having no business of her own to attend to.

No, that was not true. She had the business of finding her sister. Grimly, she set herself to this task. Loan had given her an address. Trang made her way there slowly, distracted. Everything seemed larger, busier, faster. Down a long, dim hallway, behind the last door on the right, she found Loan on a mattress on the floor, covered by a thin, gray sheet, a damp cloth over her forehead. At first Trang thought she was asleep, so she crept in as silently as she could, her shoes left at the threshold. There was barely space for anything else; the room was almost as small as the bookstall. But there was a tiny window that leaked in a trickle of light, and the floor was not dirt but covered with dull green squares of linoleum. This was not what she had envisioned for her sister.

And when Loan sat up awkwardly, pushing her butt against the wall and pushing her pillow behind her back, Trang sank to her knees and closed her eyes to shut out the sight of the small but unmistakable bump in her sister's belly.

"Are you praying for me? Don't bother," Loan scoffed. Though her words were laced with scorn, her voice was flat and lifeless. "No, it's not John Wesley's child, before you ask. He's long gone. I left him, if you want to know the truth. He was not the man I thought he was. Before you tell me that I should have known better, I did know better. I knew he was weak and vain, and a liar and a scoundrel. I knew all that. But he loved me; that was all I cared about. I thought it was all I needed. Perhaps this is the part where you condemn me: that I did not stand by my man. But you see, I did not love him. I found that I could not love a man who could not protect me, could not give me a safe and cherished life as he had promised. This child. I don't know whose it is. There were so many."

Loan's words lashed her, and she submitted to the stinging rebuke. When silence fell, she continued to kneel, head bowed. She stayed frozen in that position even when the sobs came, quietly, like the last drops of rain after a monsoon, fatigued, defeated. *Lord . . . oh Father . . . help us, Lord . . . strength, forgiveness, grace . . .* The words of prayer would not string together in Trang's mind; they kept breaking and scattering into the dusty corners of the room. What would Father Martin say? A shiver of unease rippled down her spine. She could almost hear his voice whispering in her ears: *Sin. Sister. Sister. Sin.* How closely those words echoed each other in English.

My sister. Oh, my sister, my sister, my sister.

The first week was the hardest. The doctor had ordered complete bed rest, or Loan would lose the baby. Trang calculated the time she would have to stay away from Huế. Four months. She would have to tell the neighbor shopkeepers to keep an eye on her bookstall. But she had no illusions: The shop would be emptied by the time she got back. There was no helping that. Loan needed her here. It was curious, she thought. Loan's usual relentless pragmatism did not seem to extend to her current situation. Trang found herself stealthily wondering, for she could not think it directly, why her sister did not do the practical thing now and disobey the doctor's orders in the hope of avoiding an outcome she could not possibly want or be able to provide for. But she did not ask Loan about this; even thinking it a little bit brought waves of shame, made her sick to her stomach, to tell the truth. God made her vomit up her shame as punishment for these thoughts, and for the dreams that invaded her at night as she curled up against Loan on the thin mattress, closed her eyes, and slipped into Father Martin's arms in the darkness once again.

During the day she shopped and cooked; she massaged Loan's legs and kept her hair tidy. She wiped down the small room; she read aloud, mostly romance stories, for Loan could not endure the Bible. She longed for her copy of *Jane Eyre*, anything that could take her mind away from this small, hot room. A scene of Jane tramping along the bracing English countryside, perhaps. The damp green earth and the endless horizon. Shadows darkened beneath her sister's eyes. Loan was listless and silent most days. Trang herself grew morose. She could not help it: She felt tired and resentful, but she hid her feelings. It would have been unchristian to do otherwise. But she counted the days. Each one that finally passed meant she was closer to going back to Huế, back to her bookstall. Back to Father Martin. She had not spoken to or heard from him since their last exchange of letters. When she got back, she vowed, she would remedy that. She would confess. She would beg his forgiveness. He would give it to her. For she was the one who had led him into temptation, and if he had succumbed, it was not his fault. He was generous, he was caring, he had not meant to . . . Here she stalled. Because she did not know what his heart wanted. Yet she could not bring herself to regret anything. She only regretted the loss of his warmth, the pulsing urgency of skin against skin.

"Trang! The rice is burning!"

They pushed the window and door open and fanned the smoky air with their hands. "Dreamer! What were you dreaming about?" Loan scolded, settling back onto the mattress with her palm against her side.

"Nothing. I was just tired."

Loan's eyes narrowed as she scrutinized her sister's face. "You're so distracted. What's on your mind?"

Trang started to panic. Loan was always such a good mind reader. She read all her sister's secrets like a book. Loan did not look convinced, but she said nothing more. She closed her eyes and leaned back wearily against the wall. Trang closed her own eyes and tried to rest, but she found herself growing more restless, angry even. She wanted Loan to open her eyes and see her, really see her. *Look at me!* She raged inside. *You are not the only one. I'm here, and I have put my life on hold to nurse you, because you think you are the only one who matters. You think only of yourself. You have ruined many lives, not just your own, but others will pay the cost of it. I will pay the cost of it. You do not deserve him; you never deserved him.*

"It's *him*, isn't it?"

Trang's eyes flew open. Loan was staring right at her, doing as she had secretly wished: *Look at me. I see you.* And Trang felt so bare and violated that she would have slapped her sister across the face if she had not kept her fingers tightly bunched by her side.

"I don't know what you mean," she said coldly.

"Your priest, your Father Martin. You've always had a crush, but it's more than that, isn't it? He's the . . . oh, Trang! He's the father."

She didn't know where she was going when she ran out of the rented room. *Anywhere but here!* But everywhere she went, Loan's words followed: *He's the father.* Her mind whirled, refusing to acknowledge what her body knew: the tightening in her belly, the mornings of nausea, the sensitivity in her breasts. Part of her had even thought she was just mirroring Loan's condition: When they'd lived together, she remembered now, their menses had synchronized. *He's the father.* She could no longer hide it from herself. Loan's flash of insight had shattered her world, broken everything dear and sacred in her heart. Was it only sisters that could know each other like that, hurt each other like that? Trang knew this wasn't Loan's fault, but she could not forgive her. Her feet took her aimlessly about the city, to an open market where rows of fish piled on ice mocked her with their cloudy stares. The sun was starting to sink, but that wasn't why she suddenly felt a chill, then an unnamed panic. Something was wrong; she sensed it as a buzzing in her head, then all over her body. She started to run. She had to get back.

When she flung open the door to the room, her breath froze in her throat. Loan stared back in dismay. Her hair draped haphazardly about her shoulders, her hands clutched at her abdomen. Trang felt a sudden, sympathetic spasm in her own stomach, like a blow from within, as if the life she had denied now asserted itself with a vengeance, a demand for recognition. She stared at Loan's mouth, stiffened in a rictus of pain. She could not speak, could not find the words of dismay and remorse as she stared at the lines of red delicately crisscrossing her ankles below the loose pajama bottoms, stared and stared at the blood pooling at her sister's feet.

The baby was finally asleep. His round face, closed in milk-soaked bliss, was a miracle, she thought. How could anything be so perfect? But it was a relief to look away, to expand her attention beyond the small world of the two of them, if it was even possible for there to be a world beyond the two of them. When she looked out the bus window, all she could see was the wash of rain glazing the pane. Beyond the frame of shimmery water, bits of road and buildings, pieces of a broken world, flashed by. No, the world was not broken—she was. And the only thing that held her together was this child who needed her, could not survive without her. Otherwise she would have thrown herself under a bus, she would have jumped into the Sài Gòn River. And Loan would have slapped her hard across the face just now: "I know you are thinking that again. Stop it. Stop it right now, or I will slap you again and again until you come to your senses." She could have used a hard slap from Loan. She had to slap herself instead, but it was not the same. Not the same as Loan pressing her skin against her face, soothing the sting, mingling her tears with Trang's, whispering fiercely in her ears: "This is *our* baby. We will raise him together. I will send money every month. You are not alone. You are never alone, because I am here for you."

Loan had been there every step of the way after she had recovered from her miscarriage. Loan was there holding her hand tightly during the labor, so tightly, like the time she had ferociously locked onto Trang's hand before the nuns had finally separated them. She was there to hold the baby for weeks and even feed him from her own breasts swollen from unused milk until Trang could finally bear to touch him. But once she did, she could not put him down. She would not let Loan take him to raise in Sài Gòn, but in the end, she did allow her sister to take something else. The child would return with Trang to Huế as her nephew: the illegitimate son of the profligate sister who could not be burdened by a child in her pursuit of a hedonistic lifestyle. Only the two of them would know the real burden that Loan had taken from Trang: the load of shame that Loan would now bear from afar, piled on by jealous neighbors and self-righteous gossips and ignorant busybodies—in short, everybody. But Loan had shrugged it off: "They can all go eat dog shit. This child *is* mine. He is ours."

Trang laid her cheek on the baby's downy head. Her tears made a quiet rainfall on the nest of dark silky hair. She cried for the baby who would never call her Má. She cried for her sins, the ones of the past and the ones she would carry forward into the future, the life of lies to come. She cried because she finally understood why Father Martin loved Loan.

Chapter Three

Huế, 1994—Vinh

"Go faster, Đức!" He is flowing in a thick sea of bright, pulsing life. The current sweeps them all along at a steady pace, and he has time to stare at a school of uniformed girls boldly plunging into the stream of traffic, causing bikes, pedicabs, scooters, and cars to split and surge around the giggling pod. It's barely a ripple in the gushing stream of movement. Here and there pedestrians dart through the traffic in expertly timed spurts. He's glad he's on wheels, rolling, rushing, roaring down the long boulevard that runs along the canal until it joins the Perfume River.

He likes it when Đức, the neighboring stall owner's oldest son, lets him ride on the handlebars of his bike. He is crashing against the wind; he spreads his arms. Đức says, "Put your arms down—I can't see." Soon so many people are stepping into the road that Đức has no choice but to slow down. Now the wind dies, now movement slows to a trickle. The boy riding on the handlebars feels dimmed and blunted. He longs for speed. He wants a bike of his own: His aunt said he can ride her old rusty scooter when he gets older. So he counts the days till getting old enough, wondering when that will be. He's eight, though he looks like he's five, he's told. He dreams of Vespas.

"Okay, hop off now."

"Thanks, Đức."

"Be helpful to your aunt. Bye!"

"Bye-bye!"

There's his aunt's bookstall on the other side. He steps into the stream of traffic to cross. *Oh, that silver Vespa!*—Oww! He's flat on his back, the sky pressing down.

"Look before you cross, Little Worm."

"I did look!"

An old man looks down on him. It's just the spy. That's what his aunt calls him: the old man with the notebook who does nothing all day but walk up and down beside the canal, looking at the row of shops and bookstalls lining the other side of the boulevard, occasionally jotting a note into his small book.

"You were looking at the Vespa, not at the idiot that would have run you over if I hadn't pulled you back."

"Mr. Spy, how much do you think a silver Vespa like that costs?"

"How should I know? I'm only a spy, as you say, not a bike rental business."

"But don't you know everything from all your spying? Isn't that information in your notebook?"

"Humph. What's in my notebook isn't any of your business. Now get off your backside and don't make me have to save your skin again."

"Bye, Mr. Spy."

"Goodbye, Little Worm."

This time he makes it safely across. Thankfully, his aunt was busy with a customer and didn't see any of that. She doesn't like the spy for some reason. Doesn't like when her nephew plays spy. *You will not be a spy. You will go to school; you will become an engineer, or a diplomat, or a writer.* In his mind, he morphs into a figure holding a hammer and a screwdriver and fixing something that has a lot of cogs and wires; then he is holding a pencil and a pad of paper. He doesn't know what a diplomat is or what they would hold. He turns into an astronaut, a cowboy, a truck driver. He could be any of those things. But first, school. He doesn't much like school. He likes to help out at the bookstall. He keeps the postcards shiny, wiping them with a cloth as he studies them, and he keeps the books neatly stacked. He sits on the sill of the open window and calls out: "Buy here! Cheapest! Buy now!" But most of the time, he just likes to sit on the floor of the bookstall next to his aunt's legs and look at his comic books.

"What did I tell you about looking carefully before you go into the street?"

"You saw that?"

"I see everything."

"Like the spy?" His eyes open wide.

"No, not like that fool."

It's just him and his aunt. And the other vendors on either side who offer him a treat now and then. He's not sure he likes them. They look at him in a shifty way when they think he is not looking. He knows it's because his hair is lighter and his eyes a little rounder, and he tries to unround them by squinting until his aunt says she will take him to have his eyes checked for glasses, and then he stops. There are other children like him at school. One other, a girl with light-brown hair and pale eyes. They should be friends, his aunt says, but he avoids her. He knows that it won't make the other kids like him better, so he and the other remain two little islands in a vast, lonely ocean.

"I'm sorry. I'll be more careful next time, Auntie."

She freezes. "What did you call me?"

"Auntie."

She goes very still.

Once, when spying, he heard the vendors talking about his mother, who is away in Sài Gòn, and how she was a bad woman, and this upset him so much, and when he told his aunt, she went quiet and still. Then she gathered all the money they had made that day, and they went out and bought matches and a little gasoline, and she promised that they would burn down all their shops: the liars. He got frightened and broke off and ran to Father M. *She is going to burn down the street!* And Father M hurried over and spoke to her, and she cried, then gave him the matches and gasoline, and she took Vinh by the hand and they went home to their tiny room in the back of the church where Father M let them stay in return for his aunt's daily cleaning and polishing of the sanctuary. Father M wanted to give them more, he knew, because he had spied on them arguing, his aunt saying no, always no, this was all they would take, and it was already too much.

"Why did you call me that?" He doesn't understand why she's this upset about a word.

"Father M told me that I shouldn't call you Má anymore because you're my aunt."

"He said that? When?"

"The other day, after Mass."

He can feel a shiver go through his aunt's stiff body, like she's trying to keep something from breaking out of her. Then she starts breathing very fast, almost panting. "Stay here a moment," she says. "I'll be right back."

"Where are you going?"

"I just have to speak to Father Martin for a moment."

Sometimes he wonders if his mother is as puzzling as his aunt, the way she is happy one minute, then sad, then angry the next. Mostly she is happy, and that makes him happy. But then she gets this way. She looks at him like she is going to tell him a story, and he waits for it because he loves stories. His favorite is the one about the dragon who marries the fairy who gives birth to one hundred children who become the first people of Vietnam. His mother, he likes to think, is really a beautiful fairy who married a dragon, then went away after giving birth to him. His aunt is not beautiful enough to marry a dragon. But just now, she looks mad enough to kill one.

Huế, 1994—Trang

Why should he not call me Má? Why should Father Martin stop him? How could he deny her this one small consolation in a life that somehow felt like a shadow of a life, a mockery of her dreams. They were a family, but she was the only one who knew it. By the time he turned four, she had had enough. "Call me Má," she had told Vinh. "I am your Má here and she is your Má over there."

Loan wrote a letter to them once a month, which they read while looking at Loan's photograph. He made a habit of focusing intently on his mother's features during these times. *She is so pretty.* He would look at her eyes. She would smile and look back at him. *She is talking to me.* Her voice, oddly, sounded like his aunt's.

"But everyone calls you my auntie."

"Yes, I am your auntie, but I take care of you, so I am also your mother."

She was simply deaf to him unless he called her Má. Just hearing that syllable come out of his mouth. It was more than a sound: It was a lifeline out of her dark phases. Sensitive soul that he was, he caught that right away. They were so close, they felt each other's moods. Really, it didn't take long at all to train him.

But all that undone by his father! Trang hurried down the boulevard, hardly noticing the bloom of colors swelling the air. It was April, the end of the dry season. The summer tourists would be flocking in soon. It made her so happy when they stopped to chat a bit after perusing her stack of bootlegged books and old postcards. Three years ago, right next to her bookstall, an American woman had almost fainted after one such exchange. Trang had played the savior: hailing a pedicab, accompanying the woman and her husband back to their hotel, berating the incompetent hotel staff, reviving the tourist herself by pinching the pressure points between the woman's eyes. It was thrilling to be in the middle of the action, taking charge, helping them. Then, in the next moment, having sent all the staff away, Trang was the only one left in the room with the couple. They were looking expectantly at her. All her confidence had vanished. She stuttered. Her English seemed to have disappeared as well. And she saw in a flash how ridiculous she was. Of course they did not see her as a savior, as a knight to the rescue. All those

English fairy tales had deceived her, as Loan had always warned her they would. She blushed. In her shame she started backing out toward the door while apologizing for her presumption in trying to help, sorry for her uselessness, her imposition. She longed to be back in the safety and obscurity of her bookstall.

The husband interrupted her flustered thoughts. "Would you like to join us for dinner later?" *What?* "We want to thank you for your kind help."

This was what Father Martin must have meant, she thought, when he said that Christianity was everywhere. They must be Christians. It popped out of her mouth: "Are you Christians?"

They laughed. "No, we're Jewish. But we're hungry," the woman said. "Will you join us?"

"No, no, of course not, I can't, I am too busy." She fled. But she could not hide even from herself how pleased and surprised she was at the invitation. To be invited to dinner by Americans!

That was three years ago. Every summer she was eager to see if they would come back. Maybe this time, this summer, they would. And she would be there, with shiny new postcards and more up-to-date books about touring Vietnam. And she would be wearing new clothes: a crisp white blouse. Yes, I will come to dinner.

Trang opened the door of the church building. So quiet at this hour. Mass not for another hour. Yes, she was capable. She had saved the American woman on her own. Where would Father Martin be? She headed for his office at the back of the building. Yes, she had done it on her own. She had raised her son. She was a mother, not an aunt. What right did Father Martin have to say Vinh could not call her Má? Her hand on the doorknob paused, but she took a deep breath to brace herself. A son had the right to call his mother Má. Her feelings swelled; she thought her heart might burst from the surge of rage and longing that coursed through that organ that moment at those words: *my son.* She had meant to knock first, but the momentum of her feelings pushed her right through the door. How dare you tell my son—

The words ready to pour from her heart instead froze in her throat. *Oh no. Oh no no no.* She sank to the ground beside the slumped form. She wrapped her arms around the still shoulders, buried her face in his collar. *I will never. I will always. The past he never knew, the future they never had.* She rocked and moaned, rocked and moaned. That was how the first parishioners to arrive at the church found them.

"Take more soup."

"No, Trang, I've had enough."

A little gruffness in his voice. He was getting a little cranky. That was a good sign. A nurse came in to take his blood pressure. Father Martin was gruff with her as well. Trang exchanged silent glances with the nurse: The patient is cranky. That's good.

What a week it had been. She had been at the hospital day and night. The doctors and nurses were a little terrified of her. She translated for Father Martin when needed; when she spoke on his behalf, she added her own opinions as an extension of his voice. Throughout, Father Martin had been docile and willing to let her take charge. She had never felt more energized in her life. She only left his side to care for Vinh, to greet him after school and spend an hour or two with him in the bookstall. Then she left to bring food to Father Martin, for he could not be subjected to the poor feeding at the hospital. He needed special phở soup and soft vermicelli noodles mixed with tofu and shrimp. He needed his arms and legs rubbed to restore the circulation, he needed the dents in his pillow beaten out. He needed to have his nurses told to be quiet and to come back later to take his temperature and blood pressure because he was napping right now, couldn't they see with their own eyes? She left again to feed Vinh, who was watching the store and doing homework. Later she put him to bed in their small room at the back of the church. Then she rushed right back to the hospital. She had a mat on the floor. Luckily Vinh was not afraid to be alone, though she felt conflicted. As soon as Father Martin was stable, she promised herself, she would go back to sleeping with her son. Today the patient was cranky. She would be able to go back soon.

"We almost lost you," the Western doctor said cheerfully. Dr. Rogers had a big red nose and runny pale-blue eyes. He used to come to church to talk avidly with Father Martin about theology. Dr. Rogers had been a seminary student before he switched to medicine. Trang didn't like him. He called her "dear" absently when he remembered that she was in the room. "You're better now, but you can't go on as you have, you know." Dr. Rogers was American, from the South, he said, which was why his speech had a kind of stretchy quality that Trang found hard to follow. *Ten. A. See.* That was where he was from. "You work too hard, and the climate here is bad. You were lucky this time, but it can't go on like this." Why did doctors become more cheerful when delivering bad news? she wondered. Just now, the doctor had his hands in the pockets of his white coat while he rocked a little on his feet as if he were just discussing the weather with Father Martin.

Father Martin sighed. "I know, Frank, but there's so much to do. And I . . . I feel a connection to this place, these people."

Was Trang imagining it, or did he look quickly over at her when he said that? Her heart quickened.

"If you want an early death, then by all means stay on," said Dr. Rogers. "But there's a chopper ready to leave the air base next week, and I highly recommend that you wrap up here and be on it." If she'd had a stick, she would have rammed it into his runny left eye, and oh, that was very unchristian, but that was how much she hated him at that moment.

After Dr. Rogers left the room, Trang continued to sit quietly in the corner. But inside the solemn, still form there was a raging storm. Inside was a battle of emotions threatening to erupt.

"Trang, come here please."

She was at his side in an instant. Father Martin took her hand, sending shivers down her spine. It had been ages, a lifetime ago, since she had felt his hand upon any part of her body. Fragments of a memory glimmered like the light from a lit candle. That night at the church. *An offering to Saint Abha, from the velvety darkness, Saint Abha speaking of a sea voyage, a rebirth; in the darkness a hand caressing her face,* Loan, you are here, *no I am—fingers on her lips, shush, breath against her face, forgetting who she was, forgetting everything but that voyage together in the sea of darkness.*

She closed her eyes, but the tears seeped out beneath the lids.

"My child," he said. "Please. We knew this day might come."

No, she had not known that; she had refused to know it, ignored the coughing, the paleness, the canceled Masses. She had brought soups, tinctures (kindly returned), small charms left in the corners of his room, said extra prayers. Really, it was like having a second child. (Later this period would rush back to her often. How she wanted to protect him in his vulnerability. To keep him close and care for him this way was the only means she had to express the love that he would never know she felt for him.) But it was tiring. Motherhood. And now, the prospect of Father Martin leaving them, leaving her to do it all on her own. Loan sent money every month. That was not the same thing as having a mother and a father. Knowing the father was nearby even if he himself did not know it. Her body still ached for him, but she had learned to push that down, to ignore it. To find reward in his solicitude for the boy who was his son. Even if . . . even if that regard came from his belief that it was Loan's child. And even if he secretly wondered if it was his child too.

He had confessed as much to her once.

"There's just one thing. I want to do something for the child. To help you, Trang. You are a saint for raising your sister's child, and you must not be alone in this. I must help."

"Please, there is no need. Loan sends money. And you are kind to us and take an interest in his education." He often stopped by the bookstall to quiz Vinh on his reading and math. *Okay, little man, how about eleven times eleven?* She smiled at Vinh's swift and correct answer, his proud grin. He had memorized the times table up to twelve times twelve. Father Martin was proud too; she could tell when he mirrored Vinh's grin and tousled his hair. He had given them so much: the clothes from church donations, the extra cleaning job at the church that justified the tiny room in the back where they slept.

"I want to help," Father Martin said. "I feel responsible for his education, his future. I mean, we are all responsible for the parentless children brought into this world. But as I only have the modest resources to help one child, why not this one, who is so precious to our community?"

Trang had no words. She was stunned by his generosity. At the same time, a part of her objected: *Vinh is not parentless.*

"I want to help," Father Martin repeated. "For his sake and yours. For hers too." She thought she might have heard him say, but she wasn't sure: "And for my sake."

He did not say her name. He never did, anymore. And yet she knew: Her sister's name lived behind his lips, his eyes, when he looked at Vinh.

"There is just one thing I want you to do."

"Anything, Trang. You know I would give you anything you asked for."

"Please tell Vinh he can call me Má."

Silence. Father Martin dropped her hand, and he went still. Suddenly, she was afraid in a way distinct from her heartrending fear of losing him. He seemed to come back to himself as from a reverie. A little shake, like shrugging on a coat, as he put his pastor persona back on.

"My child."

Lord help us, she thought.

"My child."

"I have nothing." She rushed in to stop his words. "Why he can't call me Má? Why I can't have one small thing? I love him so much!"

He pressed her hands firmly. "I love him, too, but he does not call me Father. Not *his* father. He is a son to all of us. But Loan is his mother, his real mother. And it would be wrong and sinful to deny that.

And when I leave here"—he patted her shuddering shoulders—"I need to know that he will be cared for despite all the sins that brought him into the world. He is innocent, and must not suffer from our . . . lapses. That is owed to the child, and to his unfortunate mother."

Oh, her heart was stabbed, and the knife ripped down, splitting that organ in two. He would leave, and he would take with him a picture of Loan to live in his heart, and he would never know who was the real mother of their child. No. No, Loan could not have everything. She would rip up that image of her in his heart if nothing else.

"Loan never love you," she said softly. *She does not care for you at all, and her actions do not center around your existence,* she thought. *You are nothing to her.*

He closed his eyes and moved his hands farther away from hers.

She pressed on. She could no more stop herself than she could have held back a tidal wave. "I lied, we lied. Vinh is not her child."

His breathing was shallow, and his skin very pale, but she knew he was listening. "He is *my* son, not Loan's."

There. Where was the thunderclap, why was the floor not cracked open, spilling them into hell?

"Oh, my child," he said kindly, gently. "I know you wish it to be so. But do not let dreams supplant reality." His voice dropped, almost to a whisper. "She did love me, as I loved her. The woman who loved me that night was real. She did not sin alone, and I have often wondered if she was protecting me from the knowledge of the fruit of that sinning."

She thought she would die. She thought she would not survive if Father Martin left without knowing the truth. "That was not Loan," she whispered. "That was me."

He was so still. Was he dead? But now his eyes were open and staring at her. "You? That night? It wasn't her?" She saw horror in his eyes. "Why?"

She stuttered, "Because you never see me. I could never get you to see *me.*"

"It was all a lie."

Only through deception did you ever see me truly, she thought. But what she saw now was the door of his heart closing, not opening, to her. And before she was forced to see it slam in her face, shut her out completely, she fled the sickroom. Within the battering whirlwind of thoughts that followed her, one stood out like a beacon: He could condemn her for a thousand faults and deceptions—she was envious, impatient, judgmental, impractical, ignorant. She was a sinner. But she wasn't a liar, not about that long-ago night, not about the love that she felt, that she would always feel, that had afterward sheltered them, held them, covered them like a blanket, like a skin, like eternity.

All that a lie?

Never.

Never.

He was leaving today. He was leaving, and she would not think of it. Her heart was closed down, her heart was dead. She would not think of it. He was leaving today. Vinh seemed to sense her turmoil, and stayed silent by her side, had been that way since he returned from school. He sat on his high stool and looked out at the stream of people and bicycles flowing past their shop. Every now and then she felt his eyes upon her as she grieved behind a stoic mask. At four o'clock, he slipped off the stool and said he had to go to the church. Her heart skipped a beat. Now?

"Yes, Father M said to come by."

"He told you that?"

"He sent a note to school. He's going away, and he wants to say goodbye to me. Why is he going?"

She pressed her eyes shut and clenched her fists to keep her feelings in. It took all her strength. But then she was calm. "It's for his health. He's going back to the United States to rest and heal from his sickness."

"Will he come back?"

"I don't know."

"I hope so," Vinh said, "because who will lead the services?"

"They will find someone," she said.

"It won't be the same."

She had no answer to that. Nothing will ever be the same again, she wanted to cry.

"Go, then. Say goodbye. And tell him . . ."

He waited.

"Nothing. Just go."

What was there to say? That it had been the happiest eight years of her life, that she could ask for nothing more. Except for it to go on. To go on raising their son together, even if he hadn't known that was what he was doing. When he brought a sack of clothes donated by Western churches, he always sorted out the jeans and T-shirts and sneakers that Vinh loved. They were always too big for him, but he cherished them. And books for her. Ragged paperbacks. Never romances. He took care to curate her reading, to make sure only chaste books were given: histories, biographies, never fiction, but sometimes poetry. She loved the poetry. She did not tell him that the poetry was sometimes even more salacious and heart pounding than the romances. E. E. Cummings, Verlaine, Sylvia Plath. She loved them. Though they didn't have the special place in her heart that *Jane Eyre* did. Jane had been there for so long now that she was part of Trang.

The comfortable domestic rhythm with Father Martin had taken a while to establish itself. When she had first returned to Huế, tiny baby in her arms, everyone had accepted her story immediately. Of course it was Loan's baby. Her lifestyle, after all. And how selfless of the aunt to take on the sister's burden of raising the child. It was easy. But Father Martin had been silent and distant. Then one day, a month after she returned, he came to the bookstall as she was closing. It had been a long day, and the sun had already set, bringing a coolness that eased her tiredness. As she was lifting Vinh from his basket in the corner, preparing to wrap him into a sling around her back, Father Martin walked up and held out his arms. "Let me take the child, Trang." Astonished, she handed over the small, squirming bundle. He took it gently and studied the tiny face closely. Then with a sigh he gently handed the baby back. At first she felt awkward.

Then she rearranged the picture in her head: A family walks home.

"You are remarkable, Trang." Father Martin had noticed that she couldn't stop smiling as they walked.

"What? Me?"

"Yes, you. Here you are, gladly taking up the sins and burdens of others as if they were your own. Others run away or hide or deny the truth, but not you. You give what you have, however little that is. Remarkable."

They stopped at the house where Trang and the baby shared a corner of a room with several other families. Father Martin paused. "You deserve better, Trang. You deserve help. You will not live in this squalor."

It wasn't bad, actually. She liked the company, the warm bodies close together in sleep. It was crowded, but clean.

"You will come live in the church."

So Father Martin had spread his wings over them and sheltered them in the small room at the back of the church, and she had earned her keep there by cleaning when she was done at the bookstall. She took care of his church as a way of taking care of him. Of loving him, she saw now. And they tried not to be there at all during the day, only late at night after she had closed the bookstall, when she would wake up Vinh from his mat on the floor of the shack, pressed up against one side so there was barely room to move, and they would walk back in the dark to a room about the twice the size of the bookstall but with a real bed and mattress. Luxury. There would follow another hour of cleaning before Trang lay down beside Vinh and fell asleep the moment she closed her eyes. They were both gone before the church doors opened for early-morning Mass. Like ghosts.

Would the new pastor allow them to stay? And where was the boy now? The afternoon was drawing to a close. The heat was lifting, and there was a general sense of loosening, unwinding, letting go of the day's grip. Would they have to go back to a packed and crowded room with no privacy, bodies everywhere? It could be worse, she reminded herself. She had saved a little bit, and that plus Loan's money could get them something perhaps for just themselves. But it wouldn't be the same.

Nothing would ever be the same again. But what was the point of crying over it? When did anything ever go the way one wished? One had no choice about anything: conceived in a land of windswept fields and prosperity, or born in a country of heat and war. The man one loved, who was lawfully bound to another. The man one loved, who loved someone else. Your life already written as a story with the ending in place. If only she could rewrite the narrative, set characters down different paths. Then where would she be? That question jolted her. She thought not of Father Martin but of her son. If she was in a world that didn't have Vinh, she would search every pathway to get him back. She would blow up the story, jump time and space to find him. For that was the miracle: Nothing ever worked out the way one wished, true, but the thing one didn't know to wish for, like a son who sat beside you in the bookstall and counted motorbikes all day—the unwished-for miracles of daily life—wasn't that all one needed?

She would even miss the crazy old spy across the street if he were to disappear one day. *Look at that fool dashing into the busy street. He will get run over this time, for sure. He's really lost it now, and oh my, is he coming* here?

"They're gone!"

"Gone? Who?"

"He took the boy. He took your son!"

Later she would remember that she ran out of the bookstall so fast she left a slipper behind. Later she would remember trembling so hard she could barely balance on the rusty scooter as it wove crazily through the crowded boulevard on the way to the airfield while she clung to the back of the spy's jacket, barely able to breathe. Later, she would remember that he had said *your son*.

Huế, 1994—Vinh

There's his aunt, so small! And oh, the spy, and their motorbike! He waves and shouts, and they are looking up, and his aunt raises her arms to the sky as if she is getting ready to catch him if he falls from the helicopter. "Don't worry," he shouts, "I won't fall!" Not like that time he climbed the linden tree to retrieve the bound kite and slipped and broke his arm. He had never seen his aunt so distraught. Even the spy had said to him after the cast came off, "Don't do that to your aunt again," as if she were the one who had broken a bone. "There she is, there she is," he says now as he tugs on Father M's arm, but Father M is looking out the other side of the helicopter and rubbing his prayer beads and mumbling. So he waves and waves on his own as his aunt and the spy shrink into tiny dots, and the buildings and trees pull farther away, and oh, there is the bookstall. How small it is! He barely recognizes it, except it is the smallest one in the row of shops and stalls. But he waves to it, as he promised his aunt he would do if he ever flew, as she'd told him she's done in her dreams, over the rooftops of Huế, over the top of their own bookstall. He waves and waves as they soar over the Perfume River, and nobody waves back.

Chapter Four

Upstate New York, 1996

Jack Malone had taken his cap, the one Father M gave him as a souvenir two years ago when they arrived in the United States. But he wasn't going to fight to get it back. Or cry. That would definitely make it worse. He kept looking at it stuffed into the back pocket of Jack Malone's pants, where the rim was getting crushed. It was a stupid cap, with the once-white threads of the **USA** lettering gray and worn. But wearing it reminded him of rising in the giant metallic bird, the ground dropping away, his aunt's raised arms, the bookstall tiny as a matchbook below. Sometimes he still felt groundless. Actually, he always felt groundless. Father M said it would get easier. He knew that Father M wasn't *his* father, but he clung to him nevertheless. There was no one else. Father M had even shared his name with Vinh, because he said that he needed one; everyone needed a proper last name. So he wasn't just Vinh anymore—he was Vinh Martin.

Jack Malone had taken Vinh Martin's cap, and now he raised his hand and asked to use the restroom. Vinh did the same thing a few moments later. He knew what to do. Outside the classroom he saw Malone strolling down the empty corridor, hands in his pockets, not in any kind of hurry to get back. Vinh moved on silent feet, tackled him, threw himself at the back of Malone's legs, got him to the ground, grabbed his cap, got up to dash—right into the arms of Father X.

"You will come with me."

"But it was mine. He stole it!"

"No, sir, he's lying, sir. I wasn't doing anything. He hit me from behind, damn sneak."

"That's enough, Malone. Get on with you. Come with me, Martin!"

Instinctively he glanced over his shoulder; had another boy entered the fray? It always took him a moment to attach the name Martin to himself. At Father X's desk, he was given a small chalkboard and piece of chalk. The other boys stared curiously at Vinh standing by Father X's desk.

"Write this down: 'lazy, deceitful, liar, unsporting, *biter*,' according to the good Christian woman who has fostered you for two years among her own family." That was Aunt Marie—Father M's sister, the good Christian woman. Vinh lived with her and her twins. She was the one who had told Father X that he was a biter, and Vinh wondered how she could be called a good Christian woman when that was a lie: The twins were the ones who bit, and kicked, pinched, and spat at him when no one was looking. He had learned to stay silent, avoid them, though that seemed to exasperate her as much as his presence. *What's wrong with you, it's not normal to be so quiet, what are you thinking, are you secretly hating us behind your yellow face?* She never talked to him like that when Father M was visiting, and Vinh never said anything. He only asked when he would be able to return to live with Father M.

Now, in the drab classroom that felt like a cell, the boys jeered. He felt he might faint from mortification. The board was hung around his neck, and he was ordered to stand on top of a stool at the front of the classroom. From this height Vinh looked at the sea of hateful faces below. He heard every titter, suppressed laugh, look of amusement and contempt. He was not blubbering, yet, because he was still in shock at the exposure, as if a rock had been lifted and he had been yanked out of darkness and exhibited under a glaring light. Too stunned to fully react. Then just when the numbness was wearing off, the class was over and the boys dismissed for their recess break.

"Not you," Father X said pointedly to Vinh. "You stay up here for the rest of the day."

The empty classroom was somehow worse, for he was alone with his thoughts: Father M would never come and take him away now. A boy entered and walked toward the front of the room, book in hand. As he approached his stool, the boy looked him right in his eyes, and not in a jeering or curious or contemptuous way. It was a calm look that indicated the boy clearly saw him. And there was a challenge in that look as well, as if to say, Well, and there you are—what of it? Is it the end of the world?

Yes, Vinh wanted to shout, it is the end of everything! If the floor could open up and swallow me right into hell, let it happen now!

Eye roll that said it all: What drama. Will you let them make your world so small?

It stopped Vinh's breath. It dammed up his tears. And then the boy passed, placed his book on Father X's desk, turned, and walked out of the classroom.

Kenneth Dawson. Kenny. He was an older student, Vinh recalled, too old for this grade, but kept behind even though clearly more advanced and smarter than anyone else in the room. Used as an example of sloth and ineptitude: "Keep messing up, boys, and end up like Dawson here, held behind and still with the kiddie classes." Dawson never showed offense. He took it all calmly, politely, bowed his head, tucked it back into his book. It was why Vinh had never really noticed him much before, and indeed, when the class returned, there was Dawson in his customary corner, deep in a book. He never looked at Vinh again. But Vinh looked nowhere else, and did not attend to the returning students who hurled insults and laughs before the teacher arrived, throwing things, crumpled paper, erasers, a textbook that just missed his head, and then sudden stillness and hush as the teacher entered. Vinh found that he didn't care about any of it. Because Kenneth Dawson had looked him in the eye. Someone had seen him. And somehow, Vinh felt strong enough to keep standing.

The hard part was that inner curve in the ear, and if he didn't shade it just right, then the little pocket of space would flatten and the whole ear would collapse into a muddy patch. He pressed his pencil into the spot to darken it, and the craters of the inner ear opened up, suggesting depth. Now the part he was yearning to sketch: the way the dark-brown strands tucked behind the ear curled at the tip of the lobe in springy half circles. He might have made them springier and curlier than they really were because it felt like he was touching them when he was drawing them, and he put his longing into the image: It made you *want* to reach out, pull gently, watch them spring back to the side of this face. He watched Kenny carelessly loop a ringlet behind his ear, his face never leaving the pages of the damn book. *Look up, look at me!* Kenny kept reading. He seemed far away. The sketch Vinh drew made Kenny look like he was deep in his own world, unaware of the burning gaze upon him. All his sketches had this feeling of something just out of reach. His pictures were mostly memories of another time, another country, where faces resembled his own. One face in particular. It was not a beautiful face, and though he had the rudimentary skills to make it so, he preferred its plainness. He had sketched that one over and over again.

"What are you reading?"

Kenny sighed. But he answered patiently, as he always did. "It's a book on philosophy and religion: an argument about the existence of God."

"Is it interesting?"

"It is to me, though you might find it a bit dry."

He knew for sure he would, but now that he had Kenny's attention, he would pretend he was fascinated.

"Who wins the argument?"

Well, so-and-so makes sound points, but in the end so-and-so says such-and-such and Vinh was no longer listening, just watching Kenny's expression of deep thought and how he flushed a bit as he got into the argument and how his clear gray eyes looked into the distance and the pupils made little darts back and forth as he described the defeat of one scholar by the other: It was like he was there, watching them battle to death, and he was rooting for one while admiring the fight put up by the other. Then Kenny stopped speaking.

"You didn't hear a word of that."

Guilt. "Of course I did!" Sigh. Another boy might have challenged the claim. Kenny accepted it without judgment. His eye caught Vinh's sketchbook. Father M had gifted it to him on one of his rare, brief visits. It was nice to draw pictures without bars of lines running through them.

"Let's see your latest drawing, then."

He gave Kenny the sketchbook shyly.

"Hmm. Not bad at all, Martin. You are really improving."

A flush of warmth at the praise. Kenny flipped farther back into the pages of the sketchbook. "Who's this?"

"Oh. My aunt."

"Hmm. Very interesting, how you've drawn her."

"She's not very pretty," Vinh said defensively.

"What of that? Where is this place?" The sketch showed a woman looking out a window, or opening: a blur of street, the open sky.

"I used to live there," Vinh said quietly. Kenny gave him a look but said no more as he handed back the sketchbook.

As he did so, he was overtaken by a fit of coughing that ended with the older boy gasping for breath. Vinh looked on anxiously until Kenny's breathing returned to normal. His pale face looked even paler, but his voice was steady as he admonished Vinh not to overreact.

"I'm fine. Allergies. Asthma." He waved his hand impatiently. "Body stuff. Not important."

Vinh wondered how the body could be unimportant. "If there's no body, there's no you, Kenny!"

"Not true, Martin. The body is just a random vessel. Your true self, the one created by God, is for all time and beyond any body."

It was hard to understand. "But how would I draw *you*, then?"

Kenny smiled. "Look," he said, sweeping his arm over the school grounds and beyond to the meadow separated by the stone fence and beyond that to the trees, and the fields, and the hills.

"Draw the landscape?"

Kenny nodded. "And the sunset, or a bird, or a bottle by the side of the road. You would find me everywhere, in anything. Just look around. There it is. Because it's not what you see that matters. It's how you see it."

Vinh shook his head. "But I like you just the way you are."

"The trouble, Martin, is that you're far too emotional and impulsive; you have no self-control. I've been watching you."

Vinh glowed with the thought that Kenny had observed him, deemed him worthy of observation, but he was abashed that he was found wanting in patience and self-mastery. "I'm going to be more like you, Kenny," he vowed.

"Reading is important, definitely, but why are these things exclusive to each other, and why should you imitate others when you have your own talent to cultivate?" The older boy smiled and ruffled Vinh's hair. He pulled a book out of his bag. He always had the book bag with him, and it was always filled with an abundance of books. "You might like this one."

Vinh opened the cover gamely. Two pages in, he set it aside and picked up his sketchbook instead. Kenny merely smiled without looking up from his own book, his stillness making it easy for Vinh to study how the light sharpened his profile but softened the tightness that usually rimmed his eyes (Kenny needed glasses, was always squinting). A few quick lines corrected the problem—and now Kenny had round spectacles on his face and could see perfectly, at least on the page. Satisfied, Vinh shut the sketchbook, lay back, and let his thoughts drift with the clouds overhead. He didn't remember closing his eyes, but when they snapped open, it was dark enough for him to see stars instead of clouds in the sky. Beside him, Kenny lay with his book opened at the spine upon his chest, gently rising and falling with each breath.

"Wake up, wake up—we missed the bell!"

Fortunately, it was Father Q who met them at the door (if it had been Father X, it would not have gone well for them). Father Q laughed and told them they had missed dinner, but "Come on then, I've got something in my room." They followed him. Father Q was a favorite, and he was kind to everyone, but particularly to Kenny. Vinh noticed how they leaned toward each other in their eagerness to gather every drop of their discussion of some obscure theologian. It made his head spin to try to follow their talk, and after a while, Vinh gave up and just watched their faces. In their eagerness for intellectual food, they left most of the meal of sandwiches and stale cookies untouched. But Kenny, Vinh noticed, became expansive, glowed. Vinh could hear the passion in his voice, even though he didn't understand what he was talking about, and he could see how much Father Q admired him as he nodded, his blue eyes twinkling behind dark-rimmed glasses. In the end, Father Q broke off to urge Kenny to eat, wrapping up the leftovers in paper and tucking the packets in the boys' pockets.

"Well, then, it's late. Off to bed, you two." He might have been talking to a log. Vinh couldn't move: He was so full and tired and happy. He had a groggy perception of being lifted by the strong arms of Father O, who had popped in to ask Father Q a question, of being carried down the hall to the junior boys' dormitories while Kenny was sent off to the senior boys' room, of the hushed voices of Father O and Father Q.

"Should he be allowed to spend so much time with Dawson? Doesn't he know how sick . . ."

"Hush, O'Malley, there's no harm, and no need for him to know." Heavy sigh. "It will happen when it happens; all in good time; all in God's hands . . ."

More murmurs . . . soothing rhythms of steps going upstairs, cool sheets, but not cool enough to stimulate him awake, soft pillow, the silence between the suspirations of air from the rows of sleeping boys, sighing, turning, dreaming, breathing in, out, in, out.

The end of February brought an ill wind, cold and damp. It blew over the marshy fields and settled in the school and crept down one's neck despite the upturned collars and the heat cranked up (despite the grumbling of the headmaster about costs) at Father Q's insistence. And yet the old furnace could only do so much, and the students huddled with extra sweaters and scarves wrapped up to their chins as they worked at their desks in the schoolrooms, stopping to blow on their fingers. Then one by one they began to fall ill. It started with young Alfred Marks, who threw up in the middle of the night and cried for his mother, and then it spread to the rest of the junior ward within days. Then the senior students started to cough and sneeze and feel nauseated and drained. The faculty and staff were not immune. Parents swept in and retrieved their loved ones, and the rest were packed off wherever possible to extended family in the area. The teachers too packed up and shipped out. The staff was down to a skeleton crew. Father Q remained. A hired nurse took care of the bedridden, and the hospital sent over a doctor to look in at the request of Father Q. But really, there was nothing to be done but to let the illness run its course.

Those who had escaped sickness, about a half dozen, with no one to impede or reprimand them in any way, ran wild. Vinh was one of them. Whenever he could, he would try to slip past the nurse to say hello to Kenny at his bed by the window. Sometimes he would wave up from the grounds and see a thin hand wave back behind the pane. But most days Kenny lay with his eyes closed, sleeping. Vinh checked in on him once in the morning after the nurse had made her rounds, and once more in the evening after the nurse had made her rounds again. In between, he had the run of the school. With Jack Malone's departure, the pecking order had fallen away. The remaining boys were left totally unsupervised. Vinh wandered, ate apples, looked at the clouds, tried to sketch other boys. Tried not to think about how much he missed Kenny.

He lay in his bed staring at the ceiling. He thought about what he had seen that day in the abandoned shack when he took the shortcut behind the tennis courts. That was kissing, he was sure of it. Faces squished together. Eyes squeezed shut. Strange panting, moaning sounds. Bodies rubbing against each other. Then, as he watched, pants dropped. Roger Oakum's shockingly white behind. He couldn't see but *felt* the pink protuberance in front, as his own suddenly swelled and filled his pants. He remembered. He felt a ringing in his ears and his own breath breaking in sharp gasping intakes and expulsions. And he couldn't tear his eyes away even though he knew he would go blind from seeing this. Wasn't that what Father M had said: to witness sin was to partake in it, and the Lord's punishment for it was to banish sight so that the sinner dwelled in eternal darkness, the better to think on one's filth, one's reveling in filth, to live in shit and shame and darkness forever? Shit and shame and darkness. Shit, shame, darkness. His hands moved to the rhythm in the dark, beneath his sheets; the words pounded in his head; he saw again Roger Oakum's head flung back, mouth open, eyes glassy, as Wilson Ross dropped to his knees and kissed the soft, pale bud, kissed and licked and stroked with his tongue until it sprouted into a firm, smooth shoot, and Wilson filled his mouth with the grassy taste and warmth and fullness of it, and remembering this, Vinh squeezed his own eyes tight, copying the look of pained bliss on Roger's face as Wilson swallowed him up, his breath huffing faster and faster until he felt dizzy, on the verge of passing out.

His whole body tingled. How many prayers to not die? To not end up in hell, in the filth and shame and darkness? He would stay awake all night to say them. But near dawn he fell asleep. When he woke up, he was still alive. He was alive, and it was a new world. It was a beautiful, fragile, awful, wonderful world, because it was the only one there was. His faith was gone.

He could still fake it, but he knew it was only show. Did everyone else know too? Were they all faking it as well? He looked closely at the remaining teachers and thought he detected sly, knowing winks directed at him.

At first it was shocking; then he felt like a member of a secret club. Only one person he knew for sure was not a member of this club: Kenny. Kenny was so smart and wise, yet Kenny was wrong about God. It went round and round in his head, confusing him. He was careful to avoid Kenny for the next week. Sometimes Father Q would seek him out and tell him that his young friend could use some company . . . hinting. But he couldn't.

Then, one night, he startled awake and knew he had to get to Kenny. In the dark, in bare feet, he found his way through the near-empty dormitory to the infirmary. It was empty of occupants except for a lone figure in a small bed in the back pushed up against a window. It was through this window that Vinh and Kenny would wave to each other. They were too far away to talk. But Vinh would stand there, for twenty minutes sometimes, peering up. Sometimes he would lie on his back when his neck got tired. He was able to sketch on his back, and he would hold up his drawings for Kenny to view, and Kenny would give an approving nod or thumbs-up. So it would go until a teacher eventually came by and moved him along. Vinh had not gone to the window for a while. He slipped into the narrow bed.

"Your feet are so cold. Why didn't you put on your slippers?"

"Sorry," Vinh whispered. "I'll try not to touch you with them."

"It's okay. It feels good. I'm so hot."

Vinh put his hand on Kenny's head. "Wow, you *are* hot. You can use my feet as ice packs for your head."

"Ha ha," said Kenny. "I missed you. Why did you stop coming to the window?"

Vinh was silent for a long time, but he knew that Kenny knew he wasn't asleep, that he was just pretending. Finally, he whispered, "There's no God, Kenny."

"Now why do you say that, silly?"

"Because I sinned and He didn't strike me down."

Long silence. Then: "Do you think that is God's purpose, to punish the sinners?"

"Isn't it?"

"That is the devil's job, perhaps. But He has bigger plans for you than that."

Vinh perked up. "For me? What?"

"I couldn't possibly say, little friend." Sigh. "I only know the plan He has for me."

"What plan, Kenny? Tell me."

Long silence.

"He's calling me home, Vinh. I'm going home. Soon."

"I thought you didn't have a home, Kenny."

Laugh. Cough. Minutes to recover from the racking heaves.

"Everyone has a home, Martin, though sometimes it takes a while to find it, to return to it. I'm going home. At last. Sooner perhaps than I might have wanted. But I'm ready. So ready to join Him. It's the only thing I've ever wanted."

Vinh didn't know or understand what Kenny was saying, but he found tears streaming down his face. He began to sob. "Kenny, tell Him you can't go yet."

"Silly. I don't have a choice. But even if I did, I would choose this. I would always choose this." The darkness of the room was gradually diluted by the thin morning light. Vinh could see Kenny's face, how it glowed with heat and fervor. "I think I hear the distant music, a brightness there." He watched as Kenny's eyes opened wide and his voice dropped in awe. "Oh, if you could see . . . you would never be afraid again . . . no one would ever be afraid . . . He comes. He comes for me. It's like a mote of light, at first, then more, millions of them combining into a stream, a river. An ocean. Yes. Yes."

Kenny closed his eyes and seemed very far away, as if he had started the journey. His breaths came slowly, and Vinh counted every one of them. The counting soothed him; the breaths were gentle; he found himself drifting on the river of light and warmth Kenny had made for them, one arm wrapped around his friend.

Upstate New York, 2004

What would Kenny have said? "Trust in the Lord to guide you."

He still missed Kenny. He knew better now, but he used to think of Kenny as going home to live in a country far, far away. *I'm going home.* A country far, far away where people he loved lived. They never visited him. After a while, he stopped waiting for them to. Though he was more than ready to leave the school, part of him was afraid of losing Kenny when he did. This was the only home he knew. He often dreamed of what lay beyond the gates, of opening them wide and stepping out. And that day was finally here. He was graduating.

No other boy had taken Kenny's place. Though he didn't think of Kenny as he thought of the other boys. He had avoided the abandoned shack behind the tennis courts. He had avoided all kinds of places: the last stall in the lavatory on the second floor of the science building, the storage room in the corner of the gymnasium, the empty bedroom of the brother who had died in bed and whose position they had never replaced. He avoided side-glances, knuckles brushing against his own in the hallway. He even stopped sketching for a time because he found he kept drawing pouting lower lips, downy hair above upper lips, sloping eyebrows, elbows curved on desks, muscled arms peeking from rolled-up shirtsleeves. But lately he had picked up his sketchbook again, had found pleasure in sketching a quick view, in a brother hurrying across the fields, bent against a strong wind, one hand holding down a hat in danger of flying off. He was intrigued by how much more he could convey by leaving out details and clear lines. Moods and emotions could be captured by shading and composition. The brother in the windy field almost looked like part of the landscape. The more details he left out, the more feeling came in. He was slowly finding Kenny through abstract sketches . . . the feeling of him: his seriousness and innocence, his looking far off as he had a conversation with God, that tingling feeling when he turned his eyes on Vinh. How penetrating that vague look could turn: sharpening into a dagger that pieced your soul and saw you to your core. It was thrilling to be stripped so bare.

Most of his drawings were done over breaks, especially the longer summer interims. The school was his home; he had no other. The brothers were rather fond of him; they liked his quiet, obedient demeanor; he earned part of his keep through tutoring; he even had a class or two of the younger boys. He bothered no one; he was a model student and boarder; he was at every prayer meeting, even the optional ones. Here was a convert. They didn't know he came to find Kenny, to feel him. Kenny had loved God; Vinh tried to be close to God to be close to Kenny. So he sat and waited. He never felt anything.

He was graduating. He didn't know why he was so nervous as he paced the hallway outside the headmaster's office. Father M was in there chatting with the headmaster. Wasn't this the visit he had always been waiting for? Of course, there had been brief check-ins, at least one lengthy letter a couple of times a year—mostly dull affairs chronicling the trials and tribulations of a cleric's life in smallish suburban districts—and an annual "I'll be by at the end of term for lunch." How he had lain awake the whole week prior to those lunches, always miserable silent affairs in the end, as he yearned for and never got . . . something. Some offer-to-come-and-live-with-him kind of thing.

The door flew open in mid-conversation, the two gray-haired men laughing as they emerged from the room. Smiles still lingered on their faces as they turned their gaze on him. Father M looked just the same as when Vinh had seen him a year ago. Perhaps a bit grayer. Smile the same: more a pressing of the lips with a downward turn at the corners, and eyes always a bit distant, as if it was hard to focus directly upon oneself. Those pale-blue orbs were now semifocused on him. He gestured him into the office that the brother had vacated for their use. The men waved goodbye to each other. Vinh entered and sat at the edge of the leather armchair facing the desk.

"I hear good things about you, young man."

"Thank you, sir."

"Come now, we are not that formal, are we?"

"No, Father."

That was a complex look that crossed his face, Vinh thought. A mixture of pleased and repulsed, hard to describe: like when Vinh ate sweet-and-sour pork for the first time when Father M had taken him out for lunch on their last visit.

"I heard about your acceptance to several prestigious universities with strong religious and clerical programs," he said.

"I don't know," Vinh said, "what my plans are. I got this internship at a law firm in Boston last week."

Father M frowned. "Come, that one can't be a serious consideration."

"There's a small stipend. I can't afford college, even with a full scholarship. There's housing and all that."

That was hurt that flickered across Father M's face. "Did you not think, given our long association, that I would not fail to help you?"

If it came to that, Vinh thought. Then he came out with it: "To be honest, I'm not really sure what our association is, Father. I don't want to presume."

Father M looked sad. He brushed his gray hair back with one hand. "Think of us as family, Vinh."

Oh. Did family tuck you away in a boarding school and only visit once a year? Vinh was glad enough not to see "Aunt" Marie and the boys anymore. They must have been college-bound seniors at this point. But he had missed Father M. For years after the helicopter ride—the bookstall contracting to a matchbook size, then disappearing in a land-scape of blurs—Father M was the only solid thing he could cling to. He felt groundless then. Now. At sea. He wasn't his *real* father. Yet he was an anchor.

"The point is, Vinh, I feel responsible for you; I brought you to this country to give you opportunities you would not have had otherwise. And going to college is one of them. Especially a college that will help you in your path to religious training."

Here it was. He took a deep breath. "I'm not sure I want religious training, Father."

Silence. "Then, of course, you are still young and wish to explore. But some of those small liberal arts colleges are rather a waste of time. Fiction is frivolous. So is art. God will wait, of course, but why keep him waiting, especially when doors are open? What I mean to say is: I will make it possible, financially, for you to take the right path." He looked very pleased with himself after he had made the offer.

"Yes, Father. Thank you, Father."

At the bus depot he examined the envelope, which was stamped and addressed to Father M, but not yet sealed. The bus to Boston was delayed, so he opened the envelope and read the letter one more time. He opened the metal lip of the blue mailbox. The jaw hung open, hungry. But he hesitated. What was the point? Father M would know soon enough that he had not chosen the path to divinity school. And all the other stuff he had written: *I'm sorry I'm a disappointment to you. I wish you had not picked me—why did you? Are you really my father?* He had needed to say it. Did Father M need to hear it? He let the lid of the box close without feeding it. The last call for boarding echoed in the near-empty waiting room. He dropped the letter into a trash bin and boarded the bus.

As the bus pulls away, he closes his eyes and feels a curious sensation of weightlessness. The bus is rising, the ground dropping away as it lifts over the highway, over the cars and houses and antlike people below looking up and waving as he rises higher and higher, and if he were to open his eyes now, he would be hovering at the same level as the clouds. The soothing hum of spinning blades stutters. A choking sound. The engine cuts out. For one second more the craft hangs suspended in a sea of cloudy silence. Then plunges. Eyelids slam back, body jerks, bracing for the crash. Panting. On the seat beside him, the zoned-out teenager wired into his earbuds, hoodie over his eyes, doesn't seem to notice as Vinh huffs out air, waiting for his breath to catch up to itself, for the thumping of his heart to settle.

He takes another breath.

The wheels of the bus grind reassuringly along solid asphalt. *What is there to be afraid of?* he chides himself. It's just the world out there. But he looks out the window again, half expecting to see a sea of clouds.

Jane Eyre Rochester, 1857–1975

"I am no bird; and no net ensnares me."

Chapter One

Tonkin, 1946, First Indochina War

Jane

Jane

Jane

I remember the call from what felt like an impossible distance. I remember the heat, how it smoldered in my head until my skull swelled and burst. I step out of my smoking skin into a new country, steaming, green. Everywhere, vegetation the size of small huts, leaves like grooved spades, flowers larger than my head. I weave around the strange plants like an ant, almost drowning in the heavy, moist air. It is all so different from England's thin, dry atmosphere. Each step I take sinks my slippers farther into the damp ground. I can only conclude that I'm dead. The fever took my life, and I wander now in the Lord's land.

No. I am here, fully awake, all my physical senses alight. I fight my way through the dense branches and strangling vines, ankle-catching roots. Sweat blinds me, phantom insects sting me, and knife-sharp thorns stab and slice my skin. I have never battled a jungle before, and I am surely losing. Nothing stays still in this bewildering setting; I step aside to avoid a column of marching trees. I blink, and they turn into a row of men.

I am so astonished that I simply freeze and stare. Each, as he silently, swiftly passes, turns an indifferent, blank-eyed glance at me. None stop to question or assist. Their vacant stares stream right through me as if

I'm not there. I note how they do not fight the jungle, as I did, but advance as if carried by a current. I see in a flash how the jungle is a river—not an unyielding obstacle, but a flowing force: To move forward is to submit to its course. It carries me.

Shouts and shots wake me from my amazement. I hear snatches of French, surely a friendly language. Yet instinctively I bolt after the vanishing crew, attaching myself to the tail end of the ghostly marchers. I do as they do: find the opening, flow around barriers, veer along an invisible path determined by the jungle itself and not by my own will. Behind me, the crashing tumult grows more remote as the jungle swallows us up. I try to keep the last man within my sight, but his ragged tunic flakes, hardens into bark, and when I blink, all I see is a tree. I am alone once more. Amazement and panic give way eventually to dull forbearance. The tedious work of moving onward still lies before me, and I undertake it, but admittedly with more ease now than before. The odd men that the jungle threw up taught me how to navigate the tangled terrain, and I give myself to it until it chooses to eject me some hours later into a clearing.

After so much time winding through its bowels, one might expect to feel freedom and relief upon release, but on the contrary, I suddenly feel abandoned and exposed, as if the jungle has been a friend, a comrade in arms, a protective lover that held me, hid me, absorbed me into itself. With trepidation I take in the view. What strange beauty lies before me: an emerald field ripples, sparkles, spreads. It is a sea, it is grass—it is neither, I realize, but stem upon stem of some grain spiking a sheet of water. Here and there bent figures in coned hats work the flooded fields. Such openness. Before my eyes, the toiling figures stop working and quietly fade into the field. The mud squelches between my bare toes, for I have long ago lost those useless embroidered slippers, and I too feel that field of green beauty calling me to return to it. It slowly drains the life from me, absorbs me, just one of many, like the little islands of grassy stalks, and as it sucks me back into the earth, I give myself to it. The jungle, the fields, this land, this water, I let it claim me.

Suddenly, the temperature drops, a mist rises, and through it a figure appears on the far edge of the field. We stare at each other across that cloudy reach. He reaches out a hand. I hear him call my name with such sadness, anguish, longing.

Jane

Jane

Jane

His call is a lifeline thrown out to me. I grasp it and follow it home.

Ferndean, 1857

"If she is to regain her health, Rochester, she must submit to bed rest. Wandering in the mist at dawn: That is strictly prohibited."

"Trust me, sir, had I known her intent, I would have arrested her progress ere she reached the gate. Rest assured, she will not slip past my guard again."

And so it went, back and forth, those agitated male voices. Finally, they left the room and closed the door, and it was quiet once more, quiet in my head. I basked in the stillness, the wide airiness of a room free of the volume taken up by two gentlemen, one of them in a foul mood. The room felt peaceful, open, not unlike the moment the jungle spat me out into the open field stretched beneath a beating sun. I longed to return to that floating green field, but I only saw emptiness behind my closed lids. Eventually the door opened and he entered, alone. He did not go to his chair in the corner, but stood glowering over my bed, arms crossed. All this I knew, even with my eyes shut.

"Cease your ruse, Madam; you are quite awake."

I did not deny it, nor did I answer as I turned on my side, away from him. The low growl I heard could have been anger, exasperation, or despair. I was past caring. I heard him crossing the room restlessly, his heavy footsteps vibrating against the floor. The percussive pacing jangled my nerves, but I forced my body to stay still. At last he stopped, again, by my bedside. "Do you hate me so much that you would throw your life away to escape our marriage?"

That was unkind, and I could not forbear responding to the injustice of the accusation. I turned and opened my mouth, and was brought short at the sight of the ring that he held in his palm. I remembered now: I had taken it off. But it was in fear of losing it, for I had grown so thin from the fevers that it had slid alarmingly past my knuckle when I had bent to pick up some dropped item on the floor. I had laid the ring on the bedside table for safekeeping. I looked at the slim iron circle in his palm. I knew he had wanted a gold band set with rose-cut diamonds, sapphires, emeralds. At every point I had resisted him, his scowls, his accusations of devilish obstinacy. But on that quiet morning, with only the parson and clerk present at the ceremony, he had slipped the plain band adorned with a single rare ruby onto my finger as he said his vows. Later I had the ruby removed and cherished the ring even more for its plainness.

He took my hand now and slid the ring on again, going still when he saw how easily it passed along my finger. He took the ring off. He held it in the palm of his hand and stared at it. Then he bunched his hand around it, letting his forehead sink to his fist. "Did I not lose a son too? Do not tell me that a mother feels the death of a child more deeply than a father, that grief drives her mad, heats her brain, sends her running out into storms searching, but he survives intact. If my own mind does not shatter, my heart does. William is gone. Can we not grieve together and preserve what we still have—each other? What will I do? Tell me. What will I do, Jane, if I lose you as well?"

If words could reach through madness, his would have. But it was not madness. I saw them: the ragged militia fleeing through the jungle. Somehow, I was connected to them. Somehow, they were connected to William. And at once, they somehow had the feel of the daydreams I used to entertain during moments in my domestic duties when the hours seemed to extend inexorably and to insist on repeating—daydreams of a life of travel and adventure in foreign lands in service to God alongside St. John. Those daydreams sometimes seeped into my night dreams, unfurling in vivid, bold colors and searing emotions that woke me, breathless, tearful, alarming poor Edward. His fear turning to wrath and jealousy: "Do you wish you had decided differently, Jane? Would you have been happier as a missionary's wife?"

"I will never stop searching for him," I said very softly, awake now in my room as Edward stared at the ring in his palm. As I stared, too, my mind suddenly splintered off along different paths, my quest branching in flashes of a jungle, an ocean voyage, a desert crossing, as I searched and searched, but forgot what, who, I was searching for. My thoughts snapped back to the present when I felt the back of my hand grow warm and wet. While he wept, Rochester did not let go of my hand as his shoulders shook silently in defeat.

Our tears paved the way for a truce in the days that followed. Edward brought the ring back on a gold chain, which I wore around my neck. I no longer stepped through time and space. When I slept, my dreams were just dreams. Yet I insisted, still, that had been no dream of the jungle. I was certain of its reality. I had touched, smelled, heard, tasted that strange land. I had marched with those men who had materialized from the trees, flowed through the jungle, then morphed back into bark and wooden trunks.

It was a fever dream, they told me, a vision from my overheated imagination. My illness. It was a world that had unfolded from my longing, from a need to find him so great that I had broken through my smoking body into that strange country: a jungle of my own making. I had to get back.

Edward was away. He was rebuilding the main house, the one that had been destroyed in the fire. He was determined that our days at Ferndean be done. But for me this was the place of my return and redemption.

It was here that I found him, my master; here that we brought the two broken halves of our lives together and made ourselves whole again.

Reader, when I married him, I did not expect another, final miracle. Not his mostly recovered sight, the partial use of his damaged limb with the aid of a wooden prosthetic. Rather, the new life we created together: a being so precious, so fragile that the jealous spirits snatched him away after five years of bliss. They told me it was wrong to grieve so. Edward held me for hours and days and said we would try again, that we would have a family. But I knew, even before the doctor told us the risk was too great for my fragile condition, that William Edward St. John Rochester was the only child we would ever have. Our son.

We had not thought we needed him. He was extra. We had already reached the summit of gratitude at recovering love in the late summer of our life together. How he sweetened the end of that summer! How flowers, birds, warmth lingered and green days were not yet edged with brown. How Edward coddled the boy. And though I tried to be stern to his antics, I was a shame to the profession of governess. Indeed, I rebelled against that role. I was a mother, not a governess! As mother I could indulge. But it was more than that. For a governess, there is the satisfaction of guiding and improving a young mind. And then there is something else altogether. When I reunited with Edward across a world of painful separation, I thought then, even with his reduced con- dition, that my happiness was complete. I never expected that sitting quietly reading while my son drew pictures by my feet would constitute a level of warmth and contentment as blissful as romantic passion; that motherhood could equally ignite a degree of ferocious protectiveness frightening in its uncompromising intensity. I was his mother; that was all. That was everything. Nor could I decide whether motherhood had subverted or liberated my nature. It was the excess of love, in the end, that undid us all. For when it ended—when his little body was buried on the hilltop beneath the linden tree where he used to play, because I could not bear for him to lie in the cemetery behind the church, his least favorite place, restless lad, to be—when it ended, so did all summers.

They say autumn is a graceful season, full of burnished color in fields and woods; flash of feather, scale, fur in the animal world; the steady stockpiling of food and fuel in readiness for a long period of cold to come. But that first autumn following William's departure was a harbinger of all the winters that were to come. Should we not meet it boldly instead of hiding and trembling? Edward was stern. He would not allow my mind to quietly slip off to at least contemplate that possibility. Before I learned to master the subtle tells of my face, he could always detect my mind's direction and attempt to redirect my thoughts.

Becoming ill was a relief from his solicitude. I sank into the first fevers with an almost ecstatic release. Then that last fever that had awakened a sense of purpose. *I must return.*

The hired woman was stout, red faced, gruff, but not unkind. My jailer. I had said as much to Edward, and he had growled at me that he would hire ten such if I continued to abuse my health. Hannah's large, red, competent hands straightened my pillow, shepherded spoonfuls of broth to my chapped lips, laid cool cloths on my head. Every touch, every ministration was a trial. But I endured the good Hannah. I could wait. I had practiced.

It happened again just after I had put down a copy of *Gulliver's Travels.* The wild adventures affirmed the possibility of worlds beyond our own. Gulliver's morphing body confirmed that bodies were flexible, strange things. I was seated by the window after my bath, wrapped in a large toweling robe, cleaned and scrubbed and waiting for Hannah to return.

And then I saw them.

The marchers in the jungle.

From my view at the window, I could see them slipping into the woods at the far edge of the field. I half rose from my seat; my breath came hard and fast. And then Hannah entered with a warm drink in her hands. She helped me into the bed.

"Take your sleeping draft now, like a good dear."

When her back was turned, I poured some of my sleeping draft into her tea. I smiled compliantly at her as she settled into her chair with a heavy sigh. When her breathing turned smooth and even with an occasional snuff and grunt, I threw the covers off and bolted upright.

Ferndean, 1857 / Điện Biên Phủ, 1954

I got as far as the pond.

Normally no more than a sheet of water between field and woods, it was now, due to a recent deluge of late-spring rain, a veritable river dividing me from the far bank, too wide to skirt around without wasting a great deal of energy and time. The wind blew through my hair as I contemplated the situation. I had left in such haste that my hat remained hanging from its hook at the house when I made my escape on silent feet, the good Hannah snoring placidly. At any rate, I had no need of it. Or a cloak. These things would simply be in the way if I forged into the pond, for that was what I had decided to do. To reach him. It was not very deep; the water would only come up to my chest. I had lifted my skirts to my knees, ready to plunge in, when I remembered the little boat. It was in truth a raft, lashed together for William's entertainment just a summer ago. It barely floated, but the making of it had taxed Edward's ingenuity and delighted William for hours. I had watched from a grassy knoll, resting among the ruins of our picnic lunch, feeling a heavy breeze caress my face. Utter satisfaction.

And where do you want to go, William? Beyond. To the orchard? Farther. The top of the hill. Why? To be closer to the stars; to see to the other side of the world, what's there. Oh, away from us, our little home? I think, William, when you've been to the other side of the world, you will see that there is nothing better than the home you have now. But young and already restless as you are, you will not be satisfied until you have seen it all for yourself. Your mother is quite right, young man, so it is best that we get started at once.

I remembered. I had to return. I felt a crushing ache in my throat. Strange how happiness can choke. I breathed in the chilled, damp air and felt my airway loosen.

The raft was still there. I dragged it from its burial place beneath a pile of moldy, wet leaves. I also retrieved a long branch to help navigate across to the other bank. The raft wobbled as I stepped tentatively onto the lashed barks, but it held together as it drifted across the water. On solid ground again, I made my way toward the hill. An urgency propelled me now, and I ignored my quavering knees. The skies darkened, and the air stirred ominously, whipping my face with small pellets of ice. When I looked back behind me, the sheet of water rippled and swelled, arching like the back of an animal. I heard a distant rumble of thunder just as I reached the hill. It came from the earth, not the sky, vibrating beneath my feet, a steady, muffled beat. Edward was coming, his horse's hooves tearing up grass and dirt. But I was already climbing. Soon I crested the hill.

I aimed for the lone linden tree as for a beacon in a stormy night at sea.

Yet the moment I reach the hilltop, a dark fog suddenly descends upon the summit, and I am plunged into darkness. Nor am I alone. All around me I sense a stirring, a suppressed sighing. I reach my hands out blindly, and they encounter rough bark. A tree, many trees, I see now by the dawning light. A forest covers what was once a bare hilltop. The woods writhe and twist and spit out people who dash about in great confusion. In the dim light I can make out men using poles to carry long mounted guns between the trees. Everywhere I look I see more and more men, more and more weapons. They step lightly around me, and no one speaks to me, as before. Their faces are grimly set on their tasks, and I can see that it is a brutal one. No road or machinery eases their way: They bear it all piece by piece with sheer will and bent backs. Whom do they fight? An outpost, a fort at the bottom of the surrounding mountains. A cornered lion holding off an army of swarming ants. The enemy is outnumbered yet far from helpless. The fort bristles with armored carriages, great guns, exploding shells, holding off the attackers. The men on the mountain shoot back at them. On the ground, others charge forward. Gunfire from the fort punches holes in their ranks and they scatter, then re-form and charge again. The carnage is devastating. No one can possibly survive.

And then I see him.

He is young, so young to be a soldier, no longer a child, but still so young, his whole life before him. How different he looks. If I were only looking with my eyes I would see a Chinaman, not tall, not sturdy, a farmer's son, conscripted, frightened, undernourished. Days of marching to get here were followed by weeks of digging in the tunnels, another common foot soldier helping to haul the supplies and weapons, all underfed, untrained, ill prepared to take on that formidable force below.

William.

He looks at me, but there is no recognition in his face, only a resigned look, an expression that seems to accept an inevitable outcome.

I am not a harbinger of death, I tell him. *You need not die. Not today. This army is heroic, but what it tries to do is impossible. Go home. Live.*

His eyes are glazed, and he speaks quietly, as to himself. I understand him. "It is not my own life—it belongs to my family, which belongs to this country, which is ours. They say we can kill this French lion, even if we are ants. It is cut off from the others, and there are more of us."

There is nothing you can do, I plead with him. *Slip away in the confusion. Return to your village, your home.*

"I saw my childhood friend die. From an explosive. We used to ride on the broad back of the water buffalo together. We would try to push each other off. I always ended up in the mud. So many dead. How can I go back alive when they are all dead? No one will be there to help with the rice harvest. The women will have to do it by themselves. My sisters. My mother and aunts and grandmother too. She is old, but she still works every day. At the end of the day, your back is achy; your legs feel rubbery and your feet shriveled and itchy from standing in the drained mud, but when you stand up, you see the whole land, how it ripples and shines when it meets the sky. It's ours. We shaped it, we love it. No one will take it from us."

He charges right through my misty body. I pin my eyes on his back and try to fix my sight on him, but he disappears into the sea of rushing soldiers. They all blend into a single wave as they pour down the mountain.

It's raining red.

I try to hold the red rain as it runs down my face, hands, and fingers. I don't even feel the explosion that rocks me, tears me from my body, flings me into the sky, higher, higher, until I am spinning with the stars. I'm flying. It is so peaceful up here, far from war and death. In the sea of clouds. Below are pinpricks of humanity, little flitting lights like fireflies. Little flickers of light bend over a shimmering field, wearing cone-shaped hats. I see them, the mothers, the sisters, the aunts and grandmothers. The old women wave to me. I wave back and continue west. Fields turn to mountains, to forests, cities, towns, meadows, a house, a hill, a tree, a woman kneeling on the ground. The man beside her, head bowed. Together they look at a small grave under the linden tree. They are so sad. There is so much sadness and pain and death in this world. Why do we keep coming back to it?

I turn my face to the stars.

Chapter Two

Ferndean, 1858

There was no reasoning with Edward after my trip to William's grave in the storm. The simple Hannah was dismissed and replaced by the good Mrs. Lodge, the widow of Reverend Josiah Lodge, the late curate of the neighboring county. She lived in modest accommodations in the shire. Having relinquished her spousal duties at the rectory, she had now taken it upon herself to offer her services to Edward as my companion and nurse, refusing any recompense for her pains. Payment would have been preferable for me, for then she could've been dismissed, but Edward could find no caretaker for any fee to come to this gloomy, isolated fen and care for a recalcitrant, uncooperative patient. Moreover, it was clear that not fees but the position of caretaker to an esteemed gentleman's wife offered social if not economic advantages, as her position had declined after the curate's death.

Pillar-like in bristling black muslin, Mrs. Lodge was a creature of singular patience and watchfulness, an obstacle indeed to my attempts to elude her, outwit her, or adulterate her beverages with sleeping drafts as I had done with the simple Hannah. Edward disliked her as well and found excuses to exit the room at her entrance. Her simpering mannerisms were enough to drive anyone out, and yet the prospect of having me wander off on my own once more was equally intolerable to him. "I will care for you day and night myself," he vowed, "as soon as the new house is finished."

Much of his time was taken up there. For Thornfield was being rebuilt, and construction had been underway for some time. It was near ready. It should have been done years ago, but we had delayed, and I knew he blamed himself. In truth, neither one of us had felt hurried to return to that former setting of trials, horror, and death. And William had loved the farm here. Now Edward was determined that we would start anew; that our lives would begin again properly, leaving behind the fetid marsh air of Ferndean and the sad memory of William's illness and death. Though he did not say it, I knew he also hoped, against reason, that a fresh start would mean another family, or, barring that, quiet days where I could lay my mourning to rest. He feared for my mind as much as my body: "If you were to go mad, Jane, I would hold you gently in my arms to prevent your harming yourself, for it would not be your fault." Yet I sensed that he thought my madness generated from an unseemly grief, my refusal to let go. Nor was he entirely wrong, for I absolutely refused to let go, not out of grief, but out of certainty that William's life was not finished. That it was my task to recover my son.

That task was hindered by the unwanted ministrations of Mrs. Lodge. "Leave it all to me, sir": She dismissed nearly all the help, and thus any potential allies for my cause. Only a surly cook, a pair of housekeepers, and a half-blind gardener remained, all held firmly under her thumb. Worse, she was starting to convince Edward that I raved and lied, though he did not judge me for it. "If she trespasses upon your dignity or comfort, Jane, you must inform me at once. Caretaker she may be, but I will not brook insolence from any on your behalf, my darling." When I informed Edward of all the ways that the good Mrs. Lodge trampled upon my dignity and discomfited me, he was vague as to how he would redress these ills, nor did he contrive to dismiss her. "Bear with her but a bit longer, Jane. Thornfield is near completion. Be assured that she will not accompany us there."

Unhappy as I was with Edward's response, I could not fault him entirely. I knew that he suffered because of me, for I had found the remnants of a half-burnt letter in his library; only the bottom half of the paper was legible, but it spoke a world of pain.

> . . . counsel, though well meant, I soundly reject . . . not the same Jane I married, but do I not know first-hand how people are changed and shaped by tragedy . . . did she not save me from the hell of my own self? Then I will do the same for her . . . not in your benevolent asylum attended by your sisters of mercy . . . I will care for her myself . . . though day by day I see her beautiful, firm mind warped by cunning, and I admit it, I am afraid, but determined to keep her safe . . . she is still there . . . the obsession has obscured but not entirely destroyed her essence . . . she is still there . . .

Shortly after I discovered that fragment, I confronted him. Edward struggled with his vision still, having lost much of his eyesight from the fire at Thornfield, and I had often assisted him with his letters. Looking at his uneven scrawl, I was moved that he had tried on his own to express his concerns over me. "Edward," I said, accosting him in his study, "if it's a missive to the asylum that you wish to write in regard to me, let me help you." I held out the burnt letter.

He paused and became very still, regarding me sharply. Finally, he took the paper. "Help me to put you away, Jane?"

"Even were you to do so, it would be because you thought it best, and I would not resist you."

His next pause was even longer and became a little terrifying. "The day you forbear to resist me is the day I know you are truly gone, my love. But perhaps this is your cunning attempt to see what plans I have in store for you that you might write a counter missive nullifying my orders."

I smiled. "You have found me out, my dear."

He smiled as well, with an edge of relief, I thought, at the corners of his mouth. For this was a shadow of how we used to banter, to negotiate our differences—how small and minor they seemed now—over how to discipline the boy (*no dinner tonight for that rascal; but Edward, just a piece of pie—it's his favorite!*); his future; his play (*he is too young to ride; bosh, I was on a horse at age five*). Edward pulled me onto his lap, and this, too, I had missed: his smell of leather and tobacco, running my fingers through his coarse mane of hair, graying now at the temples.

"Will you really immure me in a house for the mad?"

"Jane, Jane, Jane," he whispered. "I would rather go completely blind, I would rather lose the use of my right hand as well as the left, if only. Please, Jane, for my sake, stay with me in this world . . . in whatever capacity. Stay."

He was dramatic. But I could hear his pain. "Oh, Edward. I wish, oh how I wish I could." But a world without William, I thought to myself—I did not think I could stay in that world. I would tear up that world, or I would tear up myself trying to reach him. Edward clutched my hand harder, as if he could hear my thoughts, feel me slipping away. And he was not wrong: I had slipped beyond this room, this house, the wide fields; on the other side of an ocean I soared, I felt I could go even farther, but before I did, I looked down, and from the height of the sky, I saw a home, a hearth, a husband and wife clutching each other in grief.

Yet his broken words worked upon me, kept me quiet for a time. In my silence, I longed for him. I missed the warmth, weight, nearness of his body. After my bout of recent fever, Edward had taken up a separate bedroom so that I in particular might rest without disturbance. Though

I loathed to admit as much, it was soothing to be away from Edward's constant anxiety over me. I lay awake plotting over the war between the cunning Mrs. Lodge and myself. To that end I made a significant advance the day I discovered her weak spot.

Mrs. Lodge was a Christian, but a peculiarly superstitious one. She believed I indulged in witchery, though she knew better than to accuse me of such and certainly to say anything to Edward. She laid crosses all about the house, many of them made of metal. She hung an iron horseshoe above the front door. She even endeavored to get Edward to put metal bars on the windows, but he roared that he would not turn the house into a jail, and especially not when he was about to tear it to the ground anyhow, as soon as Thornfield was completed.

Yet helpless I was not, entirely. If she believed I indulged in witchery, I indulged and even encouraged her belief whenever I could. I walked backward; I always contrived to have an uneven number of objects about: seven candles, three pillows, thirteen rolls of yarn. She responded by taking away my knitting, leaving me without a single stick of light. I was not overly discomfited by these acts, though I was certain she wished I felt their absence more keenly than I did. I hated knitting; I preferred sitting in the dark. But she seriously overstepped her bounds one day, I felt, when she contrived to dress me in souvenirs of her superstition. She offered me the "gift" of a bracelet, a broad band of elaborately wrought metal. It was a gauntlet, a cuff, I would say, a manacle. "It will keep you grounded from your fanciful flights, Madam. The metal will secure you." Edward laughed outright at the claim when I complained. I refused to have it near me. Yet it did give me pause. If metal "grounded" me, perhaps that was the reason I wasn't able to escape my body to find William. Something kept me imprisoned here. Perhaps the good Mrs. Lodge was right.

One late morning when the house was quiet and Edward was away, I sat by the window as was my wont and pondered. Mrs. Lodge was resting in her room next door. My book, *Gulliver's Travels*, was laid aside. This was where I had sat when I last set eyes on those ragged marchers at the edge of the field. I had not seen them since, though I had sat at this very spot every day since. What was different then? That day, as this day, at this hour, I had just bathed. At that time, it was a washing meant to diminish the heat in my fevered body. I was not ill now, but now, as then, I was still lounging in my dressing gown, having just replaced my ring necklace around my throat. *My ring necklace.* That day I had forgotten it, as I often did; it generally lay covered by the shawls constantly wrapped about my shoulders against the pervasive chill of Ferndean. Could this small iron ring be the lock that kept me imprisoned in my own time? I could not condone Mrs. Lodge's superstitious beliefs, yet had I not discovered at this very seat, looking out on a view I had seen a thousand times by now, seeing it terribly morph, that the laws of time, space, and nature were illusions? Surely, the divide between this reality and another was merely a veil. But how to lift that veil at my command? For I could not bear to be at the mercy of such chance transportations. I preferred to believe that it was my *need* that tore up the workings of the universe, and in this regard, Mrs. Lodge's notions of an alternative set of principles that ruled the world were not that far off after all. I was desperate. I chose to believe. Slowly I unclasped the necklace and laid it aside.

Then I proceeded to wait.

Phú Yên Province, 1965

The planet spins on its axis and tips the world upside down, spilling the oceans upon the earth, turning the ground beneath my feet to liquid. Here, men drown on land. Flashes of battle cross my vision. Here, men who look like brothers fight each other, and only differences in uniforms, or sometimes lack of uniforms, distinguish one side from another. I find myself allied with the ones who fight with hatred and despair, who have something to lose, something to save, over the ones who are ruthless and savage. The invaders, I guess. And everywhere, so much water. England has never seen so much water. But then, I am not in England anymore. I have indeed escaped!

I must find shelter from this downpour.

I stumble toward a shadowy structure. It is a hut, part of the soaked thatch roof intact enough to provide an umbrella of sorts. I huddle beneath this dubious patch of dryness for half the day. I can barely see my hand beyond the length of my outstretched arm. Finally the rain begins to taper, to dwindle. It stops at last. And that's when I see them.

They emerge from the far edge of the field as in a dream. They are as silent and ragged as the first time—no, I am mistaken. These wretched souls are not soldiers on a march. They are men and women and children with sacks and bundles on their heads, shoulders, backs, the detritus of their homes that they carry with them as they tread steadfastly, sorrowfully away from whatever calamity turned them into desperate wanderers.

I slip into their stream.

A small boy with dark, luminous eyes offers me a bit of his rice cake when his mother is not looking. This tender gesture raises a surprising pang deep in my belly, a memory of hunger more than an actual feeling of it, but I smile at him and shake my head. I can see from the hollowness of his cheeks and the sharpness of his collarbone how hunger has eaten him. They are all hungry, starving. But except for the moment when the boy looked directly at me and offered me food, I feel nothing of my own body's needs. Truly, I must be but a shade here. Other bodies have a materiality so certain I can smell it: They travel with a beast in their midst, a water buffalo, I believe, with round, placid eyes that seem to take me in. As it does not shun my presence, I find myself walking beside it companionably.

Before long we spy a column of smoke in the distance. The convoy stops, and there is concerned chatter among them. As a group they suddenly veer off from their current path. At the same moment, I feel a tug deep within my semisolid body that is unmistakably connected to that distant site that they are now hurrying to avoid. What is there? Whatever it is, I cannot resist an urgent summons. My fellow travelers do not look back as I part ways with them, not even the little boy with the rice cake. Eventually the mist clears and I am able to see, to see with amazement and horror, a scene of utter carnage and annihilation. I press back against a wall at the sound of approaching voices.

"Any captured spies?" The voice is authoritative yet youthful. An officer?

"No sir." The reply is flat.

"But then how can we goddamn tell?"

"We have to go with what they say, sir."

"What do they say, then?"

"Half ran away. The other half resisted and had to be neutralized."

"Kids?"

"They're all trained as spies and informants, sir."

"Do they have to loot? It makes us look like savages."

"They're doing a search, sir."

As they speak, a soldier drags an old man from a demolished hut and throws him to the ground. He starts kicking and cursing the old peasant, who curls into a ball and howls until another vicious kick to the head renders him silent. This soldier looks different from the ones who are speaking. He could have been one of the villagers himself; the old man could have been his father.

"At least make them stop killing everyone, Sergeant. We need to bring some back to the interrogation center." The young officer again.

"Yes sir."

"Fuck all this—fuck this whole damn war."

The young officer speaks in the flat accent of an American. His anger seems directed more at the senseless violence than a particular foe. His face is twisted in disgust, deep brows lowering over piercing eyes—can it be? He appears older than the young black-haired soldier I saw last time, but that frown mirrors the one Edward takes on when confronted with the follies and disappointments of humanity. It has not yet acquired a sardonic edge, as if to say, What else could one expect? But one day soon, with many repetitions of these brutal events, confronted with the depravity of human nature, that edge will come, sorrowing a mother's heart, that final loss of innocence.

I take a step forward. Then another.

William! I call his name, but the officer does not hear or see me. *William, I'm here! See me.* His eyes widen. *Yes, it's me! I've found you at last. You are not dead as they say.* His jaw drops. Of course he does not expect to see me here. I reach out pleadingly. A startled, strangled sound rips from his throat, and I have the oddest sensation that even though his eyes lock upon mine, he is not so much seeing me as seeing through me, beyond me. I turn my head in time to see the old peasant who had lain prone on the ground now charging toward me with a rifle in his hands. The rusty blade of a bayonet extends from the rifle, and the tip of it glimmers as he charges with a cry, and I cry out as well. For a moment his eyes open wide with terror as they meet mine and, yes, they do see me. But then he blinks and clamps the lids shut, and the momentum of his blind charge drives the point of the bayonet forward even as I fling myself upon William to shield him. The weapon punches through my abdomen and drills into William's stomach. I feel only the merest pinpricks. The peasant is stabbing. Stabbing William. My useless hands fail to stem the flood of bleeding. I am nothing but air as I watch William die beneath me. Again. And nothing but a shroud, a mist, drapes over his body, and weeps and weeps and weeps.

Ferndean, 1858

"If you want her to live, sir, if that is your objective, then you have no other choice but to carry it out as I've suggested." Mrs. Lodge was arguing with Edward when I awoke.

"I will never imprison her. I would sooner cut off my remaining hand and blind my other eye."

"Much help that would do you or her, sir. It is not a prison to keep the body safe. Look how we found her: skirts torn, shoes caked with mud and filth, face and hands all scratched and bloody. We may not be so lucky next time; she may wander off and never return. We must secure the helpless body when the mind flies off. It is lovingly done, sir. Hire others if you wish, but none but myself will come: They think this place haunted."

Silence. Then, a roar of fury lanced with despair and grief. "Do as you will, but I will not be here to witness it, and when the new house is finished, there will be no dungeons or barred windows, and only I will be prisoner—to her constant watch—and I will do so willingly with all my heart and breath!"

A wrenching groan, half sob, broken off, a flurry of stamping feet down the stairs, a door banging so hard the whole house shuddered. I sat up. I felt something cold upon my neck. My hand reached to my throat, and I found there an iron cross on an iron chain with no clasp. It had been soldered on. To keep me anchored. And I realized I was not in my own bed, but in a narrow one, in a smaller room. I tried the door and found it bolted. I ran to the barred window—*iron bars*—and looking far below, for I must have been put in one of the previously unused attic rooms, I saw Edward on his horse, fleeing from the house as if from the fiery inferno of hell itself.

Chapter Three

Ferndean, 1858

I am an ant doing my part, carrying a bundle of wood. No, they are rifles bundled up with wood on my head as I follow behind the others with similar burdens, carrying food, fuel, one behind the other, along the dirt trail so narrow that only one at a time can go through. Bicycles wheel along, carrying heavier artillery. Ahead and behind me are men, some in uniform, women, even older children. Like ants we are pulled by a single purpose greater than each singular life, and the burden is light because our belief carries us. Sometimes the trail disappears, splits around a huge crater. We weave around, hidden beneath the dense canopy. We make a new trail with our feet as we pass. We are the trail. We are one, pulled along by a thread of urgency impossible to deny, the thread leading to a light, a blinding light that explodes behind my eyes.

Light shatters the darkness as the drapes are drawn back.

"'Tis high time to arise."

I kept my eyes shut, my body still.

"The Lord knows you are not asleep. And I do as well."

Insufferable how the woman presumes to know as much as the Lord.

"Leave me another hour, Mrs. Lodge. I am exhausted. I barely slept for the demon thoughts in my brain plaguing me through the night. I think you must increase the dosage to ease my burning thoughts."

Mrs. Lodge frowned. "You are already taking the maximum dosage that the doctor prescribed."

"He is a charlatan," I protested, "and not to be trusted."

She paused and perused me. And I read her thoughts: *Nor do I trust you.* "Why do you tell him you are well, have no devilish thoughts and sleep soundly through the night, then?"

"Why, to rid myself of his tiresome services, of course. Do you think such as he could bring me any relief?"

She concurred: "Not *he.*"

"Perhaps that is why he recommends such a small dose," I pressed. "He believes I am merely whimsical."

"He does not know how you really are," she allowed, "not like I do."

"No one sees through me as you do."

She beamed at my blandishments. "We'll double the dosage tonight, then."

Really, it was too easy. I cut out a bit of felt and concealed it beneath my tongue, where it soaked up the sleeping draft when I pretended to drink it. This I wrung out carefully into a small vial when Mrs. Lodge had left the room. The vial was a quarter full by now. Soon I would have enough to incapacitate a small water buffalo. I smiled to myself at the thought as I peered at the precious accumulation of drops, then quickly hid the vial in the inner pocket of my apron before Mrs. Lodge returned.

The second part of my plan was a bit more difficult: I needed to convince Edward to command Mrs. Lodge to take me out on walks. This was not easy, as Edward was so often away supervising the reconstruction of Thornfield. But at last, he returned of an evening, and came up to the attic to sit with me, as was his wont on these occasions. He fretted, however, at an obstacle in the construction that threatened to delay its completion another fortnight. "Really, Edward," I soothed him, "what is the hurry? I am quite comfortable here. Indeed, I dread leaving this familiar, safe room. Here, I am like a wild bird come to rest in its eyrie high above the turbulent world."

Edward smiled at me. "My little bird, indeed. What I would not do to keep you safe from the turbulent world."

"Then proceed no further with your plans to remove us from our home. Here we are well away from that fraught and changing world. Here, within these four walls, six steps from the window to the door, six more to return to my starting point, repeated for hours until my mind becomes numb and I am tired enough to rest, day in and day out, is all the world I need. Indeed, I no longer look out the window."

His lids shuttered slowly, and when he opened them, he looked about as if seeing the gloomy room for the first time. His features darkened and hardened as a picture formed in his mind, the picture I had given him: of an inmate pacing his cell, slowing losing touch with the outside world and coming to love his prison. He excused himself shortly thereafter.

The very next day Mrs. Lodge started taking me out on short walks about the grounds.

At first the walks were confined to ten minutes and only as far as to the hedges along the road. But it was a start, and I restrained myself from asking for more, pretending, instead, to desire otherwise. I complained at having to go out, but appeared to be more compliant and to sleep better for having endured the outing. Indeed, Mrs. Lodge came to advocate the daily outdoor exercise when she saw how I was more agreeable for the remainder of the day, took my sleeping draft without fuss, seemed to sleep and to wake on a more regular basis. None of this was difficult to contrive. The only difficulty was to go slower than I wished in order to allay suspicion. Timing was all. In another three days it would be the beginning of September, and the new house would be complete. It was also the time when the tinker who passed through this area was expected to return. Mrs. Lodge, who was not from these particular parts, did not know of this annual migration.

We had now reached that point in our route where we rested beneath a shady oak before turning around. It was along the tinker's route. This morning I had seen from my high eyrie a glimpse of his cart and had calculated the hours until his arrival at the point in the road where we rested. My quest was to arrest his progress before he reached the house. As we sat I reached for the bottle of lemon water we had taken to bringing for refreshment and quietly opened it, carelessly spilling some on Mrs. Lodge's lap, for which I apologized profusely. While she fussed and wiped at her skirts, I quickly found the vial in my pocket, opened it and tipped its contents into the bottle, and offered her what remained of the unspilled portion in return for her forgiveness, which she grudgingly granted. I watched as she swallowed the entire contents greedily, for it was a warm day, and continued to observe as her chin sank to her neck, her head rolled to one side, and her breath began to slow to a scratching rasp just as the tinker's cart swung around the bend.

For the frugal management of any household, a tinker is among all itinerate tradesman the most valuable. His work, though crude, is truly magical: Where there was a hole, an absence, he generates a patch, a presence, thus healing the pot and making it once again useful and whole. *Alas that his tools are not fit to solder the hole in my heart.* Yet among the instruments of his profession was one that would benefit me greatly: smoother of rough edges, severer of unwanted bonds, the humble but indispensable file.

I rose to meet the tinker.

Border of Laos and Cambodia, 1968 / Ferndean, 1858

The trail has grown. It is no longer just a narrow path cobbling the way for a string of human haulers and bicycle transports. It is wide enough now for vehicles. Ahead, an explosion rips apart the seams of the world. We scatter and duck as dirt and debris pound over us. Then silence, and I gape at the crater when I reach it: a hole as large as a pond. Already, workers are shoveling, filling in the void, diverting around the ragged edge to get traffic moving both ways again. It has slowed down progress along the trail, but it has not stopped the movement. It is broken, but it still moves. And moves. There are now two lanes, coming and going, day and night. Vehicles hurtle south down the narrow road, in darkness to avoid detection. Other vehicles returning north bring bodies home for burial. I feel them around me, the fleeting souls. Wandering. Like me.

I woke up with a start. I was in my bed, still. It was a dream, not a jump. For that was what I called them now: *jumps* in time, space, between lives. Or perhaps I was there, perhaps I *jumped* but hadn't been able to get a foothold, to stay for more than a glimpse. I did not feel the bodily exhaustion I had felt in the past when returning from such journeys. Only a vague disquiet, as a distant witness, not a participant. It had the quality of a dream. I was there, but not quite there. I was getting closer. With the iron cross necklace gone, sawn off with the help of the tinker's tool, I could sense it. I must just bide my time and not arouse Mrs. Lodge's suspicions. I stroked my naked throat and smiled to myself. For no locked door could stop me now.

And yet I did not vanish! To my chagrin, day after day I was still in Ferndean. It seemed I could not will it: I was taken when I was needed. But of what use was I? I had failed to save William twice now. Perhaps I was never meant to prevent his death, only to witness it, over and over again. Perhaps this was my penance, my private hell and eternal punishment for the crime of forgoing a life of godly good works with St. John to indulge in one of romance and love and a family, undeserved and against all odds. William was taken to clarify this lesson, at the height of my felicity, as if to confirm its illusion, to throw me down to the depths of hell, as if to say: *Here, Jane, is what happens when you think women such as you deserve happiness, the love of the most passionate and original*

man ever met, a child of wonder conceived in redemption. There, and there, and there is the outcome of your misguided hope.

Who spoke to me thus? Was it a vengeful God? A little St. John dwelling in my soul? Then another voice intruded, one filled with quiet gaiety, a child's voice: *someday, somewhere, somehow* . . . Against all reason, my heart grew lighter.

When I raised my head, I had jumped.

Southern Huế, 1968

"You shouldn't be here," he whispers. "What are you?" Not *who* are you. *You see me?* I kneel over him; his blood stains my clothes. He is bleeding out before my eyes. "Am I already dead? Are you a ghost? Or an angel?" His labored breath catches. "You just sort of appeared. Did you hear the explosion? I've been calling out for hours. Didn't expect anyone to come." My eyes roam over the piles of rubble. It's some sort of urban battleground. This man before me is not William. But he sees me. "I don't want to die." *Talk of death—what nonsense.* I speak to him briskly, though the words feel shaky as they leave my mouth. *You are very much alive, young man, but you will not be for long in your condition if you remain there unattended by your compatriots.* "Please help me, please help me." He is fading before my eyes, and what can I do? Though he seems to see me, his compatriots do not, so I cannot compel them to come to the soldier's aid. The sounds of gun battle seem more distant now, the fight edging away. Soon the wounded soldier will be another corpse.

Did I say that aloud? For his hands grip my arm with a solidity that shocks me. I feel embodied in a way I have not before in this land. "Help me get up, help me get to them."

I must find William. I do not know how much time I have here; time is slipping away. There is so much death all around me. But there is only one person's death—stopping it—that matters to me. Even so,

I find myself reluctantly drawn to what is here, the one before me, the one who needs me now. Is it the need that causes the metamorphosis? For a moment, there is a blurring, a doubling. The face of the stranger becomes the face of my son—then that moment shatters. The face before me resolves. The soldier's skin is dark and rough under my touch, and though I know he is not William, I do not move my hand, savoring the pressure and warmth of contact. Uncertainty returns. From prior jumps I've learned to study the soldiers' faces, the pale ones and the dark ones, for I have come to know that William can be embodied in the form of any age, race, or nation. I have also come to know with more certitude than ever that while the exterior covering may affect how one's life is lived, how one is able to live, it is what happens within that sustains life itself.

That life is bleeding out of the boy in my arms, and there is no time to ruminate. I need strips of cloth to bandage his stomach. My petticoat does well enough. "Water, please, miss." I find a drinking container in his pack and hold it to his lips. He takes a few sips, and then his eyes start to close, but I shake him until they open again. *And now get up,* I say. *Get up now.* He blinks at me. His speech is slurry as he begs me to go get help. *I cannot,* I tell him. *They do not see or hear me. Yet you do. Why is that?* "Because I believe in you. My grandma always said there are dead folks all around us, the restless ones. But most people don't see 'em. Except sometimes, if they're gonna die soon. Oh Lord, I don't want to die." *You will not die,* I tell him sternly. *For I am not a ghost. Merely a . . . time traveler. And it is not your time to die. Get up.* I speak with a certainty that surprises me. I am not a useless ghost. I am giving a lifeline to the boy, and the unexpected connection holds me to this world and to a sense of myself. I help him to his feet, relishing the weight on my shoulders where I had felt weightless and insubstantial. We take halting steps toward the distant sound of gunfire. "What's your name, miss?" *I am Jane.* "I'm Sam. Samuel J. Parker." *Tell me about your grandmother, Samuel.* "Oh, you'd like her. She's a tough little thing, like you. Always wears long old-fashioned dresses like the one you got on. Always on my case. 'You do better, Samuel J. Parker,' she'd say, 'or I'll whup you.' She pretty much raised me. I tell everyone I joined the marines to get away from her." He laughs ruefully. "I'd give anything to see her again. If I make it. If I don't fucking die first in fucking Vietnam." He clutches his stomach and shivers. We are closer to his comrades, but not close enough. *Samuel,* I say, *your grandmother will surely whup you well if you do not convey your pitiable form forward.* "You mean my sorry ass? Too ladylike to say it? Sorry ass! You all, come and get my sorry ass!" he shouts.

"Parker, that you? Parker, shit, man!"

"We need a medevac!"

"We need cover."

"Move it, move, move, move!"

I drift away as his comrades surround him. But at the last moment, I turn, and his eyes are on me. His hands faintly rise in farewell, and I smile and wave back briefly. I am torn between two immensities. A life saved. But what of the other life, the one I sought to save? What was it that Samuel had said? The dead are all around us. Why this life and not that one? Samuel. William.

I felt so grounded bandaging the young soldier, but now, again, drifting, I'm unsure whether I'm solid. Suddenly, I feel that I have gotten it all wrong: I have not fallen out of time. Instead, the opposite is true: I have fallen into some great, chaotic amalgam of lives and events, lost souls, searchers. It is a storm, blowing me along with all the rest of the debris of progress. What future it is blowing me toward I cannot see. I only see William's face. And so much confusion, as I look back desperately to undo the dark disaster that set me along this course, the singular catastrophe of my son's death.

I must return. I must go forward.

I cannot discern my direction. But for a brief moment the hand of another touched mine, amid the storm. For a moment, in the eye of the storm, I was at peace.

Chapter Four

Ferndean, 1858

I sat up, gasping, in my bed. My bed in the attic. Moonlight leaked in through the barred windows, striping the bare floors. It was so bright I had no need for candles, which I was forbidden anyhow. Did I just return, or had I been back a fortnight? William. Samuel.

I could see in the moonlight that there was no blood on my hands, no dirt on my skirts; my petticoat was intact, untorn. I was fully dressed. I remembered that I had taken to sleeping in my clothes, for of course I could not be wandering in foreign countries out of time in my nightgown! Unseemly! And when they tried to intervene, I howled like a wolf, a trick I'd learned that turned the visages of those around me into such grim, harrowed masks that I could laugh, often did, but it allowed me to be left alone in my perceived eccentricities.

I shivered. Mrs. Lodge had put out the fire before she left the room for the night. The fire was for her own comfort in the chilled autumn nights. No fire for me, however, just as there was no light. It made for some discomfort and inconvenience, for now after Mrs. Lodge had left, I had to proceed in the darkness and cold. But there was moonlight, and even when there was not, I had gotten into the practice of slipping out of my bed and feeling my way about through my senses alone.

I shifted a warm ember from the ashes of the banked fire and carefully revived it, blowing gently until it started to glow, a spark of redness gleaming from its depth. I set it carefully in the middle of my bed. For had I not learned: When you remove a thing from its habitual environment, when it touches upon a new thing, it extends its matter; its essence is released from form, which after all can never be contained forever, will dissolve eventually into air, merge with time, become the nothing and everything of space. What is form but an illusion? Our essence can embody anything. Did I not learn that as I sought out William in all his different forms? Had I not seen for myself how form is but a temporary hold on time, how a trail can become a road, how a land, a nation can divide, come together, cleave, reach yet again for unity? Mutability is existence.

And now the time had arrived for another change. Be victorious or be vanquished; exult in triumph or succumb to terror. The conqueror approaches, and among the conquered all is panic and despair, and those who can, flee, leaving behind all those who can't . . . *for we cannot take them all, Jane, the ghosts of our loved ones; they will be left behind.* Edward had said this with grim sorrow. I knew he was right. The end of Ferndean would be the end of my adventuring: When we left here, I would never find my way back to that strange and beautiful and terrifying land, find my way back to William.

So I would ensure that I did not come back. Tonight would truly be the last night. I imagined the ember upstairs embracing the threads; a small flame was born. I wished I could take it with me to light the dark hallways, but then I realized I did not need it. My bare feet knew the way.

I crept to the locked door. My fingers skimmed the floor and found the crack at the edge of the wall where I had hidden a slim iron instrument. For in addition to sawing off my metal cross, the tinker, for the exchange of a cameo brooch, had given me a tool for picking locks. The trade might have seemed unequal, but not in my eyes. This instrument I slid into the keyhole while I listened for clicks and tumbles, felt for resistance and yield. The lock sprang.

I opened the door.

How still the house was! Each night I had passed through the house, it had become emptier, tables and chairs draped in white sheets, empty spaces where some of the furniture had been removed already to Thornfield. Tomorrow, the few remaining servants and I would follow. I trod like a phantom beneath wrapped chandeliers. Door after door. I tried them one by one. Not a sound. Nothing but the sighs of the sleepers, restless, frowning through dreams. I gazed upon the closed face of one of the sleepers, and my fingers lightly caressed a dark lock on the broad forehead. I recalled the heated conversation we had exchanged that morning:

"In that new house will there be a slightly larger attic, Edward?" I had asked. "Indeed, though the walls will be farther apart, will not all Thornfield be my new prison?"

His face had darkened, then blanched. "Do you think so ill of me, as one who would imprison his own wife?"

"Have you not done it, before?"

"Not to you, Jane!"

"And how am I living now?"

"You must not harm yourself, and what of how *I* live?" He swore; he left in a rage to attend to final details of our removal.

Edward. Dear. So attentive to details and yet he had forgotten to blow out his bedside candle. So careless. A breeze could stretch that flame, a finger of it reaching to caress the edge of the curtain by his bed. His eyes, closed in sleep, rendered his expression a look of peace that I seldom saw on his face these days. How I ached to run my hands through that mane of unkempt hair, still mostly black into his late middle age. But I feared to wake him. So I bent quietly over, kissed the air above his cheek, and blew out the flame.

I moved on. Another door. Sometimes another sleeper. Yet another door. Door after door. I opened and closed them one by one. Oh, it made me laugh, this house of endless doors, and how that laugh echoed in the empty corridors. I had not yet found the one I needed, the one that opened not upon a room, a sleeper, but upon a world. There was one I had not yet tried, one that divided the top floor from the roof, and to this one I now made my way. At the top of the stairs I saw light leaking from the bottom edge of the closed portal. What lay on the other side? Sunlight blazing over a canopy of trees? Spreading fields of floating green shoots? A bustling city filled with the sounds of a foreign tongue? William, waiting for me? One step and I would be in the middle of it.

I opened the door.

Sài Gòn, April 29, 1975

I pass through a haunted city seething with empty streets and hidden eyes. A city constricted with anticipation and fear. A dark-haired boy brushes past me, then turns his head, body still propelled forward but eyes widening as he stares at me for a moment before swiveling his gaze ahead, not stopping, only slowing down when he dashes past a lone open café where a man sits by himself with a glass of amber liquid on the table. The boy points an accusing finger at the man, shouting: Go home! America, go home! His high, sharp voice is derisive and bitter. The man, reaching for his glass, freezes as the boy runs past. I drift toward the man, the American. I seat myself across the table from him. He shakes out a white stick from a squashed packet and lights one end with a flame that snickers out of a slim metallic tube. His shadow stretches mournfully behind him. He isn't William.

A waiter appears with a sweating bottle and refills the man's empty glass. Will you be leaving soon?

I'm staying, damn it. Got friends in the French embassy promised to put me up. Smoke blows from his mouth. I've been covering this war for ten years. Not leaving yet, not until I get the end of the story.

The waiter wipes the table and keeps his thoughts to himself. Look here, the seated man says, pulling out a piece of paper from his pocket. I was in Phan Rang last week with a bunch of other journalists.

Found some graffiti written on the walls. I wrote some of it down. Can you read it?

The waiter peers at the writing. Just names, dates, sir.

Nothing dirty?

Here's the name of a village. That one says *wait for me, mother and little sister.* Hmm, that could also be *girlfriend* or *lover.* This one. He pauses. *Vietnam . . . I weep.*

I hear the sorrow and longing in the words that the waiter deciphered and linger on one word: *Vietnam.* The name of this place?

The waiter hands the scrap of paper back to the American, who folds it up and puts it back into his pocket. The waiter has never once looked at me, but he shudders as he returns to the back of the shop. The street begins to fill with people who slip silently out of doorways and move with hurried, purposeful steps; vehicles start to crowd the streets. Without warning, one of them screeches to a halt right by the table where we sit.

You two, the driver shouts.

The man cocks his head. You talking to me?

The waiter is nowhere in sight.

You and your lady friend can't be here.

The man peers behind him in confusion. What lady? I'm a journalist; I'm staying for my story. I'm not going anywhere.

What story?

How it all goes down, how Vietnam ends.

You stay at your own risk, sir. And you don't need to be here to write the end. All you need to say is we cut and ran, that's it: done. They made us liars and cowards, but I've got my orders.

The journalist leans back, puffing smoke. Got to see it. World's got to see it.

Get in, the driver says, I'll take you both back to the embassy, along with the others I have to round up. Let's go, Miss. He looks at me closely for the first time, stops talking, eyes widen. Oh, it's you.

The journalist is perplexed by that statement as he glances back and forth between me and the driver. Who in hell are you talking to? *Samuel,* I say, *dear boy, you survived.*

Though he is hardly a boy now, I think as I look fondly upon the familiar face, careworn, hardened, no sign of the frightened, panicked soldier in the city ruins. But alive. I smile, and he smiles back a wide grin that wrings a boyish expression from an older man's face. Just talking to an old friend, he says to the bemused journalist. But I have to go; can I give you a lift, ma'am? He gets out and opens the door of his vehicle for me. Welcome to my jeep.

We leave the baffled journalist squinting after us. The streets suddenly dim as passing clouds blanket the sun, bringing relief from the glaring brightness, though the heat remains oppressively heavy. Might get a bit of rain, Samuel mutters. That will help. *With what, Samuel?* With the bombing. He nods with satisfaction as a light mist starts to drizzle down. That will make it harder for the bastards, he says.

I do not understand it; I will never understand it. I can only accept that it happens. And because it does, there must be a reason, scientific, religious, philosophical. And if there is not, then I am a madwoman, a phantom, or a dream.

Samuel, I ask, *am I a ghost?* You don't know? *And yet, with you, I feel solid, alive.* Then maybe I'm the dead one, he says cheerfully. *You look very well, Samuel,* I say gravely. Well, you had a hand in it, he replies. Would have been pushing up daisies after Huế if you hadn't gotten me off my butt. I never told anybody about you. Well, one person. I was passing through medical in '73 for a minor wound, and some kid was recovering from a shot to his leg and looked like he could use a distraction.

He pauses. He's somewhere else, watching himself tell the story to the young soldier who listens with glassy-eyed wonder at a tale of angels, ghosts, saviors wandering the battlefield.

Samuel continues, Maybe I should have told more; mighta gotten me a crazy pass out of the war. In truth, I have wondered about my own sanity as well, I confess. You sure are crazy to be here. But I am too. I was wondering if I'd see you again. They stitched me up after Huế, gave me a purple medal. I was all ready to sign the exit papers, head back to Georgia. And then I just couldn't do it. At home I got restless, couldn't settle. It was like I wasn't done.

I kept hearing in my head: *I must return.*

So I did a second tour, and a third. Got promoted. I'm a staff sergeant now. Normally I wouldn't be doing grunt work like driving around picking up strays, but we're taxed here, and no one knows the streets of Sài Gòn like I do. But today, seeing you, something clicked. Like, maybe this is what I was waiting for. What are you doing here, Miss Jane? *The same as you, Samuel, a thing left undone.* Guess we'll do it together, then, he says, laughing, since it worked so well the last time.

As we move, the road starts to fill with people and other vehicles, some, like the one we are riding, powered by a kind of internal mechanism; some with only two wheels, moved, it seems, only by the power of the rider's pumping legs. Curfew's over, Samuel mutters as he jabs at the middle of his wheel and emits a piercing honk. I hear a roar overhead, and looking up I see a most amazing sight: A large, wingless iron bird with a crown of spinning blades hovers, then alights on the rooftop of a tall building. People start running from the streets to the building. Some are already converged on the rooftop, beckoning, crying, pushing and shoving to board the bird, clinging to the sides of a doorless opening or grabbing the bars below the bird as it begins to lift back into the sky. I gasp as it sputters and jerks, tearing away from the desperate boarders, some still dangling from the bars below it. They drop, one by one, back onto the rooftop, but a determined young man continues to cling to the rising bird. And the young man is not alone: Another grasps his ankle, and another the ankle of the one below, creating a human chain of determined desperation. But the weight of that despair is too much for the first man. His grip breaks, and he falls back upon the other two on the rooftop. The bird spins away. I am clutching my chest in horror when my eyes meet Samuel's. He is shaking his head.

Well, that's another way to die here, he says as he swings his attention back to the road.

We are moving along the road, yet the next moment a stutter in time lands us in front of an imposing building, with no sense of having come upon it. There's the embassy, Samuel says. More people arrive; a wall of bodies blocks the entrance. A woman pushes into the middle of the crowd and shoves a bundle forward.

This American baby. You take, you take American baby.

No one moves to take the child, a small thing, perhaps a year old, an amalgamation of features that freezes my attention: light, gingery hair; golden-brown skin; dark seed-shaped eyes, so bright and luminous when I look into them.

I gasp. Looking into them is like falling through time. I am running across a field of fresh-cut grass, holding a small, sticky hand, laughter bubbling from lips reddened from gobbling wild raspberries, small head lightly jostled against Edward's broad shoulders as he carries the sleeping child home, to the father and the mother who love him so much, the mother whose heart is broken as she kneels over his grave and cannot find the strength to ever rise again. I pull back with a shock.

Oh, Samuel. Take the child, please. What? The woman, face contorted with sorrow and panic, shoves the child against Samuel's chest, but his arms remain slack at his side. *Samuel,* I cry, *this child must live! Please, take the child now!*

I blink. Another skip in time pitches me forward, in increments of minutes, hours, it seems, instead of years, centuries. To my relief, I see Samuel holding the child. As the door to another of those giant iron birds starts to close, Samuel presses up to it with the child, ducking below the spinning blades. He hands the child to the soldier at the door, who automatically takes it and immediately turns and hands it off to another pair of arms behind him within the body of the bird. I cannot see who takes the child in the end. Samuel does not look back once he's handed off the small form. Fall back! Gusts of air raise my long skirts off the ground, and the iron bird rises. Cries of don't forget us, come back for us! I hear their cries, I see their despair and longing as the bird flies away.

And I feel an inconsolable ache.

What will happen to them now? The hope: a better life, away from here. I feel what that mother feels. And more. I'm back in that storm of time, loss, searching. I feel what everyone torn from their country, their home, feels, and what anyone who has lost a loved one and knows not their fate feels—will they survive, will they be loved, will they be able to live? But as the onlookers, faces raised in awe and longing, fear and desire, track the rising bird, Samuel is pulling me.

Let's go, he whispers in my ear, that was the last one, let's go, let's go.

Another hop in time, and we are on the rooftop of the embassy building. Now the night stretches endlessly, a reversal of the prior frantic, speeding time. The soldiers are bored, but vigilant, tense, apprehensive, an unspoken refusal to give in to the fear, yet it is there all around them. They are all wondering, perhaps, *Will this be where I die?* We're the last Americans in Vietnam, Samuel says. I stand beside him as he looks out over the roof. We see flares, fires, and he points north at distant flames. That's the air base, he says, and over there, Biên Hòa. Sorrow in his voice. *You will miss this place,* I say. If I get out . . . yeah, he admits.

I'm so ready now to leave, especially after tonight. Disgust in his voice, wistfulness. But I can't help thinking that part of me's always gonna be here. Three tours. Feels like more than half my life.

That look again: He's somewhere else, thinking about how many lives he's lived in this one, in this war.

Of course something gets left behind, he says, and something in the tone freezes me to his words. He tosses the remainder of his smoking stick over the roof. Who knows, maybe even some kids. The way everyone was fucking around over here, sex practically free, there's gotta be a lot of babies come out of it. Maybe even some of mine. I don't know.

Silence.

And what about you, Miss Jane? Did you get what you came for? *Yes, Samuel,* I tell him. *With your help, I did.* He smiles. So we're even. I knew there was a reason I had to come back.

A thread of light begins to mark the eastern horizon. It turns into a band of whitish gray, then rich opal; blue and pink, salmon, bronze ribbons streamer the sky, a bolted bulge of gold so bright and beautiful one can only look upon it with reverent silence. But the quiet is broken by the muffled sounds of people beneath, working their way up. As the dawn unfolds, specks begin to appear in the southeastern sky. Is it? Yes. Another gleaming iron bird.

Everyone on board, let's go!

I hear cracks of firearms. I pull out of Samuel's grip. *Goodbye, Samuel.* You're not coming? *No, my work here is done, as is yours. Go now.* He nods, turns, runs to the iron bird now lowering on the landing platform. We are suddenly surrounded by smoke . . . cries . . . can't see a goddamn thing . . . that tear gas getting sucked back to us . . . pilot, go! I see their distress and know there is one more thing I must do. It is not Samuel's day to die. I climb to the edge of the roof. Miss Jane, what the fuck! *Goodbye, Samuel.* I remember when he was a young, scared soldier. Roar of blades beating the air. Miss Jane, for god's sake, don't jump, take my hand, Miss Jane! Jane!

Edward's anguished face. You are not in your right mind, Jane, take my hand! Smoke and flames all around me. I hardly need the candle in my hands. How I long to ease his fear and dread. But there is one more thing I must do.

I look down on the grounds of Ferndean, but it is a city that rises up when I step off the edge. I don't drop. My skirts flare open and catch a wind that lifts me up. I float above the city, leading the iron bird. And then they are free of the blinding smoke; we are in the clear morning sky, the city flaming below, shrinking to dots of light, wisps of smoke, patches of gray and green.

The open sea ahead.

Sài Gòn, April 30, 1975 / Huế, 1985 / Ferndean, 1857

Floating. The iron bird has flown off over the sea, but I linger along the shoreline. The clouds clear; I see that rubble has been cleared too, roads restored, cities rebuilt. On the midpoint of the coast, I peek inside a tiny shack where a woman lies on a pallet on the dirt floor. She is asleep. Dreaming of my country, of England, of green hills north of London, near a small town, on a hillside, a quiet place near a farm, where a child used to run and play, a favorite place, quiet now, no laughter or sound today, only two people quietly standing before a small stone marker. In her dream I drop a bit closer to see the writing on the gravestone. *Jane Eyre Rochester, beloved wife of Edward and mother of William Edward St. John Rochester.* The man stares at the inscription, one hand hidden inside his waistcoat, the other clutching the hand of the small dark-haired boy, wide eyed, who looks up suddenly and waves at me. I wave back, almost overwhelmed by a surge of joy. My child lives! Will the child remember the mother who gave him up, the mother who will lose him? Will he know how a mother will travel across time and space to find him? Does it matter? He lives, and I can rest at last. My travels are done, my work accomplished, and the dream of my existence can now be laid to rest alongside my body beneath that gentle bed of earth and its loving marker.

But then the man looks up, and it is as if he can see me, and yet not see me, for he shouts blindly into the sky, *I will find you—maybe not in this world, not in this time, but if you are there in another, I will find you.*

With that, I feel myself falling back into life.

Boston, 1912

She had not been there a moment ago. But there she was now, staring right at him. He nodded nervously, hoping she would move on soon. She nodded back. He didn't know what to do after that, so he waited. *Go away.* Instead, she crossed the street and peered at him from the top of the alley. He kicked the brick away as he retreated behind the back door. Safely barricaded, he leaned his ear against the door, listening. A knock. The doorknob rattling from without. Another knock.

Hesitantly, he opened the door to meet her eye. *"Fermé! Désolé!"*

He found French words sputtering from his mouth, and he was hardly surprised, as he was always thinking about how to get back to France, a country he had barely set foot upon before having to leave. When his long shift ended at this quiet hour before Boston awoke, the cool, still dawn air made him think of Paris as he imagined it must be like at this time of day. Paris at dawn is like a woman slowly waking. He had read that in a poem. But the real woman before him shattered that metaphor with her haggard, hollowed cheeks and her intense stare. A real woman does not wake like a Paris morning at all, he realized. *Do poets always lie?*

They stared at each other. It was a jolt to his system to be suddenly noticed; he felt himself becoming uncomfortably solid and wondered when he had gotten so used to transparency. Most people here looked at him only enough to register that he was a foreigner; then their eyes slid over his foreign face to something more familiar, and he felt his own face fading a little more each time until these days he was pretty much a ghost wandering about the busy metropolis, invisible, alone.

She murmured something, then held up a single bedraggled lavender kid glove. She pointed to her mouth, then waved the limp glove. He took this to be a universal gesture of barter.

"This is all I have. Though its mate is lost, the remaining one is dear to me."

She is starving, he realized.

I will regret this, he thought as he opened the door wider. *And what will I do with a single glove?* She stepped in with a look of gratitude and sank down on the chair that he had pulled out for her. Once seated, she closed her eyes and breathed in the rich, yeasty fumes of recent baking. Her entire body seemed to absorb her surroundings. *I have been hungry, exhausted, and alone as well.* He set down a plate of rolls, the sweet, buttery, folded rolls that the hotel was famous for. Sometimes he would cut the dough into triangles instead of squares and roll and bend them into croissant shapes, making him think of Paris.

He sat. In spite of himself. She smiled at him as he looked down. At some point she had placed her glove on the table. It lay there demurely, the knuckle of the pinkie finger bent awkwardly at the top joint; it was remarkably expressive even in its shabby, handless state. It came upon him suddenly that he would treasure this glove forever.

He gently nudged the plate toward her.

"Thank you," she said.

English. Unfortunately, his English was bad, worse even than his French. He nodded.

"I have not eaten all day."

She shredded a buttery roll as his gaze intensified. *She is not beautiful,* he thought. She was what they called "plain." But her face was remarkably malleable, so that when she spoke, even though her words were incomprehensible, the meaning was somehow conveyed through the intense luminosity of her eyes and the expressiveness of her lips.

By the time his focus shifted from these thoughts back to the table, she was finished with the roll. He pushed another one toward her. She shook her head at the glove.

"I have nothing more to trade."

She's saying that she doesn't have anything more to exchange, he thought, again reading her eyes. He pushed the roll closer to her. She slowly picked it up and began to tear off pieces, stuffing them nervously into her mouth.

"I saw your face from across the alley." She was speaking between swallows. Her hands went still. "I've seen your countrymen." She frowned. "At least, I suppose those were your countrymen that I saw in the jungle. It was yesterday." She paused. "It was many years ago." She looked into his eyes; alarmed, he stifled an impulse to bolt. "It didn't happen; it was a dream. Or a prediction: It is going to happen."

She is saying that she has fallen out of time, he thought. He knew that feeling. When he first arrived in Boston, it was like being dropped into another world—so different were the sounds, the tastes, the movements, the air. And now the dull bewilderment of the city's profound indifference to his existence, which, day by day, had made him into a living ghost. She must be a ghost herself, he thought, to recognize another ghost.

She raised her small, pale hand and examined it as if affirming its solidity. She murmured, "Are we not all human? All made the same, with hands and feet, hearts and minds? Yet all they see is that you are different, that you don't belong, that you are poor, and so you do not matter." She was indignant. "Everyone matters. You are not the sum of your possessions, for those can be taken from you. You are what you believe, what you do. They had nothing, your countrymen. In my dreams, my predictions. But they went on. I don't know what kept them moving. Not fear or hope. Necessity, I think. They were set on some path; they moved forward in order to live." She stretched her arm forward and lightly touched the back of his hand, sending delightful shivers down his spine. "Thank you for your kindness. I would have starved without your charity."

At the door, she turned and inquired, "What is your name, sir?"

His milk name was Nguyễn Sinh Cung. Later, when he finally made it to Paris, he would be called Nguyễn Tất Thành, but he would also begin writing passionate, furtive letters in his head denouncing Western imperialism, signed under the name of Nguyễn Ái Quốc. Someday, he thought, he would write them down and send them out. *Someday, I will have another name that the world will never forget.*

She nodded. "I'm Jane," she said, stepping out into the Boston morning that was not like a woman waking. He held the glove to his nose and breathed its fading scent of grass and cinnamon. When he looked again, the Englishwoman was gone.

In a time to come, when he was old and tired, when he was falling in and out of dreams as he waited in the bomb shelter for the drone and shudder of the American planes to pass, when he thought of death, and woke, afraid that his hopes for a liberated, united Vietnam would die along with him, Hồ Chí Minh would take the glove out, feel its soft, worn leather, smell a whiff of yeast, and remember her. And he would force himself to take a breath, and then another.

He would make himself move forward.

Vinh Trần Martin, 2008

"ALL MY HEART IS YOURS . . . IT BELONGS TO YOU; AND WITH YOU IT WOULD REMAIN, WERE FATE TO EXILE THE REST OF ME FROM YOUR PRESENCE FOREVER."

Chapter One

Boston, 2008

Porn as the first thing to hit your eyeballs when you wake up guarantees the rest of the day will go downhill from there. True that, but he's already skimming through last October's issue from Danny's dumped *Playboy* collection. Danny gets all his porn on the internet these days, but Vinh prefers the glossy pages, how he can manipulate the magazine so that the light glazes the surface, making half the image go invisible. Seeing all the hot stuff is the *point*, Danny huffs indignantly, but there's such a thing as too much to see, Vinh argues. (Like, he would rather unsee Danny's hairy butt—though he doesn't mind hairy butts in general—crossing the apartment to get to the bathroom after sex with his girlfriend. Behind closed doors, thank God.) It's an ongoing argument that they have as they cross paths during night guard duty at the museum: Seeing is overrated; there are your other senses, Vinh schools him. What he doesn't explain to Danny is that while he's not really that interested in the feminine curves, veiling half the image in a sheet of light allows his eye to linger on an inner thigh or a delicate bulge of calf muscle, that his imagination sketches in the rest, lengthens, thickens, hardens parts here and there, until a whole other kind of body reveals itself in his mind. He knows Danny wouldn't get it. Vinh's never discussed his preferences with his roommate/coworker. Danny's a good guy, but in many ways they are worlds apart. *Don't jizz all over the pages.*

I might want these back some day. Vinh tries not to imagine that there's a slightly tacky feel at the edges as he holds the image up in one hand while doing his business with the other. His brain jolts, and his eyes roll up behind his closed lids as he milks the seizure through the last pulse. Deep sigh, and then all too soon having to face the emptiness of the rest of the day.

Right. It's already two. Time to roll out of bed, shower. In the bathroom he strips off his T-shirt and makes the mistake of catching his reflection in the mirror over the sink. He hates mirrors. He doesn't like seeing himself, his body. He finds it embarrassing, so unlike the bodies he desires—though lately he's caught a certain look from guys, and some women, a look that hooks his eyes, then dips down, then back up. That only makes the body stuff more stressful, though. It's why he avoids reflective surfaces and is so annoyed at catching a glimpse of himself now. But this morning he's annoyed that he's annoyed. *Grow up!* Okay, he'll look. But he can't take it all in at once. He starts at his navel. He thinks about how some navels have an enchanting line of curly tendrils leading down farther to a woolly, springy spread. His own navel sprouts no such enticing line of hair, and it is also mostly smooth skin over his chest and back, which does nothing to camouflage the ridges of his rib cage. He wishes some of the hair on his furry legs would migrate up his body, up to his face, and give some boost to his beardless chin, the pathetic trace of a mustache he's been trying to grow, though it's mainly because he wishes he had something to hide behind. His roommate's girlfriend once told him: *You've got amazing cheekbones.* He would duck his head and could barely look her in the eyes after that until Danny told him to chill, *She's not into you,* and what a relief that was. His mop of dark hair finally brought under control by the Korean barber who trimmed back the sides, leaving the strands on top longer, layered, hanging over his forehead. He'd always thought he looked kind of plain, but Jonathan had told him, *No, you look like a treat to be devoured. Slowly.*

Blink. Thoughts scatter. *I'm right here, right now,* he reminds himself sternly.

Finish shower, go get breakfast/lunch. Purpose propels him forward; lukewarm water leaves him feeling half cleaned, the humid air leaching any remaining sense of freshness right out of him, corned beef sandwich and coffee settling in his stomach; all this moves him along until the momentum leaves him stranded on the park bench, emotionally depleted, crushed paper bag in hand, staring at the trees in their fullness, just starting to brown at the tips of their leaves. *This is the fullness of summer,* he thinks. The heat is peaking, the city is wilting; *what have I done today?*

He gets up and starts walking. Last night had seemed so promising when, during his shift at the Gardner, he'd sketched that drawing of the mother and child looking out on a boulevard of streaming peddlers and motorbikes. It was the first time in a long time that he had drawn anything. He pulls it out of his jacket pocket and studies the picture sketched on the back side of a flyer. This image, extracted from a half-forgotten memory, makes him feel like finding something, someone that he thought was lost forever, and losing it again. But what had Kenny said? *Draw the sunset, or a bird, or a bottle by the side of the road. You would find me everywhere, in anything. Just look around.*

He squints at something scribbled at the corner of the page. There's an address there, and it takes him a second to remember that he first grabbed this flyer to make a note of a job opening for a tutor. *That's not far from here, I think.* He looks around for a street sign.

The motorcycle swerves, skids, and spills the rider on the ground right in front of the curb just as he is stepping off.

Damn you, the rider curses as he sprawls in the dust.

He sits up shakily and wrenches his helmet off. At first glance, the black curly hair and dark eyes suggest a younger man, but the details tell him otherwise: the bits of gray in his beard and at his temples. Like Jonathan. Not as handsome as Jonathan. Yet something about those deep dark eyes, the way you feel like you could fall right into them. Vinh realizes he is staring at the stranger and dips his head apologetically.

I was speaking to the damn bike, the stranger says when Vinh leans over and offers to help. He looks dubiously at Vinh's extended hand. That doesn't look like it would support much, he scoffs; it would probably break if I put just half my weight on it. Vinh's instinct is to withdraw and hide the useless hand behind his back, but the stranger's naked rudeness somehow makes him do the opposite.

I won't leave you until I know you're okay, he says firmly. *How weird,* he thinks, *that I can speak like this to a stranger.* He's usually too shy to even make eye contact with people. Quick check to make sure he hasn't turned into someone else, which he sometimes wishes would happen. Nope. Same thin arms and skinny legs. *Same body.*

So I'm not a weight lifter, but I can at least help you get to your feet.

To his surprise, the stranger grasps his hand and allows Vinh to assist him to the curb, where he tentatively flexes his booted ankle and grimaces.

Sprain, he says with disgust, then spits into the street.

The way he limps when he experiments with putting weight on his leg makes Vinh wonder if the stranger suffers from an earlier injury. He notices Vinh observing him and scowls.

Do you make it a habit to step in front of oncoming traffic, or did you just want to get my attention?

What? I would never! Then he stops at the absurdity of the denial, the accusation. The stranger is looking at him intently, and he feels heated, and not because it's July. No one has ever looked so directly at him. Well, maybe Jonathan. But at the beginning of their relationship. Not for a while.

And where the hell did you just go that second? the stranger demands, noticing Vinh's distracted look.

As if it were any of his business. That is none of your concern, sir, he says primly. *Why do I sound like a stupid nineteenth-century parson's daughter all of a sudden?* May I offer you some water to help you recover?

The stranger waves away his offer impatiently: I'm fine, damn it; you can go.

I'm not going anywhere until I see you're all right.

Stubborn one, aren't you, he says, scowling even more. So is that what distracted you? Your doodling?

How did he know? Oh. The stranger picks up Vinh's flyer, which flew from his hands when the bike spilled in front of him. He dusts it off and examines it as Vinh squirms silently, afraid to snatch it back as he wants so badly to do. Silence. Then: Did you draw this? Vinh nods nervously. The stranger nods too. There's a story there, I'm sure.

Suddenly Vinh wonders what it would be like to share the story with this man, this stranger. He opens his mouth.

I . . .

What's this address? the stranger asks sharply, pointing to the scribble in the corner of the flyer.

Oh, nothing. Just heading there for a job thing.

Huh.

He gives Vinh an odd look, which rattles him and makes him start babbling. I mean, I don't have it yet. The job. I have to go interview for it. A tutoring gig. *Shut up,* he tells himself.

The stranger finally hands the flyer back. He smiles, like he's pleased about something. It's a smile that stirs something in Vinh, makes him want to close the distance between them, to know everything that man is thinking. *Okay,* he thinks, *now or never. Say something.*

My insurance will take care of this dent, the man says abruptly, but just in case they don't, you should take the job. And do me a favor. Pay attention next time; don't die.

He's already put his gear back on. Time's running out. Vinh tries again.

I . . .

The stranger doesn't look back when he releases the clutch and the throttle snaps, leaving Vinh in a plume of gasoline-smelling dust.

Okay. That was weird. Goodbye to you too. He checks his watch. He has three hours before his shift starts at the museum. He checks the address on the flyer again. This is where they told him to go when he called last week. Taken from a stack of ads in the Laundromat: *English lessons tutor needed for ten-year-old boy. Some knowledge of Vietnamese desirable.* Fancy Back Bay address. Odd way to hire an English tutor. Weren't there big private companies, shit like that? But he figures it made sense to put an ad there: The Vietnamese community in Boston is small. Everyone goes to that Laundromat; everyone gets their community news and hears about jobs there. Giving English lessons to a ten-year-old kid. He could do that, he guesses. No fancy degrees, no BA, that ship has sailed—has not heard from Father M since he left the boarding school. But he can speak English, even if the occasional jerk on the subway tells him to go back to China or asks where they can get "flied lice." Ha ha. Fuck off. He can't even muster the energy to say I'm Vietnamese, moron. Half. He can't even feel enough anger to flip them off. What's wrong with him? Why does he feel so tired all the time, so drained? He used to be able to paint for hours at a time while waiting for Jonathan to get home from work.

Jonathan had been a lifeline. When he had arrived at the law firm for the internship position that paid so little he couldn't afford housing, he'd had to make do with the couch in the staff lounge, hoping that his late shift would make people believe he was napping between filing. All he could think about at the time was his day-to-day survival. It made him a bit lightheaded, never getting a complete night's rest, but between the couch and the restroom, the toothbrush in his backpack, and sponge bathing in the sink, he'd managed to get by—a bit dicey that time he walked in and heard the activity in the corner stall, two pairs of expensive footwear toe to toe, one pair especially that caught his eyes: oxblood wing tip shoes. And he fled, and how restless he had been that night, how strange the dreams that had invaded his sleep. Then the next day, the lawyer, the one with silver at his temples, stopping to say hello as he poured himself a cup of coffee in the lounge, and looking down and recognizing the expensive shoes. After that, it was more casual chats over coffee breaks in the lounge, joining Jonathan at a nearby restaurant for lunch, then drinks after work, then nights at his condo, and then somehow, he had moved in. Jonathan had arranged it so smoothly that he hadn't even noticed that he was being seduced. And Jonathan had never minded the sketches and half-finished paintings all over the apartment. And also hadn't minded the brief bouts of weeping after sex; Jonathan just held him quietly until it was done. It was embarrassing. He didn't know why he did it, but Jonathan found it charming. The painting at least kept him busy on certain nights when Jonathan was out with clients. After a while he had stopped sketching and painting; it had just petered out. As well as the sex and the weeping.

He looks again at the address on the paper. Giving himself a chance to change his mind. *Maybe I can find a way to make money with my art.* No. He needs money now. *It has come to this,* he thinks. *Either I go on as I have been and die of boredom and exhaustion, or, if that's going to be my life, at least endure boredom and exhaustion in a new situation.* He likes how dramatic that sounds. It's stupid, but it helps him move forward.

He lifts the heavy brass knocker that hangs on the door, and when he lets it fall, he hears a muffled thud echoing inside. He waits a long time, heart thudding as well. Finally, he hears shuffling footsteps, and the door creaks open. Ghosts. This place gives him the creeps. He kinda likes it, though. It reminds him of the Gardner at night. A hand reaches out and beckons him inside. Not a ghost. But it takes a moment for his eyes to adjust. The parts of her clothing that are black seem to blend into the dim interior, making the parts that are white, like her large apron, appear to float in midair. Her face is a pale, floating disc. She looks sternly at him in the near dark until he finally whispers, I'm here about the tutoring job. He wasn't sure why he was whispering except that the creepy atmosphere seemed to call for a soft voice. For the boy, he says. Still, the woman doesn't say anything. Um, can I speak to his parents?

Mr. Rollins is the boy's guardian. The master is presently abroad, she says stiffly. I am Mrs. Poole. Please follow me.

He wonders what it would be like to live in this large, solitary, silent house where the occupants are called the master and the mistress. He sees tastefully worn carpets and matching armchairs that Jonathan would approve of. Exposed brick walls, a portrait of a woman in a long, old-fashioned gown mounted over the fireplace—*wait, is that an actual John Singer Sargent?* Over there, a staircase leads to a second story, maybe even a third. There are no other sounds besides their footsteps. The whole house reeks of Boston Brahmin wealth (Jonathan used to like to tell him proudly that *his* money at least was earned) but feels strangely deserted. They reach a closed door in the back, which she opens, beckoning him to follow.

The flood of sunlight blinds him when she opens the door. Blinking, he now sees a space lined with books reaching from floor to ceiling. Wheeled ladders so one can reach the highest shelves. A large round table, dark and polished, makes an island in the center of the room. It is bracketed by two stiff armchairs. In one corner is a huge globe (he prefers to think of them as small worlds) held up by encircling arms of wood. It's all impressive but not very inviting. His guide leaves him there, and in the silence he turns toward the small figure, the only other person in the room. Vinh sees only the back of a head of light-brown hair as the boy stares through a window with his back to the room. Out there he can see a small rear yard that was once a beautiful garden. It's now an overgrown jungle, invasive weeds strangling an old elm tree and choking the flower beds, shattered stone urns scattered about. Time stands still. And the child standing at the window looking out at the ruin of the garden seems to be part of the arrested setting. The wrongness of it freezes him to the spot for a moment, makes him wince, like a sudden jagged pain between the eyes. There's no way a kid that young should be facing backward, stuck in time, when his whole life is ahead of him.

Hey there, he says quietly. No response. So, um, we're kinda from the same country, he continues. What's your name? The kid doesn't answer. Brat. Maybe he doesn't know any English? He digs into his memory for the Vietnamese that he hasn't spoken since Father M brought him to the States.

The boy finally turns around to face him. I'm Michael, he says in flawless, unaccented English. Vinh blushes. *What does the kid need me for, then?* Between his perfect English and his light-brown hair, he would not have guessed the child was Vietnamese if the advertisement had not hinted so.

He catches himself doing what others have done to him, what annoyed him so much in the past: expecting him to look or be one way or another based on some assumption, and being surprised or disappointed when he fails to measure up to that expectation. *Just chill,* he tells himself. *Just talk to the kid.*

Michael, do you remember Vietnam? Your family? Michael is silent for so long that Vinh is about to repeat himself, thinking he was not heard.

I don't remember anything, Michael says coldly. He's turned back to look out the window. That is not my home. We are not the same.

Unbelievable. He's both annoyed and impressed that the kid stands his ground: Fuck off; you don't know me. And to be honest, a little bit hurt at the rejection. He says, Yeah, right. Michael keeps his back to the room as he looks out the window at the ruined garden. He does not speak again. Okay, then. Vinh's heart feels heavy as he leaves him there.

At the front door, he finds Mrs. Poole, waiting. Before he can say anything, she opens the door and nods. When he steps out, she closes it firmly on him. For a second, he feels disoriented by the passing cars, as if he's stepped back into time from an era where everything moved more slowly, without engines or electric streetlights like the ones starting to glow against the dimming sky as he makes his way home.

Is he hired? Is he not? Vinh finds himself thinking about the kid in that big, rich house all night long during his shift at the museum. He's still thinking about Michael the next day. *So did I get the job?* There's only one way to find out: He goes back to the house, same time as yesterday. Mrs. Poole answers the door again. This way. Um. So I have the job?

The master says to give it to whoever comes back.

So much for qualifications, Vinh thinks. And seriously, who in the twenty-first century calls their employer "master"?

Am I the only one who ever came back? She doesn't bother to answer as she leads the way to the library and leaves him there.

Hey, Michael. In the schoolroom, as Vinh thinks of it, the boy is standing by the window as before. As he did the last time, he ignores Vinh as he looks out. Why is this kid always facing backward? Vinh doesn't care about the kid not showing his face, but he wonders what he is supposed to teach him. Mrs. Poole had no instructions in that matter. Michael's English is already very good, way better than his at that age. There is nothing there for him to teach. Vinh stares at the silent back. There was a time, Vinh remembers, when he didn't speak much either. Even before coming to the States, he was very shy and didn't interact much with the children of the other shop workers. He spent hours alone with his most precious toy, his G.I. Joe soldier doll. Or he drew pictures of G.I. Joe in a notebook. Sometimes he would show his aunt his sketches and tell her the story they illustrated. They were bloody stories that scared his aunt, or at least she had pretended to be scared, but they were thrilling too. The muscular American hero sweeping in to save humanity. His G.I. Joe had a beard.

Do you want to hear a story? Michael ignores him. Here's one I came up with when I was about your age. It's about a G.I. Joe soldier who destroys an army of invaders from another planet all by himself. The boy shrugs. In the beginning, no one knows they are from another world, Vinh starts the story. Everyone thinks: They're only tourists. But not G.I. Joe because he peeked and saw they had green skin under the tourist clothes, and that's not right. As he tells it, he starts remembering the small details; then the story slowly unknots into a long, wayward thread of G.I. Joe's special powers. He could turn invisible if he held his breath. Most people get dizzy when they hold their breath too long, and they pass out before they can become invisible, but G.I. Joe could do it for over an hour. He could fly. He could jump around in time: If he arrived too late, he could make himself come back five minutes earlier. The stories always ended with a victorious battle, but often Vinh didn't even get that far. It's much more interesting to invent the middle.

He's been storytelling for almost fifteen minutes. Vinh feels a little breathless. Done for today, he says. Michael has not moved the entire time. But Vinh can tell he has been listening. He even thinks he heard a soft chuckle over parts of G.I. Joe's adventures. Let's get some air, Vinh proposes. He doesn't wait for an answer. There is a door in the schoolroom that opens right into the rear yard. Vinh opens it. He steps out. The garden is bigger than he thought it would be. Even in Back Bay most of the gardens are small. And when he crawls under a wall of vines, he discovers that it goes even farther back. There's a bit of a clearing in the tangle of overgrowth that's too low to stand up in but offers a secret space to sit with your knees drawn up and your head bent over, just curled into yourself. It's very quiet; even the birds sound muffled. It's like being tucked inside a little nest and he's an egg waiting to hatch, but not yet—he gets to hang out as an egg for a little while, suspended from having to be anything yet. *Really,* he thinks, *what is it about this place, this kid, this job that makes me feel like I've stepped into a fairy tale?*

He feels a touch on the back of his neck. The small hand is cold. He puts his own over it and holds it there for a moment. Then he and Michael crawl out of the secret space, and they walk back inside together.

By the end of the week, they've cleared out a corner of the backyard jungle and planted seeds saved from Mrs. Poole's meals: apple cores, cucumber bits, avocado pits, carrot tops found in the trash. On the days that it rains, they settle down in the library. They throw a sheet over the polished table and make a cave where Vinh tells Michael all the Vietnamese fairy tales he remembers. He shows Michael how to draw dragons because Michael liked the story of how the dragon lord and the fairy queen fell in love and created a great sack that opened up, spilling out a swarm of one hundred children, the first people of Vietnam. The dragons they draw have long scaled bodies and great horns and whiskers, just like Vinh used to draw them, filling page after page in notebooks in the bookstall, waiting for customers. Sometimes he can't tell whether that time is a real memory or a dream. *It's wasteful to use up so many notebooks for drawing instead of selling them,* she says, but she's smiling as she admires his picture. Vinh draws to his heart's content. That's what he remembers. *Someday the art opening will be yours, and we'll all go see it.* That was what Jonathan said after they left the gallery, and Vinh felt this exuberance, this ballooning in his chest cavity, and later, he doesn't want to think about it, the deflation, the slow leak of their relationship.

Michael asks him why he looks sad, and Vinh stops thinking of the past and looks at him. He's a good-looking boy. Only when he smiles and his eyes go up a bit at the corners might someone guess that Michael is not an all-American boy. Wait, that's messed up. Vinh frowns. Michael's a good-looking boy whether he's all American or all Vietnamese or half of each. *Stop being a dumbass,* he tells himself. *You of all people should get it.*

People tell Vinh sometimes that he can almost pass. *Pass for what?* Or is it *pass* like moving forward? Pass from one identity to another? One body to another?

I'm not sad, he tells Michael. I'm cool hanging out with you. He speaks only English with Michael. When he tries speaking a bit of Vietnamese, Michael goes vacant, as if that time of his life is a blank. Michael doesn't strive to become an American boy either. He seems satisfied with being in between. Vinh gets that. He likes Michael. He's just a little freaked out by the empty house, the missing master, his ambiguous job situation. *I'm kind of a babysitter, not a tutor.* The difference makes him anxious: He's always been cared for, by his aunt, by Jonathan, even by Father M, in his own way. He's never taken care of anyone else before. Not even himself very much. It's an odd feeling, makes him weirdly protective, which is uncomfortable. If anyone tried to hurt Michael, he would go nuclear on them. *It's just a job,* he reminds himself.

He always goes to find Mrs. Poole when he's leaving, but today she's waiting for him at the door. The master will be back tomorrow, she says. He wants to speak to you.

Chapter Two

He oversleeps. Of course he does. *That can't be an accident,* he thinks. He's never been late to meet Michael. He must be freaked out about meeting the "master," the mystery employer, who will probably fire him on the spot as soon as he sees what kind of incompetent fool has been hired. *They should have said the kid needed a babysitter. Though I'm probably not the world's greatest tutor either.* Should he even bother to show up? Well, yes, because he hasn't been paid yet. Although he wasn't sure what he would be getting paid for, except hanging out with the kid, which, if he didn't actually need the money, he would have been fine doing for free.

He's nervous as Mrs. Poole opens the door to the "master's" study. This room has always been locked; this is the first time he's been inside. Wait here, she tells him. He holds his breath as he enters. It's not like the library-schoolroom. That room feels luxurious. This one feels like a room where someone thinks and reads and dreams. There are shelves of books along the walls, but just as many piled on chairs and on the floor, as if a reader pulled them out, looked into them often, treated them like many friends in the midst of many ongoing conversations. He is intrigued. The state of the owner's books gives a brief glimpse of the reader, and Vinh wants to know more. He goes on a treasure hunt to find his employer out. He begins by examining the objects on a side table by a leather armchair. They are curious things: a pair of heavy, industrial scissors; a magnifying glass

with an ebony bone handle; a rough chunk of meteoric rock, the inside
hollowed and lined with sea-green enamel, which it looks like the "master"
uses as an ashtray. There is a sweet smell of clove lingering in the air. To his
surprise, he finds a pile of Vietnamese currency inside one drawer when he
peeks into the large oak desk. But of course, he reminds himself, the boy is
from there, and his guardian seems to have traveled through Vinh's country
and come away with these stray remnants of his time there: the bills, some
cheap postcards that one can get anywhere in Vietnam. But he pauses at
the ones of the Imperial Citadel and pagodas in Huế. Vague memory of a
rack of postcards like these, stacks of books, long, heated afternoons in a
shack. He is filling in the room's mysteries with his own story: There are
no personal pictures, no travel photographs. But what does he know of
his own story? He slides open the bottom drawer. Something rattles near
the back, and his hand pulls out a medal: George Washington on a purple
heart. When he turns it over, he reads: *For Military Merit Edward J. Rollins.*

On the floor next to the other deep leather armchair rests a half-
empty whiskey bottle. Next to it and on the seat of the chair are several
books lying face down. Vinh quickly rips a sheet of paper from a pad,
tears it up, and slips the bits between the pages to mark the reader's place
before closing and stacking the books carefully in a pile on the side table.
He feels that someone would keenly disapprove of seeing books left out
that way. He starts picking up books, even swiping the dust off the covers
with his sleeve before he catches himself. *Since when do I care about a mess?*
Honestly, being in this house makes him feel possessed—by a neat freak
now? He peeks at the titles curiously: a history of the Spanish Civil War,
a biography of a medieval surgeon, a manual on birds of the Far East.
This last one he opens as he settles into one of the leather armchairs. The
pictures captivate him. He sees himself on an eyrie, nesting in a rocky
crevice high above the crashing waves below the cliff. He feels wild and
free. The wind roars in his ears as he closes his eyes. Drifting on a current
of air, he starts to dream. He starts to remember. *It's the roar of water, it's a
rush of streaming traffic, bicycles, motorbikes, merchants shouting out, a rush
of wind, go faster, Đức, a book shack, her face—*

Throat clearing wakes him. Yet he has a feeling someone was watching him the whole time his eyes were closed, watching from the other armchair across from him. Eyes open quickly. *Oh shit.* Vinh shoots to his feet.

The man waves him down. Sit.

Vinh cautiously seats his butt on the edge of the chair. *It's him. What are the chances?*

So you're the master.

Wry smile. Is that what she calls me?

What should I call you, then?

Hmmm . . . have you considered the Tyrant? The Governor? Fearless Leader?

Seriously, you're Edward Rollins? I . . . don't know if you remember me, the guy you crashed into. Or I caused you to crash. The one who did that drawing.

Rollins looks at Vinh closely, and long enough that Vinh feels a tingle running up his spine and half catches his breath. I wouldn't forget someone like you, he finally says. I had a feeling I'd see you again when I saw my address on your picture. I see you didn't die after I left you there.

Vinh can't tell if Rollins is still annoyed or not about taking that spill because of him. Rollins points his chin around the room. Snooping, were you?

I . . . yeah. Sorry, Mr. Rollins.

Did you find anything interesting?

Vinh wants to ask him more about the Purple Heart, but it feels too invasive. No, he mumbles.

Here's where I get fired, he thinks, *and not being qualified is the least of it.*

But Ed's fine.

Oh, not fired. Vinh wonders what it would feel like to twine a curly strand of Ed's hair around his finger. Ed, *Eddy.* He's not a traditionally handsome man—rugged, almost coarse features, stubbly beard, shoulders a bit too wide for his height, and he's not a tall man. Those dark, intense eyes and brows with flecks of gray in them, though. He's kind of a gorgeous troll.

Rollins is silent, watching him slide off into a daydream. Vinh feels like he's been caught going through the man's underwear drawer. *Jeez.*

Bit of a dreamer, aren't you? Remember, that's what almost got you killed.

Sorry.

Rollins shrugs, then goes on. Michael seems to be coming along. You've brought him out of his shell, at least.

Right, Michael. Vinh feels ridiculously pleased by the compliment. He's a good kid. But maybe he deserves a real tutor. I mean, I haven't taught him anything he doesn't already know. Mostly we've been hanging out. *Did I just talk myself out of the job?*

So you don't want the job?

No! I mean, yes, I want the job. *But is it the right job for Michael?* he wonders. Respectfully, sir.

Call me Ed.

Mr. Rollins, respectfully, I think what Michael really needs is not a tutor, but, like, a companion. A friend. And I don't mean Mrs. Poole. Someone to be around for him. *Like a father,* he thinks. *Or a brother.* He watches Rollins's eyes darken as he stares back at him, and he braces himself to be eaten alive for his presumption, to be told to f—— the hell off. Long, assessing silence. *What's he thinking?*

Here are the terms for the job, he finally says. You'll quit any other jobs you have at the moment, and you'll stay here with Michael full-time through the rest of the summer until his school starts.

Stay here? he stutters. *Live with them, with him?* Somehow, his head is nodding before he's even made up his mind.

There's plenty of room; think of it as a live-in internship. Can't have you showing up late because of whatever other things are going on in your life—this is a commitment. Your job starts tomorrow.

He looks around the simple room. It's very plain compared with the other rooms in this house. There's a narrow bed and bedside table. On the dresser is a vase filled with a few flowers. A bookcase built into the wall is next to a plump armchair by the window. All in all, Vinh's pretty pleased with it. At least this is much better than being homeless, which he was on the verge of becoming when their lease expired. But Vinh doesn't get a chance to show Rollins that he doesn't get to boss him around just because he's rich, because Rollins is gone again, and no, she doesn't know when he'll be back, Mrs. Poole says. The master comes and the master goes. *What is this place?*

It doesn't take long to dump his backpack of stuff. His art is stored in Jonathan's basement. He's not even sure if he'll ever go back for his work. The one piece he still likes is the last drawing he made, on the back of the flyer. He props it up against the dresser mirror. There, home sweet home.

Vinh takes a deep breath and opens the door. Then he freezes. What was that sound? Something between sobbing and laughter. It sounds far away, yet close by at the same time. He shivers. Mrs. Poole? he calls out, peeking into the hallway. Maybe Mrs. Poole is cleaning up in the attic; all these big old houses have those, he thinks. Just as he's about to check it out, hurried footsteps sound below. The top of Mrs. Poole's head appears, then the rest of her.

Is that you? she calls out. She is out of breath. You must come down now. He's ready for you.

Mr. Rollins is back? A pang of hope.

No, the boy is in the library. He's ready for his lesson.

Mrs. Poole, is there anyone up there in the attic? I thought I heard something.

Oh goodness, there's nothing up there but storage. The door is always locked. You mustn't go wandering, young man—the master is private about his possessions. Come along.

And he has no choice but to follow, but he throws one last curious glance upward as he trails Mrs. Poole downstairs. And there, again, something like a sigh, a sigh of longing; so faint, a bare whisper in his ear. Or was that *him* sighing and the house listening? He gets so confused for a moment that he nearly trips on a step. *Either I'm going crazy or this place is haunted.*

It takes Vinh a couple of days to adjust to his new digs. At first it feels strange not to have a late guard shift at the museum every night. But then he discovers that he just ends up doing what he usually does, which is to read all night, except that he doesn't have to do it in fifteen-minute intervals between his rounds. Michael goes to bed early, and Mrs. Poole disappears to do whatever she does in some part of the house. He's pretty much on his own after that. He doesn't mind it at all, to be honest. It's peaceful.

Mostly. Then one strange night he awakes suddenly with a feeling that something is wrong. He sits up in his bed at once, heart racing. Did he hear something? The click of his door opening, then shutting? He listens closely. Nothing. But chills trip up and down his spine. Then he hears the soft thud of another door, far away, being closed. He jumps out of bed and runs out to the corridor. Instinctively, he rushes to Michael's room and opens the door. He sees at once that Michael's bed is empty. The covers are thrown back, and his pillow still holds a dent where his head had lain. In the empty corridor Vinh swivels his head in a panic and is just about to fly down the stairs when a movement at the end of the hall catches his attention. It's just the window curtains shifting in the breeze. But it's odd for that window at the end of the hallway to be open. It's not a chilly wind, but he feels his skin prickle. He goes to the window. He has no choice. Something is pulling him there. He looks out. A full moon. His heart almost stops. There is a small figure standing below, alone, looking back up at him. No, not at him, but at something above him. Michael is looking at something on the roof of the house. In a flash Vinh is down the stairs, out of the house, running around the corner to the side. He is so relieved that he catches up Michael in his arms and clutches him tightly. Michael does not resist his hug. And when Vinh looks up at the roof, nothing. Why are you out here? What are you looking at? In the aftermath of his terror, Vinh is so furious that he would have shaken the boy if he had not held back his anger.

Nothing, Michael says. But he hangs his head guiltily.

Tell me, Vinh says firmly, and no lies.

Michael turns sullen; he avoids Vinh's eyes.

It was just an angel, he mutters. Sometimes I come out to see the angel.

They don't speak of angels the next day, or after that. Vinh means to follow up. He really does, but events take a turn. Michael leaves for a two-week sleepaway camp that Vinh only finds out about when he comes across Mrs. Poole organizing the kid's tennis shoes and marking Michael's name on his T-shirt wash labels with a black Sharpie. How come nobody told me this before? What am I supposed to do for two weeks? Mrs. Poole doesn't bother to answer, and there are no instructions from Rollins. Vinh decides that he'll just carry on since nobody seems to care, and besides, he has nowhere else to go. *If he wants to pay me for two weeks to do nothing, that's his business.*

The first forty-eight hours are bliss, he isn't going to lie. He doesn't even want to call up Danny or anyone to hang out with. Not that he ever did that anyhow. Truth be told, he's discovering how much of a loner he is, now that responsibilities have been stripped away. He spends most of his days reading in bed, napping, prowling around the neighborhood in the middle of the night—it's still hard to discard his night guard schedule. Mrs. Poole is around the house, he knows, but he never sees her. He prefers it that way. But by the end of the second day, he's so bored he even considers seeking her out; maybe she needs help with the housekeeping? Maybe she wants company for when she's slipping a nip of the master's good gin? Yes, he's caught her doing it, and no, if he actually ends up joining her for a nightcap, then he might as well just kill himself. He wonders how *nightcap* got into his brain. It's not a word he ever uses; it seems to belong, like so many other things here, to another time, strangely mixed up with now.

He's saved by the sketchbook. He went into the study to find paper and pen to write a few letters for Michael at camp. Vinh didn't want Michael to be that kid who never gets mail from home. He knows what that feels like. And there, on the table, is a tablet of twelve-by-fourteen grained paper, the kind that has a sheet of tracing paper between each page so the drawings don't get smeared, and next to it a box of brand-new sharpened No. 2 to No. 6 graphite pencils. He knows this wasn't here before. Did Ed leave it behind? Now it is like he's possessed: Some force invades his body, takes his hands, makes his fingers move the pencil across the page, and hours later, when that force finally loosens its grip on him and quietly ebbs away, it's left behind pages and pages of eyes. Dark, dark eyes, fringed with long dark lashes. Penetrating, see-right-through-you eyes. *His* eyes.

It's the day before the last day of Michael's camp. The kid will be home tomorrow. Vinh flings open his bedroom door, takes one step out, and sees immediately that this day is going to be challenging. The door of the bedroom across from his is open. When he peeks inside, he sees clothes half spilling out of an unzipped travel bag. Ed is back. Vinh tries not to creep downstairs, because that would be lame—he *works* here, after all. Ed's study door is open. There he is, sitting at his desk with his feet propped up on the surface, reading a letter. He doesn't look up as Vinh walks in.

The boy's expression has gotten better. I assume you taught him that.

Michael's a smart kid; I didn't do much.

You got him to write back. That's something.

Yeah. Thanks. He's also a nice kid—he'll write back if you write first.

Maybe that's why he never wrote me, Ed says as he tosses the letter down.

But Vinh thinks Ed is pleased. Vinh is too, as a matter of fact; hearing your student praised is like getting the compliment for yourself.

So are you back for a while? Vinh asks casually. He doesn't want to sound like he cares too much.

A little bit. I'm leaving tonight.

Oh.

You seem disappointed.

No, Vinh lies, just kind of tired. I didn't sleep well last night . . . So where are you off to?

I have to go open the beach house in Delaware. You and Michael will join me there.

Okay, not what he expected.

I think that woke you up a bit. Ed smiles.

Oh, right. Yeah, nightmares have been keeping me up.

He's flustered; he tells himself to shut up. Ed looks concerned. *Why? We hardly know each other. He looked at me so strangely when he took off the helmet after the crash. Almost like he half recognized me from somewhere.* Vinh is pretty sure he had never met Ed Rollins before that moment on the street. He would definitely have known.

What was your dream? Ed asks.

Honestly, nothing, Vinh insists.

Ed walks around his desk and takes a seat in one of the armchairs. He points to the other armchair, and waits silently, arms crossed. Vinh goes over to the chair but doesn't sit. Ed frowns at him. Must you defy me at every turn? Vinh bows his head but remains standing. Eventually Ed sighs. Tell me.

The trouble is that Vinh doesn't know where to begin. With his own tumbling thoughts toward Ed himself? With the unquiet feelings? With the sound of the child crying? He decides to begin there. I heard a child cry.

A child? Perhaps you heard a stray cat.

Yes, maybe that's all it was. He had listened with all his concentration, and even left his bed to stand in the hallway for a time before returning to bed. Last night, as I was falling asleep, I heard the door open. But maybe I just heard the wind on the window from the storm. It had been a stormy night.

Go on, Vinh.

I kept my eyes shut. But then I heard a noise close to me. I woke up! I saw . . .

Yes, continue—what did you see? But it seems that Ed is very tense, and he is sitting at the edge of his seat, one hand clutching at the arm as he leans forward to hear Vinh's story.

Nothing! I didn't see anything, Vinh exclaims. It was all a dream! Was it? *Wasn't it?*

But he's glad he described the dream. Doing so seems to ease something in his mind.

Fundamentally, you're someone with a very vivid imagination. No wonder you have wild dreams.

Okay, sure. *But . . .*

Do you believe in ghosts? Ed asks right on cue, as if he can read Vinh's mind.

Vinh blinks, aroused from his reverie. Yes, he says without hesitation. Doesn't everyone?

As a matter of fact, no. But I served in Vietnam. Yeah, I'm *that* old. Though I was pretty much a kid when I faked my age to join, and I was only there for close to the end of it. That time has to do with Michael too. Anyway, another story for another time. Point is: I met someone whose life was saved by a ghost.

For this story, Vinh does finally take a seat in the armchair. Go on, he says.

It was 1968. The guy was dragged out of Huế after they were ambushed, and he was the only surviving marine left in his unit, though he thought he would end up a dead man as well. He told me the story when he was passing through medical in '73. I was there recovering from a shot in my leg, nothing as serious as what that marine had been through. He had been ripped up by some serious shrapnel. He said that a ghost had saved his life, that she all but hauled his butt off the ground and tore strips from her dress to bandage him. I told him she sounded more like his guardian angel than a ghost.

As Ed is talking, Vinh vividly pictures an angel cradling a wounded soldier. Suddenly he feels the air beating around his head, hears the flutter of wings; he's the one looking up into her fierce, unworldly eyes—how they burn with love, how his heart aches for the angel, and he is begging her not to leave him, not to let him fall. Throat clears. Ed has stopped talking.

There's an awkward silence as Vinh fights to recover himself.

Sorry, he says, just a . . . nothing, I'm fine. Go on, please. *What the hell was that?*

Ed still looks concerned, but he continues: This angel, this ghost, she made him stay awake and told him he had to live because there was something he was destined to do for her and she would haunt him for the rest of his life if he didn't. I never got a chance to ask him what he meant. I never got his name. I was young and stupid and scared and had no business being there in the first place, according to my father. He had paid good money to keep me out, but I wasn't having any of it. Perhaps part of me wanted to die in Vietnam to vex him.

Vinh wants to ask Ed about his father and why he sounds so bitter. There is so much that he doesn't know. The flood of questions is on the tip of his tongue. But he holds back, sensing somehow that asking them would unleash a storm within himself. Everything in this ghostly house feels slippery and volatile, and he feels himself slipping as well, like when he fell into Ed's story and felt his heart ache for the angel just then.

What was that? But Ed is done with storytelling, it seems. He gives Vinh a long, puzzling look. Then, as if frustrated, he stands up, still scowling, and stalks out.

Chapter Three

Bethany Beach, Delaware, 2008

Vinh never learned to swim, so he stays on shore watching when they're all at the beach, a bit envious but mostly enjoying the view of Ed's shirtless body. (They dragged him in once, Michael and Ed, two against one, no fair, tangle of arms, legs when the wave dropped on top of them, choking, sputtering, mad as hell, but couldn't help laughing, everyone looked so drenched, especially him, and then distracted by the slick heat of Ed's muscles.) Later, Ed's snoozing on his towel with a book over his face while Vinh digs in the sand with Michael. When Michael runs off to play with a group of kids, Vinh takes out his sketchbook. Thinks of the days of drawing Kenny. Cloud of sadness for a moment. Fresh page. Landscape? No way. Not when there's this luscious near nude right there. Time stands still. He finds himself adding details maybe not necessarily there . . .

Hmm. You made me taller. And younger. And hotter.

Vinh startles. Ed peering over his shoulder. *Shit.* I thought you were asleep.

You made such a racket drawing that it woke me up. Let's see—hand it over.

Reluctantly passes Ed his sketchbook. Then he remembers the nude one, but it's too late. Searches Ed's face anxiously. Will he be mad? Was it weird and invasive to draw your boss in the buff? *Of course it's weird.*

And Ed's turning page after page, pausing a bit longer on some of the pages; doesn't comment, which makes it worse. He can't look, closes his eyes. Waits for judgment.

They have been at the beach for a week, and even though he's never had a beach vacation, it's not far off from what he imagined: respectable vacationers, well-heeled children, polished young lifeguards, elderly couples walking along the shore in the early morning. Ed's gigantic beach house. It's only him, Michael, Ed, and Grace the housekeeper (not, thankfully, Mrs. Poole, who stayed behind in Boston). He wasn't sure what to expect, at first, but the three of them quickly settled into a routine. In the mornings he hung out with Michael while Ed worked in one of the empty bedrooms. He joined them on the beach after lunch, mostly lying with a book propped on his face like today . . . after stripping off his shirt.

Still waiting for judgment of his art now. Waiting.

Okay, my turn.

Ed is turning to a fresh page. He takes up the pencil. Tells Vinh sternly to be still. Vinh doesn't know which is more embarrassing: to have his secret nude drawings of Ed seen by Ed, or to have Ed sketching *him* back. Also, he didn't know that Ed could even draw. Curious. Very. The way Ed stares at him as he works is almost unbearable; it feels so intimate to be looked at like this . . . Just when it's on the edge of too much, Ed's gaze flicks down and his hands make marks. Done. Vinh can't wait to see it, reaches eagerly for the sketchbook, and what the hell is this?

I know I'm skinny, but a stick figure?

Vinh examines the sketch: The stick figure lies on its side. One stick arm bends at the elbow, propping up a circle head; the other stick arm is waving. One stick leg angles at the knee while the other stick leg stretches out lazily. It's the circle head that catches his attention. One polka-dot eye, one half-circle eye under a mop of hair represented by some scratched dashes.

What's wrong with my eyes?

You're winking.

For a stick figure, it looks pretty expressive, Vinh admits to himself, like it's . . . flirting. Like some porny guy in a magazine.

I don't think I've ever winked in my life, he tells Ed.

Really? You should try it some time. I bet you'd look really cute.

You mean I'd look really stupid.

Ed squints up one eye, one corner of his mouth quirks up as well, and he looks so comically louche that Vinh is howling, holding his sides, which hurt from laughing so hard.

What? Don't I look cute?

Now *cute*, Vinh thinks, is a word he'd never use to describe Ed Rollins. *Wolfish. Consuming. Heated.* Yes.

He finally catches his breath and opens his eyes. Ed is staring at him intently.

Vinh sits up. What?

Nothing. This is just the first time I've seen you so relaxed and happy. Oh damn, I just ruined it.

Because Vinh is now scowling self-consciously. It doesn't help that Ed tells him that's cute too. *Change the subject.* What took you so long to draw two stick arms and stick legs and a circle for the head?

Well, I guess I did stretch it out. I wanted an excuse to just stare at you back a bit.

Oh.

This one I really like.

Ed turns to the page that has a drawing of Michael looking out the library window as he did that first day that Vinh met him. Half his face is in shadows; he has a pensive, moody expression like he's looking both outward and inward at the same time.

You caught his air of being absorbed in his world. Ed nods approvingly. It makes you think of a story.

He turns the page. Vinh startles: He's placed the flyer, the one with the drawing from the Gardner, at this point in the sketchbook. He decided he wanted it with him always.

I've seen this one before, Ed says, taking the flyer out. This is another one that feels like a story. Is that your mother?

No, Vinh says reluctantly. It's my aunt. She raised me. I don't really know my mother. She kind of abandoned me, so my aunt raised me herself. And she ran this bookstall; that's where the drawing is set. It's all I really remember about Vietnam.

Hmm. Is she still there?

I never heard from her after I got to the States.

Vinh isn't sure why he's so resistant to talking about his aunt. Something feels tender and wounded in him.

Partly to change the subject and partly because he's genuinely curious, he asks, What's the story with Michael? At first Ed's quiet, and Vinh thinks he isn't going to tell him. Then he sighs.

I met this girl when I was in Vietnam. He rolls over on his back and speaks to the rolling clouds. Vinh settles beside him. After I was wounded in '73 almost as soon as I got there. After they patched me up, I was assigned to an intelligence unit. I was stationed in Huế as part of a pacification team in a small village outside the city. Our job was just to live there quietly and show the natives we were friendly. That was supposed to make the village peasants like us and discourage them from sympathizing with and aiding the Việt Cộng. They always claimed to be neutral, but you could never tell. And the more brutal they thought Americans were, the more likely they were to prefer the Communists. But it was pretty quiet the whole time I was there.

That was where I met her, Ed continues. Her name was Bi An. She was the village chief's daughter. I would see her at the hut when I went there to speak with the chief. She was so quiet; she had this uncanny ability to merge into shadows and disappear. One moment I had a glimpse of a face, and the next moment, gone, like a ghost. This went on for a while. I was determined to tame this shy, wild bird. Though sometimes I wondered if it was actually me who was being tracked and slowly broken in. If I had been older and more experienced, I might even have wondered if I was the first one . . . but I'm getting ahead of myself. I knew she followed me, though I could never actually catch her doing it. As I said, I hardly ever saw her except out of the corner of my eye—she was too good at vanishing. But I left small flowers, a square of chocolate wrapped in foil, a coin, whatever trinkets I picked up on trips into the city. I knew she took them, because they were always gone when I went back to check later. Then I found the note. It was a crude map on a scrap of paper: an arrow pointing to a storage shed on the edge of the village grounds. I went there. I waited. Every day I went there at the hottest hour of the day, when everything slowed down because of the heat and the village settled down to sleep it off. I waited. And then on the fourth day, she came.

Ed closes his eyes. He continues, It felt like a slow healing. Like a deep pit inside me slowly filled. No words, semidarkness, touch, wetness, warmth. It was enough. It was everything I needed.

And so it is, Vinh thinks, it's enough to hold a lover in the dark, in silence, in gratitude. To hold and to be held back, after warily circling each other, to finally surrender, to lay your head near the steady, beating heart of the other, and out there is a war, but here it is safe, here we are together, here we are home.

Ed's voice snaps him back to the moment. *Where did I go just then?*

It was a year; it was the end of time. Then things got bad. The war, I mean. They wanted us out of the country. There was barely time to pack. I didn't even have time to say goodbye, nor could I find her. We had only ever met in our shed, in the semidark. I left my military ID there for her to find as a promise I would come back.

I wasn't there when the whole thing went down the next year. I could only watch from afar like everyone else: the chaos, the panic, the tanks, the helicopters, the people on the embassy roof, the shame. Afterward, letters to everyone I could get ahold of working with refugees, the boat people—maybe she was with them. Maybe she got out if her boat wasn't attacked by pirates, if her leaky tub hadn't sunk to the bottom of the ocean. No word, but I never stopped thinking of her. I went back and got a GED, then went to college on the GI bill, earned degrees in programming and business, moved to California and started my own business. I had it in mind that I would be a huge success by the time I found her. That I would be able to give her everything she never had.

Ed stares off into space. *He is watching the silent years fly by,* Vinh thinks. Like birds. Time could feel that way, he knew: eternal. Then you blink and everything has changed around you while you remain the same, encased in amber.

I never stopped thinking about her, Ed continues, but there was no news, and twelve years went by like that. And finally, I decided I needed some kind of closure. I decided I would go back to Huế and look at the village where it had all begun. I don't know why. Maybe just to say goodbye to the place where a foolish young man lost his heart. That's when I found out, from the village chief, that she had left the village shortly after I did, ran off with some American priest. So there it was: my closure.

Ed takes a deep breath. Afterward, he says, when I got back to the States, I threw myself into my work, thinking to excise my pain by becoming as rich as possible. In that quest, at least, I finally succeeded. And the pain was sufficiently numbed by alcohol. And the funny thing was that the richer I got, the more miserable I became. And the more I drank.

Ed is silent for a moment. I'm skipping over a lot. What do you want to know?

Why, Vinh wonders, does he feel like Ed's being a bit cagey, like he's holding something back?

Anyway, I took a break from working and just traveled, drank, had a lot of sex, and then in 1999 somehow ended up back in Vietnam, of all places. Ed pauses again. You can probably guess what happened next: I found her again. I actually wish I never had, but she wasn't that hard to find. Almost the first seedy bar I went to in Hồ Chí Minh City, there she was. She saw me first. I didn't even recognize her when she approached me.

The years hadn't been kind. The priest was long gone, apparently. When she came back to my hotel room for a drink, it wasn't because I wanted her—God no—but I did want to help her in some way. I can't remember the rest of that night. By the time I woke up the next afternoon with a pounding headache, she was gone, and I found she had already helped herself—to all the cash in my wallet. To be honest, I was glad she took it, and I was even more glad she had left without saying goodbye.

Ed is sitting up now, scooping his hands into the sand distractedly. Vinh sits cross-legged, elbows digging into his knees, chin resting on his fists. The more agitated Ed gets, the stiller Vinh becomes as he listens. *What would you do,* he wonders, *if you were alone and poor, but your heart wanted more, wanted the loved one, wanted a bigger life, both out of reach? What would you do to get it—who would you lie to, cheat, steal from because how else were you going to survive, what choice did you have?*

Ed gives Vinh a wry look. I haven't even got to the part about Michael yet.

Actually, Vinh has been so absorbed by the story that he's almost forgotten about Michael. So where does Michael come in? he asks.

He was dumped on my doorstep about a year ago, Ed says. Well, not literally. I had to go get him at Logan. Out of the blue, eight years after our last encounter, she sent me a letter saying I needed to go get my son at the airport, that she couldn't take care of him anymore, and she was sending him to me. She must have gotten my contact info through my business card when she went through my wallet that time. There was no way I could have made a child with her, even if I had been pretty out of it that night we were last together. But on the off chance that she wasn't lying, I couldn't risk leaving some kid stranded.

I found him right away. The cardboard sign that he was holding had my name on it. I saw, too, that whatever she said, this was no kid of mine, not even close if you were going by looks. And he probably wasn't even eight, either. He was a small kid, but I was guessing he was closer to ten. I think if I had a return address, I might have done a return to sender right then and there.

A sharp laugh.

Point is, he was *somebody's* kid. There were so many like him, abandoned, left behind. That wasn't right. Even if nobody claimed him, he belonged to all of us.

Ed shrugs. I had resources. I could give him a home. That's all.

Vinh has to sit for a minute, holding his breath, because he's hit with a wave of sadness and he knows he will totally humiliate himself if he breaks out bawling, and he will if he isn't unmovable, unmoving, still, like a rock. Part of the interior landscape that doesn't move.

Seconds tick by. He tries one shaky breath. Another one. That's all right, then.

How much time has passed? Ed is asking him a question. What about you?

Me? Vinh isn't ready to have the conversation switch to him.

So who broke your heart? Was she your high school crush?

What makes you think my heart was broken?

Oh, I don't know. Maybe the way you're so skittish, and kind of avoidant, like you're holding back.

Is that what I'm doing? Vinh wonders. His name was Jonathan, and I don't really want to talk about it. *And that right there will end this talk,* Vinh thinks.

But Ed doesn't skip a beat. Not fair, but okay. But what happens if you fall in love again? Will you just run away again?

No, I would never do that, Vinh protests. It's just that I don't think I ever will anymore. I'm done with love, he adds, and he glares at Ed, daring him to say the obvious: Aren't you too young to be done with love? But why, then, does Vinh suddenly imagine that it's possible? To fall in love again.

He thinks of Ed's stick drawing, how the simple arrangement of lines and circles produced a crude figure that looked happy, and confident, and . . . Is this how Ed really sees him? It's how he's always wanted to see himself, and until today, never thought he would.

The thing is, Vinh thinks, *Ed didn't have to do it*. Maybe Ed felt sorry for himself, maybe even lied to himself about how it all went down, who was taking advantage of who, but in the end, he stepped up. He didn't have to take Michael. But he did. And yeah, maybe he's not classic dad material, but he provides. Hell, he more than provides. There he is now, running with the kite on the beach with Michael, reeling out the string to the very end of the roll—oh no! The kite escapes. They both watch ruefully as the wind snatches it up and gleefully bears it away. Now they're throwing rocks into the water. He's good with the kid, doesn't try too hard, but Vinh notices that he keeps a watchful eye out all the same, like that time Michael swam out too far and got caught in a battering wave. Vinh was still half dozing when Ed leaped to his feet and ran into the water. A few strong strokes and he hauled Michael back on shore just as the lifeguard reached the edge of the sand with his red rescue board. Ed had a few choice words for the poor sod. He didn't have to do it. He didn't have to do any of it. But he did.

It's the third draft of the note. He could hardly call it a letter. Try again. *Ed, you should know that . . . what I mean is, the thing that I really care about but I'm afraid if I say it you won't . . .* Oh God. He rips it up and throws it in the trash.

It's late afternoon, Michael has swim lessons at the pool, Ed's on a call. Vinh's walking restlessly along the edge of the shore, foamy water lapping at his feet. There's something bobbing up and down in the distance.

He squints. No way. It's the runaway kite. Now he sees.

Someone must have caught up to it and tied it to the railing of the beach steps. He can see it now: The wind keeps the kite aloft, but it's leashed, grounded. Funny, he has noticed that things have a way of coming back to this beach just when you thought you had lost them. His left flip-flop, which got swept out to sea last week. He found it a few days later, washed up on the sand. *If I lose my heart here, will it wash back on shore?*

Soft thudding footsteps behind him. It's Ed, loose white shirt unbuttoned, exposing a glorious view of curly dark chest hair, sunglasses shading his rugged face. So damn hot. Hey, don't throw away my mail. What? Ed holds up a sheet of paper that has been torn; he's carefully taped it together. Vinh feels the blood draining from his face; he's so embarrassed he thinks he might actually pass out. He forces himself to take some deep breaths. Ed looks worried now.

Vinh . . .

Give me that, Vinh gasps, snatching at the paper. It's not yours.

It's got my name on it.

It's not—just give it to me.

Don't be a baby. Tell me, why did you write this?

Vinh grabs hold of the paper, balls it up, and hurls it into the water. Then he's running, churning sand, tearing up the soles of his bare feet. He's running away just like he said to Ed he never would if he ever fell in love again. He's sprinting.

Hours later, he's ready to apologize. When he finally gets back to the house, sweaty, ashamed, embarrassed, he's ready to tell Ed he's sorry for being an ass. He's ready to tell him why he wrote the note. He doesn't care anymore. Anything is better than this wondering and wanting. He wants to know once and for all: Is he reading Ed's looks right? Is there something there? Let Ed laugh at him, let him feel sorry for him, let him. As long as Vinh just knows once and for all.

The house is very quiet. Grace says hi and tells him there are leftovers in the fridge.

Where's everybody? Vinh asks.

Michael's doing a sleepover tonight at the house next door with the twins visiting from New Jersey. Mr. Rollins says he'll be back in a few days. He's got some business to take care of.

Oh. Look who's running away now, Vinh thinks. At first he's a bit relieved. Then he's a little aggrieved.

Long, long walks along the beach don't help. Pages and pages of nude sketches don't help either. Then, at the end of the week, Ed is back. And he's not alone.

Suddenly the house is alive with noise and movement, people coming and going. Extra help from the town comes in to wax floors, take down and shake out dusty curtains, tame and manicure the lawn. Shrubbery is hastily inserted into the ground, fresh paint slapped down in the entryway. Grace's job is reduced to looking after Michael full-time and making sure he is out of the way in the evenings because a crew of cooks has taken over the kitchen, and now there are dinner parties. It's the first time the beach house has hosted houseguests. Miss Weston, a sun-bronzed middle-aged woman with tired blond hair, is given the fancy guest bedroom across from Ed. Her friends Mr. and Mrs. Thurston have another room, and the dry, witty widow Mrs. Vanderbilt another one. Other visitors, all friends of Miss Weston's, are just present for the dinner parties, which seat ten to fifteen each night.

Vinh initially keeps to his room, peeking out the window when Ed, with Miss Weston—Miranda—on his arm, strolls past on their way to long walks on the beach. It is hands down the most miserable time of Vinh's existence. But even more so when Ed starts requesting his presence at the dinner parties and after-dinner soirees. *Why would I want to see this?*

At first, he refuses. Then Ed issues a command. But after the first time, when Vinh sits in a corner seat, looking glaringly out of place in his gray hoodie, miserable and silent the whole time, Ed relents and only requires that Vinh be present for the after-dinner gatherings. At those, at least, he is able to retreat to a window seat, nearly hidden by long curtains, and observe. What he witnesses is astonishing. Vinh has never observed Ed to be a garrulous or social man, but that is what he is these evenings. He charms his guests; they circle him like moths around a light, hungry for a luminosity that shines from his core. And Vinh feels it too: a deep tug, an irresistible desire to enter into that bright orbit, to be flooded with warmth and light, to be looked at by those sparkling, dark eyes, to be lost in their gaze. Stories of war, travel, encounters with famous people and ordinary folk; it doesn't matter what the story is. He beguiles; he enchants. Miss Weston stands beside Ed holding a glass of port in one hand while the other loops casually yet possessively around Ed's arm, gazing admiringly up at him and occasionally interjecting a bon mot. Her French sucks. He's annoyed whenever she speaks, but especially when she interrupts Ed. But Ed only smiles indulgently and continues his story. Vinh doesn't even know he's hungrily leaning forward until Ed interrupts himself and looks toward the window seat.

Are you going to join us or are you going to keep hiding back there? You've probably traveled farther than any of us here. Come out and share some of your stories, Vinh.

A spotlight is shined on him. It's as if they're all part of a theatrical period piece with their parts to play, and Vinh's has just been cued. And though he's flustered and dismayed, somehow the words flow from him without effort.

Indeed not, sir. My life has been quite dull and mundane.

Miss Weston laughs condescendingly. A life of minor employment, whether here or halfway across the world, is at least a consistent story, she says brightly.

Was that the sum of his life, Vinh wonders. He does not correct her; in fact, he agrees. Ed begs to differ, but Miss Weston expertly diverts him with a proposal.

I have heard rumors that you are a gifted singer, my dear.

Those rumors are amiss, I'm afraid. I am only a tolerable baritone.

Her eyes light up; I must hear it! And though I'm only a satisfactory soprano myself, I will try to boost your performance.

But before the interested group can move across the room to the baby grand piano, Ed routs them with a counterproposal.

I say, let's not waste this lovely evening indoors, yowling like wet cats. I know just the thing: sky lanterns. Let's all make a wish, see if it comes true.

Yes, yes, let's, let's!

A perfect night for sending our wishes up to heaven! Ed adds as they walk. So that was what the hired workers unpacked and moved down to the beach earlier that day, Vinh guesses. Yes, yes, all around, enthusiastic assent, how perfectly romantic. And when Ed leans down and peers into the bright eyes of Miss Weston, and says pointedly, I want to know *your* wish in particular, there is no turning back. With heightened color and an arched back, she bats her eyelashes in compliance. And so you shall, my dear. So you shall!

Will there be no end to the surprise of Edward Rollins? A singer, a teller of expansive stories (well, that one he knows), a setter of romantic scenes. Does he know the man? As Vinh trails behind a pair of guests dressed in flowy maxi dresses and espadrilles, he can't help but overhear snatches of their conversation. *Miranda is in high form tonight. Yes, I think she'll close the deal by the end of the week at this rate. I wager by the end of tonight! What is this, the third or fourth for her? Only the third, I think, though the second hardly counts: That marriage only lasted a month! It doesn't matter how long, really. It's what she gets to keep, afterward. Oh yes, her portfolio is doing quite well. Or it was. She must be looking to cover her losses with a . . . merger.*

He is momentarily confused. *I thought they were discussing marriages, and then it was asset holdings.* It occurs to him that they are the same thing for Miss Weston. But Ed isn't a fool. Maybe he likes her, or even loves her (it hurts to think that), and if she doesn't love him back, but only wants his money, well, isn't that just what rich people do to each other all the time anyhow? In short, none of his business.

He follows behind, a shadow made even dimmer by the depletion of his spirits. He thinks there's nothing left to drain. He's wrong.

And what will she do afterward? He's tuned back into the voices.

There's an adopted son, I believe. Boarding school, of course.

Of course.

And then a top-to-bottom renovation of the Boston town house, starting with the staff.

Yes, that ghastly housekeeper will definitely have to go.

He stiffens. It's as if he knows what's coming.

And the other one, the Chinese guy.

He hangs back in the doorway, thinking to slip away in the bustle of exit, but a hand brushes against his, then moves up his arm to his shoulder. Before he can turn his head, a familiar voice whispers into his ear: You didn't think you would disappear into the night, did you? Oh no. You're coming too!

Vinh shakes his head and tries to pull away. This isn't my thing, he protests. I'm going to bed now.

Ed doesn't release him. Are you sad? Why not come and make a wish to send up to the sky—something that will make the sadness go away. Something dear to your heart. Tonight is a night of wishes: What's yours?

Does Vinh detect a note of urgency in Ed's voice? He doesn't know.

I'm not sad! I'm just tired. Please, just go and enjoy your guests. Miss Weston's waiting for you.

There she is at the edge of the wooden stairs leading down to the beach. One hand is held out impatiently. Come, Edward! Still, Ed's hand lingers on Vinh's shoulder.

You'll never know if your wish will come true if you don't send it out into the world, he says softly into Vinh's ear. He pulls Vinh along, and he has no choice but to follow, thankful for the darkness that hides his face.

At the top of the stairs, Ed finally releases him and hooks his arm around Miss Weston's. They descend the stairs together, their backs to Vinh. He could turn and flee back to the house. Lord knows he wants to. Instead, as he watches Ed lean down and speak seductively into Miss Weston's ear, as he hears her tinkling laugh and sees her face turning up to Ed's, though his whole being longs to do nothing but crawl into a dark corner and weep, instead his traitorous feet follow the lovers; his defiant eyes can't look away from their linked forms.

One by one the lit lanterns float into the sky, where they hang for a moment twinkling like distant fireflies. He hears the waves lapping at the shore. Water flows, he reminds himself, it doesn't stay still. Time to move on before I drown.

Some of the lights rise to heaven. Some of them wink out and plummet blindly into the sea.

He's leaving tomorrow, he's made up his mind. There's not much to pack. He'll go first thing in the morning, hitch a ride to the bus station. But right now he has to get through the rest of the night. He tries to sleep, twisting and turning in the smallest bedroom in the beach house, the one he chose when they first arrived. Now it seems apt that it's his: He's only the tutor, after all. Hours pass; it feels like days. No point in pretending that sleep is possible. He decides to take one last walk along the beach. At the bottom of the wooden steps, a shadow peels away. Breath stops.

Vinh.

Leave me alone.

Why the hell is he here, like he's waiting for me? Vinh wonders. But he's in no mood to talk, walks right past Ed. He starts jogging, and all along the dark wet sand dozens of tiny pale ghost crabs scatter out of his way.

Finally out of breath . . . Stop . . . following me. No. I let you run off that other time, but not this time. Why? What's the point? You're going to marry her. You're going to go live your married life and have kids and put Michael in a boarding school and—

No, I'm not doing any of that.

What? Why?

My wish. You never asked what it was. I wished for *clarity*. So I tested her. When she asked, I told her my wish was for someone who could take me as I was. Flawed. Moody. Erratic. Even if I was poor. She left the moment she thought I had lost all my investments in the real estate market crash, he says darkly. I maybe led her to believe that, and it was enough to light her heels.

You lied? You led her on, and then you lied?

Sort of. It's helpful to know where people are coming from.

That's messed up, you know that?

Yeah, I'm sick in the head, I do know that. But you see, it wasn't from her that I wanted clarity. How else, he says quietly, how else was I supposed to find out how you really feel about me?

Feel about you? I . . .

Vinh doesn't know what to think. You can't, he says, possibly feel about me what I feel about you. It's impossible.

Is it?

Ed takes a step closer; he's so close Vinh can feel his breath on his face. Then suddenly all this rage wells up in him.

That's not. *Kind.* Do you think you can dick around with me just because I'm poor and alone and useless . . . and . . . I'm still a *person* . . . a human being . . . I've got *feelings* . . .

He's pounding Ed on the chest.

I wish . . . I wish.

Tell me. Tell me what you wish, Vinh.

He wishes, and the wishes are flying all around him, pulling him into a whirlwind.

I wish I had known . . . I wish we had more time together . . . I wish I had taken her hand . . . I wish I could save him, save them all . . . I wish I knew he was happy, that he knew I didn't abandon him . . . I wish he were mine . . .

He feels the ground dropping out beneath him as the rushing column of air sucks him up into the thin atmosphere and wishes keep whispering all around him until he thinks his head is going to explode. This is it: He's losing it, he's going mad. He punches out wildly, blindly. Again and again. Ed takes the blows; he's absorbing all Vinh's fury, until it's spent, until he's sobbing and choking as Ed holds him tightly, rocking back and forth, kissing his wet face, saying over and over, Hush now, it's all right now, it's all right, everything's going to be okay. I've got you.

That's what he wished for.

To hear that.

Chapter Four

Boston, 2008 / Hà Nội, 2008

Back at the Boston house, Ed swoops his arm under Vinh's knees and carries him over the threshold. It feels dumb and wonderful. Michael will join them later: He's staying with the neighbor twins for another week at Bethany Beach, and the parents said they would bring him home. *Home. This is my home.* At first Ed wanted them to fly to Europe (I'm taking you to London; I'm taking you to Paris), but he just wants to be in this space, to know this space: his *home.*

His eyes are drawn to the Sargent over the fireplace, one of the family portraits of the Wertheimers. He knows from his time at the Gardner that Sargent was a bigwig society painter, but he likes how the artist was friends with a family that were considered outsiders for their Jewish heritage. He studies how the siblings in the portrait seem to share a closed, secret space that belongs only to them. It makes him want to paint now, to paint *us.* Not a drawing, or a sketch, but full-on color, committing stroke after stroke of his vision on stretched, primed canvas, ready to be framed, hung on a wall for everyone to see, permanent.

The paintbrush in his mind is reworking the composition now. It's Ed leaning back against the sofa, serious, sober expression, receding a bit into the background, but a powerful presence, a quiet anchor; that's him leaning on the arm of the couch, head tilted, hair falling over his eye; Michael kneeling on the floor, elbow angled on the couch seat, hand propping the side of his face, a creamy dab on the forehead where the light hits, illuminating a subtle, playful smirk. *Family Portrait. I want to paint it,* he thinks. For the first time in a long time, he can't wait to paint.

He's got more plans: They'll fix the garden. They'll take Michael and go traveling all over Europe during his school break. He feels ridiculously light and happy.

In the movies, in novels, this is the moment right before it all falls apart. It starts with something mundane, like bringing in the mail.

Two rather official-looking envelopes. Huh, one of them is addressed to *him*—who would be writing him here already? Vinh glances at the return label. It's Jonathan's law firm. *What the hell?* Whatever, he'll look at it later. The other envelope is for Ed. He goes to drop it on Ed's desk, but there's something funny about the address label. He looks more closely.

It's addressed to Mr. and Mrs. Edward Rollins. Vinh freezes. *He's married?*

It's like all the colors in his world suddenly start to run, dripping and leaking into each other until the brightness turns to drabness, all a muddy, incoherent mess. What. The. Hell. And he knows it's not cool to open Ed's mail, but he's doing it anyway, he can't help himself. He rips open the envelope, and his eyes devour the official-looking document: some review of the terms of a contract, a lot of legalese, but he worked in a law firm long enough to know his way around the terminology . . . and oh my god, Ed *is* married. He can't think; he feels dizzy and nauseated. A sound comes out of his throat, something between a choke and a sob.

There's Ed at the doorway to the study. Hey, what's going on? Are you okay? Vinh drops the papers on the desk and runs past Ed, up the stairs, into his room, slams the door.

When he wakes up later, he doesn't know how long he's slept or what time it is. He only remembers running away, slamming and locking his door, throwing himself on the bed and curling into a ball. Crying himself to sleep. And the dream.

He is walking toward Ed, who's waiting at the end of the corridor, dressed as a groom waiting for his bride, but as Vinh walks forward, Ed keeps receding like a backwater wave sucked back into the ocean as Vinh reaches desperately out, and then he's running sprinting pleading a crushing wave slams down on him he can't breathe will surely drown he pounds his fists pumps his arms breaks free now he's lifted high higher higher like that time in the helicopter with Father M looking down the earth pulling back or is he flying away up here it is peaceful he can see everything the blank ocean a long road filled with closed shops one bookstall lit up by a single light he sees a woman inside who's just woken from a bad dream thrown up on the shores of her reality flotsam jetsam of it strewn around her unsold magazines dusty textbooks the abridged copy of Jane Eyre *that's kept her up late again reading into the sticky heated nights of a late summer in Huế Vietnam quiet the end of the tourist season dark except for the flickering light of a single candle that her sister warned would burn down the bookstall one night but it is her own life unfolding in each sentence she battles to decipher searching for the meaning and whether heartbreak awaits or love whether the pious man or the passionate one she doesn't know wants to ask the young man in the sky looking down at her is it her dream or his she turns back to the book for answers turns the page.*

He's thirsty and a little lightheaded, and all he needs to think about, the only thing he wants to think about, is getting a drink of water. He listens hard at the door but doesn't hear anything. But when he opens it, there's Ed, sitting on a chair placed in the hallway directly across from his room. He must have been waiting there for hours. He stands up and follows as Vinh walks past him and down the stairs. At the bottom of the staircase, Vinh pauses, feeling suddenly lost and disoriented. Ed takes his arm and gently leads him into the study. He makes Vinh sit in an armchair as he pours him a glass of water. Then he sits back in the other chair and watches Vinh drink. This would be a comforting, homey scene if it wasn't for the fact that it is all a lie, Vinh thinks bitterly as he takes deep gulps. Looks out the window.

The family portrait he imagined earlier is in ruins, forms fragmented and dissolving into indistinguishable smears of pigment until he can't recognize anymore what's figure and what's ground.

You're married, he finally says to Ed.

Yes.

Were you ever going to tell me?

Vinh . . . yes, I was.

When?

I guess when I was sure you weren't going to run away when you knew. When you were sure enough about *us* to see that it didn't matter.

Vinh shutters his eyes. You mean, you didn't trust me.

No, that's not what I mean. I wasn't sure you trusted yourself. Yet.

This is pointless.

Why?

Because you're *married.*

That's not important.

It's important to me.

Why?

Why? Because you belong to somebody else . . . I thought you were mine.

I am yours.

Not according to those documents.

That's exactly what they are—just a bunch of documents; they have nothing to do with how I feel about you.

I can't . . . I'm sorry, I can't *do* this.

Will you listen to my story? Please, just listen to the story before you decide anything.

But he doesn't start right away, like he's collecting his thoughts. Then he sighs.

Some of this you've heard, Ed begins.

After the fiasco with Bi An, I was a mess, I won't lie. And I went on a bit of a binge, left my work, went traveling through Europe, had sex with everything on two legs. It was meant to be a path of self-destruction, but somehow, the opposite happened.

I had an AIDS scare. I was okay, but I shouldn't have been—I wasn't particularly careful, only spectacularly lucky. But I became damned careful after that. People were dying all around me, people I had come to know and love. This whole part of me that was always there but I never knew, that part of me had awakened. As I said, I owed it to Bi An, really. She released me from my rigid ideas about how love is supposed to go. It isn't supposed to go anywhere. It just finds you and overturns your life.

Vinh wonders what it would have been like if he had met Ed as a young man with a broken heart fucking his way through Europe during the AIDS crisis. *Everything on two legs. At any age, young or old, I would want him.*

I came back to the States when I ran out of money, Ed continues. One thing I learned then was that if you want to live *now* and you want to live any way you want, you need funds. And I was broke. I reconnected with my friends in tech. We had a great idea for a new start-up, but we needed seed money, and we were getting nowhere with that. I finally swallowed my pride and sought out my father; the asshole had cut me off after I quit school and joined the military instead of following the path he had planned for me. True to form, he agreed to help, but only with a lot of strings attached.

Ed stops and runs his hand through his hair, making himself look distractingly sexy. Vinh has to mentally slap himself in the face to keep focused.

You would think, Ed says ruefully, that I would have known better. The offer was this: My father was about to close on a business merger, but the other party had one deal-breaking condition. Mr. Sayre, the other owner, had a daughter with a "mental infirmity," as he called it, whom he wanted to marry off. I was the poor sod who could do it, my father told me. Like hell I would, I told him back. But they dangled the money. And it was a *lot* of money. And that didn't even include all the shares that would come to me after the merger—on the condition that I could never divorce Madeleine or else I would forfeit that fortune. It was all in the prenup that Sayre had his smarmy lawyer draw up. Why? I wanted to know. We don't even know each other. It turned out that they didn't want to institutionalize her; it wouldn't look good. What they wanted was a lavish wedding and then to dust their hands of her for good. I think I would have married her just to get her away from her awful family. But I said I needed to talk with her first. They were reluctant, afraid maybe that meeting her would change my mind.

She was an odd one, that was for sure. She seemed to live in a reality—realities—of her own. It was complicated. She was lucid at times; she was violent at others. She tried to kill her father the night of the wedding. The whole arrangement worked for her because she wanted so badly to get away from him.

Jesus, Ed.

I know. Her father was fine. Honestly she's really more a danger to herself than anything. Though it turns out this wasn't the only time she'd tried to stab someone.

Did she ever try to kill you?

Maybe. That time. I'm not sure that's what she meant to do, though. It was after the wedding, and we were traveling. I woke up and she was holding a knife at my throat. (Vinh swallows hard, feels himself instinctively reaching for his own.) I wasn't afraid. She was in a good phase at that time, and we had drifted from each other already; we both had lovers. She had this pensive look on her face as she held the knife, and she was watching me. I slowly moved her hand away, and then I gently pried each finger one by one off the handle. I did it very slowly, and waited for her to release her grip only when she felt ready to. It took a long time. When I finally got the knife away, I threw it across the room, and we were both so exhausted that we fell asleep together for the rest of the day.

Vinh is furious. He's mad at Ed for being reckless with his life. And he's mad at Madeleine for being lost in her own mind, her own reality, for not being in control of her life. And yes, he knows that's not her fault; in fact he probably knows better than most people what it's like to live on the edge of reality, those strange slips in time. A sense of other lives lived, of lives yet to be lived. But that doesn't make him less mad. Because on top of everything, there is something weirdly erotic about that whole scenario, so now he's turned on and jealous too.

Ed has stopped talking. He's observing Vinh closely. Go on, Vinh says tightly.

When we got back to Boston, she was okay for a while. Then it got bad. I found her in the attic one time, on the window ledge, and she said she was an angel; she was babbling about flying away. I got her down, but after that, I knew. I knew I couldn't give her a normal life at home no matter how hard I strained to make it happen. I couldn't. I went through the process of placing her under a guardianship. Having her deemed unfit to care for herself. It was awful. She's in the best place money can buy, in a place in Maine, on the coast. The water calms her down. I don't visit. We don't visit. Michael doesn't even know about her, any of it, though I think he has suspicions. I would see her if it helped. But the reality I bring with me seems to disturb the one she lives in. So I leave her alone. I don't want her to be hurt any more than she has been in this life.

You sound like you care about her, Vinh says. He hates that he can't keep the peevishness out of his voice. Why do you even like me?

And this, he realizes, is what lies at the heart of his insecurity. He knows why he likes Ed, but he can't understand why Ed likes *him*.

So do you just like guys like me?

What do you mean "guys like you"? I don't know anyone else like you, Vinh.

I mean, do you, like, have an Asian fetish or something?

Vinh still has a painful memory of running into one of Jonathan's exes at an art opening, of telling Jonathan afterward that he and the ex could pass for brothers; Jonathan laughing it off . . . *Yeah, maybe I have a certain taste.* And Vinh understands that people do have tastes, types. But he still felt crushed. Thinking of that now makes him want to lash out.

Do I remind you of your first love, that Vietnamese village girl?

Ed closes his eyes, takes a deep breath. When he opens them again, Vinh can't escape his penetrating glare.

No. I do not have an Asian fetish. Or something. No, you are *nothing* like Bi An. But if you mean do I think *you're* hot, *you're* special, then yes. Yes, I do.

Vinh doesn't know what to think. Okay, he says, I don't get it. Why?

I'm *not* hot. I mean, I wish I were.

I could tell you how hot you are, but I get the feeling that would embarrass you. Look, it's not just that. Ed gives him a hard look. I get the feeling that life hasn't been easy for you; you've had to struggle. You feel unworthy, which is bullshit. But you don't back down either. You're not afraid to say what you think is true, especially to me . . . I need that. But it's more than that. I can't explain it. He runs his hand through his hair as he reaches for words. It's like . . . I've known you for a long time; there's something uncannily familiar about you, like I've finally found the thing I've been looking for all my life and I didn't even know I was incomplete until you came back. You are my home. You know, if I hadn't known that you were on your way to my house that first day I met you, that I would get a chance to see you again, I wouldn't have been able to let you go.

Oh.

And here Vinh was thinking that Ed couldn't have been less interested in him that first time they met.

Ed is looking at him in a pained way. I could ask you the same, he says tensely. Do you only like me because you have a thing for older guys?

What? No! Vinh's voice breaks.

Ed's question pulls him up short. Jonathan is older, that is true. But what is also true is that he doesn't think of Ed as older. He feels the same age as Ed, honestly. He knows that would sound strange if he tried to explain it to anyone, and it's hard even to explain it to himself, but it's as if they both inhabit the same temporal space—one where they already lived a whole life together, where they already belonged to each other body, mind, and soul, and then some catastrophic event ripped them apart, flung them to different ends of the universe, and this loss, never recuperated, which no one else had ever taken the place of . . . has at last been restored. It feels, as Ed has said, like a homecoming. *Like a long journey has ended and you have finally arrived, and laid down your pack, and called out I am home, my love, I am home at last.*

Or he thought he was.

Vinh takes a deep breath. I want you to myself, he says abruptly.

The words are his, but they jolt him. He has drawn Ed in his sketchbook over and over; that meant as much as the sex. He realizes now it was another kind of madness. Was he making an impossible Ed then? An Ed that could only exist in his fantasies, out of his deepest needs? And now he's said, finally, what he wants, what he couldn't say to Jonathan. He's never felt more exposed in his life.

Vinh. I couldn't just cut ties with her. She has nobody else. I married her for her family's money, but even though that's gone—I wasn't lying when I told Miranda Weston that most of my assets went up in smoke when the housing market tanked—I'm not throwing Madeleine to the wolves. And you *do* have me. To hear you say that's what you want—do you know what that means to me? You'll always have me, even if you walk out right now. Maybe you will. I'm not exactly broke, but I'm not as rich as I was. And I'm not young. You could do better.

Shut up, Vinh says. Just shut up.

I don't want to fight anymore, Ed says. Come here.

No.

But his body moves into the shelter of those open arms that wrap around him and pull him close.

To be held like this is all he's ever wanted.

Suddenly Vinh feels very old, not age-wise, but time-wise, like he's lived this exact moment of revelation and heartbreak in another time, that temporal space he and Ed share. But the feeling vanishes, and he's back in the room, in Ed's arms. There's an ending coming that they both already know, and maybe that's why they are both clinging to each other as if they know that they've gotten to that point in the story and they don't want to think about what comes next, though it will come, this moment will come to an end, as it always does, but not yet, Vinh pleads silently. *Please, not yet.*

The early-morning light is a washed-out gray when Vinh creeps out of the house. There are only a few other travelers around at this hour at South Station. It's not hard to find an empty seat to plop down his bag and drink his bad coffee from the only vendor open. In a minute he'll take a deep breath and study the departure board, find the first bus leaving in the next hour to wherever. Right now Vinh just wants to think about nothing, to feel nothing. It's easier that way. The ticking sound attracts his attention, and he watches as the numbers and letters skim across the board as if it's a roulette wheel, falling into place to list the Northeast Corridor routes: Hartford, New York City, Philadelphia, Baltimore, Washington. Washington's the farthest, and is boarding in twenty minutes. Okay, then. He's got twenty more minutes. He has time to open the mail from Jonathan's law firm. Might as well read it now. Then afterward he can throw it out.

He likes the idea of leaving all the baggage behind him, but even so, his hands are shaky as he tears open the envelope.

> Vinny, if this finds you, then the PI I hired was worth the money. You never told me you had a rich relative. Here I've been thinking you were a poor orphan. No more. Your mother's uncle died and left a fortune to his nieces, his only remaining heirs. Our firm got contacted because that was your last known location. Yes, people are trying to find you. I took on the case immediately, for obvious reasons.
>
> Apparently your mother's uncle disappeared after the war, and everyone just assumed he had been killed. But instead he had crossed the ocean with a boatload of

other refugees and made it to the Philippines, and from there to California. Then he opened a corner store, which he grew into a chain of grocery stores, then went on into real estate and basically became very rich.

Here's the kicker. After he made a fortune, he converted all his real estate assets into gold, like he knew, the uncanny bastard—knew it was all going to collapse like a house of cards. Do you know how much money I lost?

Never mind, it hurts to think about it. His lawyers found your mother in Vietnam. Half goes to her sister, but your mother is rich even with half the inheritance. If she took it. It turned out that she didn't want it. Not for herself. She said to give it all to you. But she didn't know where you were, and when they found you, she wanted you to have this letter (see enclosed).

Anyhow, all this landed at our law firm, because as I said earlier, that was your last known location. I've had a hell of a time finding you. Why did you disappear like that? I know things weren't great with us, but we could have talked. I've arranged to open a line of credit for you, but we have a lot of paperwork to do. Who's this Rollins dude? Is he treating you okay? Be careful—he's got history, something to do with a rich heiress. Your sugar daddy has a sugar mama. You know, Vinny, we really should talk. Aside from the legal stuff. I miss you. For real. Call me.

—Jonathan

Vinh crushes the letter savagely. *You don't know anything about it. You don't know anything about him!* But Vinh also knows that he's working himself up because he's afraid to read the other letter, folded tightly still in the envelope from Jonathan—the one from his mother. Okay. Just rip the Band-Aid off.

My dearest son,

My English is bad. I am so afraid I will sound wrong to you. I wrote this with my heart, and the heart is fluent. Please read this with your heart.

(He understands what she's saying: how broken English is a reminder of the distance between them. At boarding school the others used Vinh's errors to remind him that he was an outsider. It was also a reminder for him of the cracks in himself, the cracks he had tried to cover up with perfect fluency to show that he did belong, that he wasn't broken inside. He had worked at it until his English was perfect. He still winces when people tell him his English is "so good." So he reads her letter as she asked him to, with his heart, filling in the missing articles in his mind as he reads, smoothing over scrambled syntax into eloquent, seamless sentences.)

You are the best part of my life. Maybe you don't want to hear. Maybe you won't read this letter. When you were three years old you had a great, burning fever. I thought you would die and Loan said to me over and over, just dry his tears and cool his head. That's all you need to do. I did nothing else for three days and nights, and you lived. I told Loan I could not raise you. You would be the death of me. And she laughed and said I was too serious about everything. All I had to do was dry your tears. I did that when you fell down and skinned your knees, when the other children teased you and said you were a *bụi đời*, when you said you wished you lived with your mother instead of with me, your aunt, so that no one would call you a street urchin anymore. I learned to dry my own tears. Because your Aunt Loan should have been your mother. She was the one your father really loved. I stole your father's love without his knowing. The price was never being able to tell you I am your real mother. I was really punished. Loan says none of this would matter if I were not such a dreamer. Your dreams are too big, she said, and that's why you get into trouble.

But sometimes I think that I am dreamed by someone else, that my life is someone else's dream. In my dreams I fly between worlds, in and out of different times and lives. No one else knows this, but I feel you would understand. In my dreams, I am always looking for someone who is lost to me. I had these dreams even before you were born. Maybe they were telling me that someday I would lose you. Before you were born, I wanted to leave this small shack and go into the world; I wanted a bigger life, I wanted to be loved. But when I came home to Huế with you in my arms, everything came into focus. My world was you; my purpose in life was clear: to care for you. It wasn't love that I needed; it was love that I needed to give. You were taken from me, but I never faltered from that need.

I am so sorry for the tears I did not get to dry. I let my own fall freely. I hope you have found love and that you live fully and fearlessly. May this money from my uncle add to the abundance of your life.

Your loving mother, always.

What am I doing here? he thinks. He's been in Hà Nội for over a week. The architecture is amazing: He loves the blend of French and Asian styles.

Even the food is blended: rice cake, cilantro, and fish sauce sandwiched in a crusty baguette. They are remnants of a colonialist legacy, he knows that, but right now he prefers to experience them as chance fusions—brought together out of necessity, out of inspiration—that turned out to be perfect.

He walks around Hoàn Kiếm Lakc; he visits the Hồ Chí Minh Museum. There, he has another one of those slips in time and body— they always start with a little tingle at the base of his skull. *He is back in Boston, walking by the Parker House Hotel, not too far from Jonathan's law firm, and just as he passes an alleyway, he sees a Vietnamese man wearing a flour-dusted apron talking to a small woman who looks like she has just stepped out of the nineteenth century.* The image winks out. He feels unmoored. That familiar feeling. The momentum of his earlier resolve (*I'm rich; I can go anywhere. Vietnam, here I come!*) has been replaced by a sense of uncertainty in this bustling, beautiful, familiar, strange country.

It isn't exactly the homecoming he envisioned, but it's the homecoming that is *his*. All his life he has been looking for something, something missing, and maybe it was this and here it is, but he is a foreigner here, will always be the foreigner wherever he goes. Aren't we all, he wonders, only most people are trapped in illusions of belonging. Those children, the kids that pack around the tourists, clamoring for spare change, trying to sell a package of Chiclets, sometimes a face here or there that makes him think of Michael, of himself, he wants to save every one of them, makes sketch after sketch of them in his notebook. To hold them. To set them free. In another time, in another story, that one is an entrepreneur, that one owns a chain of grocery stores in another country, that one falls in love with a man on a motorcycle who takes a spill in front of him.

It reminds him of the strange woman at the airport in Boston, when he was about to depart. She had seated herself beside him in the boarding lounge. She was an older woman, breathlessly elegant in a spotless white silk blouse and flowing black trousers. You look like you're going to pass out, she said, handing him her perfumed handkerchief. He used it to mop his sweaty forehead and temples.

Thanks. Sorry.

Keep it, she said kindly.

I'm not used to flying, he said lamely.

I don't care for it myself, she said. That's why I always travel with my coffin.

She left to board with the other first-class passengers, followed by someone who must have been her assistant, an impeccably dressed younger Asian man who dutifully carried her bag. The moment she left, he sketched her in his book. He didn't see her when the plane landed at Nội Bài International Airport.

It's been like that his whole time here: odd encounters, restless thoughts, edgy dreams.

Now, in the hotel room, he lies on the bed staring at the spinning blades of the ceiling fan. One of the blades is a little bent, adding a dull thumping sound as the fan rotates. It reminds him of the time Jonathan took him to see *Apocalypse Now* at a Francis Ford Coppola film festival. At the time he didn't get the movie, but now he feels like he understands the Martin Sheen character in the Sài Gòn hotel room, listening to the beat of the helicopter's rotor blades, having a nervous breakdown, Valkyries about to crash through the windows.

He hasn't moved all day. He's drained from that dream last night. He can't get it out of his head. It's seared into the folds and grooves of his cerebral cortex.

He's back in Boston, on top of the town house. It's burning, the building is on fire, and he watches helplessly as Ed races across the rooftop to Madeleine, who is spinning in a white nightgown, her arms flung out like wings, and in one of her twirls the hem of her nightgown catches a spark, flames ride up the fabric, and she erupts in a glorious blaze, like a bird of fire soaring into the air just as Ed catches her and they both plummet over the side of the building in a fiery arc.

He woke up in a panicked sweat, and his first thought was *I've got to call Ed.* But when you run out on someone, you don't get to call them in the middle of the night from halfway across the world to ask if they're okay. Maybe he could call the house line, get Mrs. Poole, ask her if everything is okay, if Ed is okay. He knows she would hang up on him. Or worse, what if Ed answered? Then he would have to hang up, knowing that Ed would know who was calling.

It's driving him crazy. Ed's okay, he tells himself. He would know if Ed wasn't. He would know. *How would you know, you idiot? What if he's not, what if he's crippled, blinded, dead? What if he needs me?* I would know, he thinks, I would know because there is a thread, a vein growing mutually from my heart to his, that connects us. Even across two continents. And if Ed were dead, if that lifeline were severed, then he would bleed out and die too. That's how he would know. And so it went, one thought chasing after another, all night long. He's still exhausted.

He takes out his drawing, the one he's been carrying with him this whole time, the one of the mother and child. When he first read his mother's letter, he wasn't surprised. Like he had always known, deep down. She, not the pretty one in the photograph, had always been the one who was there. He has a memory of her telling him: *Call me Má.* The sadness and pride in her voice. Hasn't he been searching for a way back to this, to her, all this time? Isn't this the missing part of him? Is he afraid of finding it? Now that he's so close? Because what if it doesn't make him whole after all? What if that isn't a sacred and safe space, the little boy and his mother, looking at the world together? Does he really want to find his way back to that? Ed is far from perfect, but he didn't leave Michael at the airport, he didn't abandon Madeleine even when most of his wealth evaporated. Vinh wonders if he could love anyone who did. Does he want to look at the world, or does he want to step into that stream of life and live it, even if it roughs him up, dashes him on the rocks, breaks his heart.

He looks at the drawing one more time; then he rips it up.

Ripping it up doesn't give him enough release from his pent-up frustration. He kicks his bag, then overturns it viciously, spilling out the contents.

What is that? A black American Express card. It's got Ed's name on it, and a note folded up and taped to the back.

You're authorized to use this.

(*The hell with that,* he thinks. *I've got my own damned money.*)

> The thought of you out in the world penniless
> drives me crazy. Use it. And when you're done running
> away, when you're finally finished with all the bullshit,
> I want you to charge it for a ticket and come home.
> Because I can never be whole without you. So I'll be
> waiting. I will always wait for you, Vinh.

It's like hearing his name shouted from across the world. He literally hears it, and his head whips around, eyes wildly searching around the room.

I'm coming!

Did he just yell that out loud? He did. He does it again; he doesn't care.

I'm coming!

He's stuffing shit back into his bag, he's checking his phone for flight schedules. It will take a bus, a cab, a long plane ride, a layover, another long plane ride, another cab. It will take thirty-seven hours. Then he'll be home.

He stops at the door. There's one more thing he needs to do first.

Epilogue

Huế, 2008

The bus arrives in Huế after the temperature breaks and the slanting rays of the sun are making shadows rather than heat. It takes a bit of wandering, but in the end, the bookstall isn't as hard to find as he thought it would be. Maybe because it stands out. It looks shabbier than the other stalls, more out of date compared to the ones on either side of it, which are filled with pallets of water, cheap umbrellas, stuffed manga toys, the usual rack of postcards of the Imperial City. The stall he's looking for looks like it belongs to another time, an age when people were still interested in stopping to browse through a stack of books. Even the splayed-out magazines look old timey, like certain issues have been kept for their colorful covers rather than their currentness. But there's something very calm and inviting about it; he knows that even if he weren't looking for this particular stall, he would have stopped to look through the books.

He doesn't approach right away. He stands on the other side of the wide street, which is quieter at this time of day, but still constantly in motion with a stream of cyclers, bikers, pedicabs, cars, dashing pedestrians, all flowing steadily onward, like time does. Until it does something else: leap, plunge, double back, freeze. He realizes what she's done. She's stopped time. She's kept one moment still: a bookstall that never changes, year in and year out; nothing new is added, maybe a few titles are changed, but the look of it, the feel of it, is purposefully constant.

So that one day I can find it again.

It's heart shattering. She's an artist, too, he thinks. It takes vision and intention to do this, to keep oneself as still as possible, to stop time. Nor was she entirely successful. Her hair is white now, her back is stooped. If she straightens up and turns around, the lady bending down to move a pile of books from the floor, he knows he'll see lines on her face, bagged eyes, mouth dragged downward at the corners.

Even art can't stop time. Nothing is permanent. But if he could just keep it going a little bit longer. If he could suspend the moment, hold back the rush of feelings, the questions he wants to ask: Was it a long day? Is she tired? Does her back hurt? But he can't hold anything back, not his watering eyes, his aching throat—*stop,* he tells himself, disgusted, *stop crying. Idiot. Just stop.* He can't, so he lets the tears flow freely. Let them come, the feelings, let them come completely. But he can do this: He can capture this fleeting, impermanent moment, not on paper or canvas, in his memory. The light right now is perfect, low and golden, giving everything an end-of-the-day glow as the day's heat subsides. Shadows lengthen, pool, highlighting that last slant of light that spills into the bookstall, gilding the sides of the bars that frame the opening. He angles his head, arranging his sight at just the right position. Now he needs for her to complete the image. Almost there. She straightens up, she turns to face the street, centered in the frame, just as the sun brushes a radiant halo around her head. For a moment, her eyes are closed. Then she looks up, gaze cutting across the stream of moving bodies and vehicles . . . *Wait for it.* Her eyes latch on to his, widen.

Suddenly, the base of his skull tingles, time, space, and body become unmoored, and he gets the feeling that if he lifts his head now (someone is watching someone is waiting) and opens his eyes, he will see across the way the one he has been watching for and waiting for all this time—the child, the parent, the lover, the friend—the lost one he has longed to see every day of his life. He lifts his head, opens his eyes.

There it is.

It's done. What to name this moment: *Mother and Child*; *Reunited Lovers*; *Self-Portrait*?

In his mind he lays down the brush. He feels exhausted, like he's been painting for ten hours straight, fifteen years running. The best art he's ever made, and no one will ever see it. In a moment it will all vanish, as elusive as a sunbeam, a wave. Kenny once said, *It's not what you see that matters. It's how you see it.* He looks. He sees. Everything that matters.

There it is.

Acknowledgments

Many people helped to make this dream a reality. First and foremost, I would like to thank my brilliant agent, Joëlle Delbourgo, for believing in this work and for her dedication in getting it out into the world. A huge thank-you goes to my editor, Emily Freidenrich, for believing in it as well, and for her tremendously insightful suggestion that helped the fourth Jane come more fully into existence. I'm also very grateful to Nicholas Machida, who advocated tirelessly for the book's fullest potential; it would not be in its current form without his phenomenal work.

Thank you to my team at Amazon Publishing, including Lydia Bowman, Julia Johnson-Viola, Becca Lee, Karah Nichols, and Zoe Norvell. Many thanks as well to Elsa Klingensmith-Parnell, Annie Sloniker, and Megan Westberg. It goes without saying that none of this would be possible without their hard work, careful attention to details, and total commitment to this project.

A special callout to the many readers of this work in all its different stages is due: Fran Lebowitz, Michelle Sterling, Andrea Nye, Robert Crane, Maddaleno Grieco, Gwen Bindas, and Christian Harrington. Their thoughtful feedback and enthusiastic responses nourished this creative journey. I want to particularly thank Joan Baranow and Mark Sullivan for being there from start to finish of this journey—their careful commentary and unwavering encouragement and support were indispensable in helping to steer this vessel to its place of final harbor.

Thank you to the Virginia Center for the Creative Arts for a residency fellowship in 2018, and to Berklee College of Music for sabbatical release in 2021 to research and write this book.

A number of historical, journalistic, and scholarly texts provided invaluable information on steamship passage, Anglican missionary practice in India, and the history of Vietnam and the Vietnam War. These include: *Passage East* by Ian Marshall and John Maxtone-Graham; *Imperial Fault Lines: Christianity and Colonial Power in India, 1818–1940* by Jeffrey Cox; *Vietnam: A History* by Stanley Karnow; *The Fall of Saigon* by David Butler; *The Sacred Willow: Four Generations in the Life of a Vietnamese Family* by Duong Van Mai Elliott; and *Ho Chi Minh: A Life* by William J. Duiker.

The most invaluable text of all, of course, was Charlotte Brontë's *Jane Eyre*. That being said, a necessary acknowledgment also goes to Virginia Woolf, whose vision and style I freely borrowed from when reimagining Jane's world.

A final note of thanks and gratitude goes to my family, Gary, Olivia, and Stella, who are the steadfast light and the enduring inspiration of *my* world.

About the Author

Photo © 2025 Kristin Palkoner

Marian Yee is a writer, scholar, and award-winning teacher. As a professor in the Liberal Arts and Sciences Department at Berklee College of Music, she teaches writing, literature, and visual studies to performing arts students. Marian's published writings include poems, reviews, and scholarly articles. *4 Janes* is her debut novel, inspired by a trip to Vietnam in 1995, where she met a street seller who was reading an abridged copy of *Jane Eyre* to learn English. The author lives in Brookline, Massachusetts, with her family.